BABY DADDY WANTED

A SMALL TOWN ROMANTIC COMEDY

CRESCENT COVE
BOOK 5

TARYN QUINN

Baby Daddy Wanted
© 2019 Taryn Quinn
Rainbow Rage Publishing
Stock Photo by Deposit Photos

Cover by LateNite Designs

First print edition: February 2021
ISBN: 978-1-940346-65-6

ACKNOWLEDGMENTS

We wouldn't be where we are today without our amazing team. Thanks, Tori, Kim, and Suzanne for all you do to make us look good. We love you madly.

Sometimes we make up fictional places that end up having the same names as actual places. These are our fictional interpretations only. Please grant us leeway if our creative vision isn't true to reality.

PLAYLIST

Into the Mystic **by Van Morrison**
What Happens In A Small Town **by Brantley Gilbert**
Stay A Little Longer **by Brothers Osborne**
Wild Love **by Ashley Monroe**
Distant Dreamer **by Duffy**
Lonely Tonight **by Blake Shelton (feat. Ashley Monroe)**
21 Summer **by Brothers Osborne**
Adore You **by Miley Cyrus**
Baby Be Crazy **by Brantley Gilbert**
I Don't Remember Me (Before You) **by Brothers Osborne**
Certain Things **by James Arthur (feat. Chasing Grace)**

FULL PLAYLIST ON SPOTIFY

To those of us who never believe we're good enough.
You are.
So very much.

ONE

Veronica Dixon: *BABY DADDY WANTED*

Single, personable woman seeking a man for the purposes of procreation. I wouldn't mind if he looks like Chris Pratt, but that's not required. No further interaction with the child is necessary, unless desired by father-to-be. Child will be created the old-fashioned way, assuming both parties agree. Contact V at **goodtothelastdrop**.

I DROPPED MY PHONE. IT CLATTERED AGAINST MY COFFEE CUP at the edge of my makeshift desk and splashed up to soak my work shirt and the sketch paper I was using. "Oh, crap." I stood and stumbled back, knocking into the pail of cement behind me. I quickly yanked off my shirt, swiping at the sticky mess.

"Watch it, Moose."

"Sorry." I turned to steady the pail.

John Gideon, my best friend and pseudo-boss, shook his head with a half grin. "Finally stripping for Mrs. Gunderson?" Suddenly, he winced. "Oh, man. Macy's thermos keeps coffee blistering hot, God bless her."

"Emphasis on the blistering."

"Go splash some water on it before it blisters for real."

"Yeah. Fu—" I swallowed the swear words. This particular client didn't like cussing. She had a comment or opinion on just about everything when it came to the Cove. Unfortunately, she was one of Gideon's best clients. She contracted at least four big projects a year. Personally, I was pretty sure she just liked to have shirtless guys in her backyard—especially Lucky. Though most women hung around to get a look at Lucky, to be honest.

And he liked to be looked at.

I shook off my phone and wiped it against my cargo pants before sliding it in my pocket. "I'm going to go change my shirt. I've got one in the truck."

Gideon nodded. "Go on inside first. We turned off the outside water, remember?"

"Yeah." I didn't want to go inside and have Mrs. Gunderson fuss over me. Or stare at me. I hissed as I wiped at the sugary coffee sticking to my chest hair. Macy at Brewed Awakening knew my weakness. Caramel toffee chocolate coffee. Tasted damn good in the cup, not so much on me.

I resisted the urge to pull out my phone again. I couldn't have read that right. Everyone in Crescent Cove checked the town Facebook page. Lost dog, lost cat, even a lost guinea pig last week. Those, I understood. But Vee posting that?

No way.

I had to be going crazy. Or maybe it was because I just wanted to see her name. It almost didn't compute. She was just Vee to all of us in town. The sweet baker and barista who worked at Brewed Awakening. Huge green eyes and soft blond hair tipped with a rainbow of colors. I never knew what color she'd be sporting when I got my daily dose of caffeine.

She was the highlight of my day.

Always.

"Stupid, Moose," I muttered and pulled my phone out again. Sure enough, there it was. An ad for an honest to God baby daddy. What was she thinking?

"Murphy Masterson, what have you done to yourself?"

I looked up from my phone and shoved it back in my pocket. "Hi, Mrs. Gunderson. I had a little accident with my coffee. Think I could wash up right quick?"

"Of course, come on in." Her bluebell eyes lit. "Can I make you another cup? I know I don't do nearly as well as Macy and Veronica, but I have one of those Keurig machines."

"Don't go to any fuss, ma'am."

"It's no fuss. Speaking of Veronica. What was she thinking posting that on the town group page? It's not a meat market."

I swallowed hard. "I don't know, Mrs. Gunderson." And I was just as surprised. God, had everyone seen it?

"But you did see it."

"It's none of my business."

"You're a good man, Moose. I appreciate that you wouldn't talk about that sweet girl out of turn, but the whole town is talking about it."

How the heck would she know? She'd been here the entire time we were working. Then again, Judy Gunderson could work a phone tree faster than the school snow day listings.

"Do you have a towel?"

"Oh, yes. I'm sorry. I'm just so distracted." She opened a drawer and handed me two plaid towels. "We've been talking about this Veronica thing all morning. I just can't believe it."

Neither could I, but I really didn't want to discuss it with Mrs. Gunderson. I took the towels with strained smile. "I'll just—"

"When you go over there for lunch, you better check on her."

Did everyone know how many times a day I went to Brewed Awakening?

"I brought my lunch."

She clucked her tongue. "You always go over for another coffee. You and John are practically addicted."

I huffed out a breath. "I'll be sure to check on Vee." I hurried down the hall to her bathroom before she could interrogate me any further. I ran the water and splashed it against my chest with a hiss. Her bathroom had been our last remodel. I didn't remember the mirror being quite so big when I'd helped Gideon put it in.

My chest was bright pink under the chest hair that spread across my pecs. What I needed was a shower and a tube of triple antibiotic. "Shit," I mumbled as I did the best I could with the tea towel she'd given me.

But while I had the space to myself, I leaned against the counter and checked my phone again. There were already eleven comments on her post and a dozen likes, hearts, and many shocked faces. Not a single reply from Vee herself though.

Had she really meant to post that to the group's main page?

She wasn't exactly the type to put all her business on Facebook, but then again, she wasn't quiet about giving her opinions. Especially when she and Macy got going. They were entertaining as hell, and I wished I had the balls to act on my feelings for her.

But to post this? It just didn't make sense.

Before I could stop myself, I messaged her using my business account. I just needed to check on her and make sure she meant to post it. That was all.

No, idiot, you just don't want her to know it's you.

Maybe then she'll notice you for the first time—ever.

My thumbs flew over my phone. Short and sweet. Just a concerned citizen.

Liar.

My finger hovered over the send button. I should be smart about this. I shouldn't send anything.

A knock at the door startled me enough that I gripped the phone tight and the swishing sound of my email sound filled the air.

"You all right in there?"

"Yes. Thank you."

"There's antiseptic in the cabinet. You may go in there and get the tube if you'd like," Mrs. Gunderson called through the door.

Well, it was too late now. Message sent. I stuffed my phone back into my pocket. "Thank you." I stared at my image in the wall-sized mirror. "Idiot," I added in an undertone.

The idiot was me, not Mrs. Gunderson.

I opened the middle section of the cabinet. Sure enough, there was some triple-antibiotic right there. All nice and organized.

Grimacing, I smeared it on. I hated the caked-on, oily residue feeling. The last time I'd had this much on my skin was after my one and only tattoo, but it did take the sting out. The double-walled coffee tumbler from Brewed Awakening definitely kept the damn coffee hot.

Then again, it did mean I had to go get another cup.

And maybe, just maybe, I'd be able to see a certain surprising woman looking for a life change.

My dick twitched in my cargos at the idea of making a baby with Veronica Dixon—the old-fashioned way. Truthfully, I'd thought of more than one biblical position involving myself and Vee. When she smiled up at me with those perfect bottle green eyes as she handed me my coffee—yeah, I definitely had more thoughts about that woman than were wise.

I just didn't know how to open my mouth.

She was so beautiful. So fucking full of light and perfection. What the hell would she want with me? Moose—just as huge and lumbering as the name suggested.

I sighed and shut the cabinet door before washing my hands and opening the door. Little Mrs. Gunderson was waiting for me in the hallway, her face pinched with worry before going slightly slack as she gazed up at me.

"My, you are a big young man."

I pressed my lips together and resisted the urge to cover my middle. There was a lot more muscle packed under the flab these days thanks to rowing, but I was still a big guy. Always had been. So much so that I made people very nervous. While Lucky was even bigger than me, somehow he seemed to have effortless athleticism.

Me? I knocked over coffee, so I looked like I'd pissed myself. Oh, and how could I forget the ointment slathered in my chest hair that made it seem as if I had mange?

Awesome.

I squeezed past Mrs. Gunderson and thanked her again before running out to my truck for the backup shirt I kept in my duffel bag. Along with my big-ass body came a whole lot of sweat. Sometimes I changed shirts before stopping into the café to get another coffee before I went home to do my real job.

The one that half the town wasn't aware of.

I loved working with Gideon's handyman service, but I definitely couldn't live off what he paid me. Being my best friend came with perks for him. I took as little as possible to keep him from feeling like he was taking advantage. Most of the time I poured the money back into supplies for him or tools to use.

Working on the crew of Gideon Gets it Done required a whole lot of hardware. And a truck.

Being a game designer, not so much. I had a sweet, high end system, blazing fast internet, and lots of time spent alone in the middle of the night in the cabin I'd helped build in the forest behind Crescent Lake.

But I liked working with Gideon. It kept me from turning into a hermit. College and the master's programs I'd flown through had taken me well and truly down that path. I'd always been painfully shy. Being the youngest boy of the five Masterson kids didn't help. I'd always been the brainy one, not the athletic one. I looked like I belonged on the football field, but I'd gotten a second helping of clumsy while my brothers took all my share of grace.

It only really mattered during Sunday dinners and in the old days, I'd been more than happy to help my mom in the kitchen while my brothers beat the crap out of each other in the backyard.

"You coming back to work or what?"

I slammed the door of my truck, tucking in my T-shirt as I strode back to the work site. The shirt was too tight, making me feel almost as exposed as earlier.

"Look at Moose with his wares on display. Trying to one up me, man?" Lucky grinned. His shirt had already gone missing with the noontime sun. He flexed his pecs and I widened my eyes. "Not for you, though you sure are cute." He winked and gestured behind me. "That was for Judy."

"Don't distract me while I'm bringing out lemonade, you rascal."

I raked my fingers through my hair, embarrassment heating my face.

"He's so cute." Lucky whomped me on the back, pushing me two steps forward. The guy was a freaking beast. "Judy, my love. I just love your lemonade."

I rolled my eyes and checked my phone at the light buzz against my thigh that signaled my usual email notification. She couldn't have replied that fast.

Sure enough, it was just a gamer newsletter. I pushed my phone back into my pocket and crossed over to help Gideon with the greenhouse windows we were installing.

Three hours later, I was still checking every notification.

Gideon was starting to give me a damn side-eye about it. I wasn't the kind of guy who was always on his phone. Then again, it wasn't every day that the girl of my dreams posted in the community group that she was looking for a baby daddy. Oh, and that she was up for the fun part of the equation as well.

Nope.

Just a regular day on the job.

"Dammit," I muttered as a screw grazed my knuckle.

"You going to join the party today, Murph? Or just daydream?"

"Sorry."

"The Vee thing, huh?"

"Christ, you know about it too?"

"Who doesn't? If I didn't hear it from Judy, I'd have heard it from Charlie and Frankie. They're worse than a horde of women when it comes to gossip."

That was true. I shook off the sting from the knuckle buster and hefted up another beam for Gideon to screw into place. "I was just surprised."

"Thinking of throwing your hat in the ring? Frankie is trying to get up the guts."

"It's not a fucking game."

He used a level then stood back to wipe sweat off his face. "Or is that why you keep checking your phone every five seconds? Did you already send her a message?"

My molars clicked shut before I could say something I'd regret.

Like the truth.

Gideon's eyebrows shot up. "I know you have a thing for her. Better get in there before someone else does."

TWO

ColtsFan69: *You're a little hottie. You sure you want a baby and not just a good hard fuck? I can give you both, but why don't we start with the second and worry about the first later? Or never? Haha.*

    HungHorse: *I'm good to the last drop too, pretty lady. Just call big John and he'll give you what you need.*

    Harley4U: *Heya, I'm that baby daddy you wanted, hun. All my swimmers are great at finding the target. Ya need proof? I've got seven kids already, all strapping sons. I breed true.*

ALL MY LIFE, I'D BELIEVED MY SWEET, BUCOLIC HOMETOWN OF Crescent Cove, New York only contained honest, hardworking, salt of the earth types like my family and friends. Some were of the slightly wackier persuasion—like my mom, and even me to a point— but all in all, the townsfolk were decent people.

But I'd missed one salient point. Among all these wonderful, homespun citizens lived a secret group of frigging horndog *freaks.*

And thanks to my misplaced post, I'd seemingly drawn them all out into the open.

At least into my inbox. Which I would need to bleach. Along with my eyes, brain, and psyche.

I had too many messages to even count them all. Before I'd posted, my inbox had contained five newsletters from different shops and places I frequented, along with a few emails from friends I still had to answer. I'd had no unread messages.

Now? The tiny number 118 blinked at me. How was that even possible? Crescent Cove wasn't even that big of a town, and surely not everyone wanted to throw their, um, hat into the ring.

And it had only been three hours since I'd posted. Barely even that. What would be the status of my inbox by tonight?

That wasn't even saying anything about my voicemails. And my Facebook messenger. And even my Facebook wall. Comments were coming in everywhere people could reach me.

Including through the front door of Brewed Awakening. You know, my job. For pity's sake, didn't people have a clue what was appropriate to discuss at work?

And yes, I'd gone down Inappropriate Lane with my accidental post—I'd meant to post on the CNY Singles' group Facebook page—but still, a person's workplace should be off-limits, right?

Not according to most of the customers who strolled up to the counter at the coffee shop today. Which of course I had to be working behind, since one of the other baristas had called off due to "bacterial some shit".

I swear, the world was out to embarrass me as much as possible. As if I wasn't already humiliated enough by my mistake.

"Victoria, surely a pretty girl like you can find a man the old-fashioned way. Why, when I was your age, my perky bosoms alone had me drawing in a long list of suitors."

I kept my head down as I filled Mrs. Conroy's order. She was one of the town's biggest busybodies, and between her and Mrs. Gunderson, they kept the gossip lines flowing.

"It's Veronica, Mrs. Conroy. Here's your lemon-raspberry petit fours and one cherry lips blow pop." I said the last part louder than necessary, pleased when she flushed from the starched collar of her blouse up to her hairline.

"Thank you, dear. But really, what were you thinking? You have to know no respectable man will want you after they hear you've had to...advertise." Mrs. Conroy made a *tsk-tsk* noise that caused heat to climb up the back of my neck. I was about to duck my head again when I threw back my shoulders.

I wasn't anyone's shrinking violet. So what if I wanted a baby and didn't want to wait forever for Mr. Right Now to storm into my world? Was that a crime?

No, it certainly was not. So, I was taking charge. Controlling my destiny. Asking for batter to make my own cake.

It was what I did. What I was good at. And I wasn't going to pretend to be contrite about it either. More people knew about my plans than I'd originally wanted, but that was okay. It must've been meant to occur this way, or it wouldn't have happened. One of Andrea Marie Fortuna Dixon's—also known as my mother's—life mantras must've rubbed off, because I believed in fate. This was destiny, my post going awry. My semen slinger was out there, just waiting, and I was going to bag him and bring him home.

Or to the Hummingbird's Nest for a night of classy sex. Whatever.

"I didn't advertise for a hookup, Mrs. Conroy. I placed an ad because I want a baby." Unfortunately, my voice carried more than I'd intended, and a couple of the guys in line behind Mrs. Conroy snickered. They were college students from the looks of things.

At least maybe *they* didn't know about my post. A girl could hope.

Mrs. Conroy shook her head and toddled off, allowing the college guys to step forward. "Tall Americano," the blond one in front said. "And my man Josh here wants me to tell you he hasn't tried to make a baby yet, but if you're asking, he's picking up the phone." Much laughter and shoving.

I ignored their antics and glanced at the dark-haired guy that must be Josh. "You want a coffee?"

He shook his head, his eyes huge and his cheeks reddening by the minute.

Inhaling a deep breath, I turned to make the Americano. It was like second nature at this point, thank God. If I'd had to do anything that required serious thought, I'd be screwed.

The next hour was more of the same. A few concerned citizens, a few jokes, a few insults. The line stretched out the door, and it wasn't just because Brewed Awakening had already built quite the reputation in town as being the place to go for funky coffee drinks and fun bakery products along with a cool atmosphere.

Now what was the big draw? Facebook's baby mama-to-be was in residence. I was practically a sideshow attraction.

Step right up, boys and girls, and take a good look at the exhibit!

As if that wasn't enough, my freaking phone kept vibrating against my ass where I'd stashed it in my back pocket. I was scared to check it. Instead of feeling excitement that maybe I'd find the man I was searching for, all I could think about was what indignity might be waiting for me now.

When the foot traffic slowed and I finally got a second to breathe, I stepped away from the counter and tipped back my head. Holy shit. Was this what my life was going to be like now?

"Ready for a break?"

The question from Macy, my boss and close friend, made my shoulders drop. I opened my eyes and sighed at her crossed arms and flattened expression. "You know."

Nodding at the swinging passthrough door that led into the reading nook, she motioned at a couple of the other workers to man the counter while we escaped. On the way, she snagged a couple bottled smoothies prepared and waiting for the afternoon yoga crowd. I took the one she offered gratefully and took a long swig.

Macy's smoothies contained a shot of espresso. They were healthy and also had a glorious caffeine kick.

Now if only mine could've also had a belt of scotch...

"All right, tell me what this hot mess express is all about." She held up a finger. "Since your indoor voice has been missing today, keep it down. Remember that we're trying to put out the fire, not burn through the pants of every horny dude in this joint."

It made me laugh when I would've said nothing could. "I'm the biggest butt of a joke that's ever lived."

"You think so? Did you miss all the longing glances from some of the most eligible men Crescent Cove has to offer? Some a little too longing for an upstanding place of business." Macy sniffed and I laughed again, reaching out to grip her hand.

"Thanks for being so cool about all this. I know it's not good having all this happen at work."

"Are you kidding me? Receipts have been up twenty percent."

I winced. "Yay. So has my humiliation level."

"Okay, so spill. What happened?"

I ran it through for her, using my indoor voice as requested. As I told the story, I ignored the occasional calls of "Yo, Vee!" or "Hey there, Veronica," from passing customers. Some I knew, some I didn't. Either way, I wasn't in the mood to be their entertainment for the afternoon.

"Okay, so you didn't mean to post it there. Where exactly did you mean to post it? And girl, did you really think this through?"

"I did think it through. I meant to post it in the CNY Singles group. I've seen some kind of similar requests..." I trailed off and set aside my half empty smoothie cup so I could bury my face in my hands. "Okay, not exactly like this, but God, Mace, you know the dating thing is such a meat market and eggs have a time limit. If I'm not fertile from the get-go, it might take awhile and—" I looked up, aghast. "And no guy is going to want to keep trying, will he? I'm such a fool."

Macy snapped her fingers and my eyes went wide. "Simmer

down. You're heading for a shame spiral, and the only ones who benefit from that are the home shopping networks and Ben & Jerry's."

"I never thought of the whole process of it. It's not super quick for most people. God, what have I done? If I delete it now, it doesn't matter. The internet is forever."

"Do you want to meet someone and try to have a baby?"

It was easy enough to answer the question when she broke it down like that. "Yes. Deep down, I do. It'd be nice if I liked the guy. Not lifetime love, just someone I could be friends with around the getting naked part." I reached for my smoothie again to wet my throat. "And maybe if it takes a little while to make it happen, he'll be okay with that. If it takes longer than he's willing to wait, well, then I'll meet someone else."

"Yes, you will. Because God knows why you want a baby with all of them crawling out of the woodwork around here—" She broke off and frowned at me. "You drank the Crescent Cove water, didn't you? I warned you."

I laughed and leaned back in the overstuffed loveseat. Macy had the comfiest furniture in her reading area. "Maybe a little. There are an awful lot of cute babies around here nowadays. And look at Rylee, just about to pop and so damn cute with it."

"Cute? She's crying hourly about ankle swelling and being too big to get off the couch."

"She just glows. And you know her baby is going to be gorgeous, what with all her and Gage's genes swimming around in there." I let out a long wistful sigh as I pictured Macy's bestie and Crescent Cove's most recent pregnant chick.

Until I got knocked up. See, I could engage in positive thinking.

"I suppose so. But it'll still be a baby. And you're responsible for them for eighteen years. More if they won't move out of your basement." Macy shuddered and tapped the side of her smoothie. "No Crescent Cove water for me, thanks."

"I get that, but I've always wanted one. Maybe two. A nice set."

"Gee, let me guess, a boy and girl?"

Macy's snark didn't bother me. I knew under it was love. And probably more snark. Like a nice sarcasm sandwich. "No, I'm not set on any particular sex. Just healthy."

"I wish I had a brother or cousin I could have help you out. Would be easier. And I suppose I wouldn't mind having you related and all. Or your brood related, which is close enough."

My eyebrows lifted. "Macy Devereaux, that almost sounds like sweet talk coming from you."

"Don't get used to it. All those dollar signs floating past my ledger today must've put me in an uncharacteristically good mood." She grinned and glanced over her shoulder. "And lookee there, the line is back out the door after a brief afternoon lull. Saddle up, cowgirl. Your latest gang of possible yogurt shooters has arrived."

I had to laugh as I straightened my crown—metaphorical as it was —and went back with her behind the counter.

I wanted to find a guy who would make a good baby daddy. This was what I wanted. Maybe not in this particular manner, but if all the extra attention sent Mr. Loaded Gun my way, well, then how could I complain? Had to put up with a little rain to get my rainbow, right?

As the afternoon wore on, I filled drink orders and boxed pastries to go, all the while keeping my smile firmly in place. The line of customers never seemed to waver, and a lot of the jokes were at my expense. But a lot of folks also asked kind, considerate questions and offered support. And Macy had my back, even if it was because her cash register had been going *ca-ching* all day long.

Everything was going to be okay.

In the midst of the hullabaloo, I thought I glimpsed a familiar face near the back of the line. He was easy enough to spot. Murphy Masterson stood head and shoulders above a lot of the people of Crescent Cove. He definitely towered over me. It wasn't just that. Murphy was sizable. A big, broad guy with plenty of muscles yet a shy nature that didn't seem to fit his brawny physique.

At least I liked to think he was shy. Maybe he wasn't that at all. Perhaps he just didn't have anything to say to me. After all, he was a serious, thoughtful man. I was like a donut with extra sprinkles. Fun, brightly colored, a sugar rush in a small package. What would a dude like Murphy see in me? But I liked talking to him just the same—or trying to, because he didn't always talk back—despite our differences. He was a bright spot in my day.

Oh, God, had he heard about the post too? Of course he had. Who hadn't?

And I was not going to stress. Nope. Not this girl.

Deliberately keeping my head averted from the endless line, I boxed up a four pack of back to school cupcakes. These were special, made for the college crowd. On one there was a little sugar Budweiser can situated on red, white, and blue frosting, on another there was a sugar iPad on sparkly buttercream frosting, and the last two held jumbo sugar cups of espresso on chocolate ganache. Macy let me do whatever crazy ideas sprung into my head.

A beer-themed cupcake? Sure, go for it.

"Here you go, Andrew. Don't study too hard. Or if you do, use these as a reward." I smiled widely at the lanky, bespectacled college junior who didn't speak much but always tipped well. I'd been a horrible student myself and had no desire to go back, but I admired those who committed to their education.

"Thanks, Vee. And um, I hope it's okay if I say any guy who gets to have a baby with you is very lucky." Andrew grabbed his box and fled before I could unstick my tongue from the floor.

By the time I sucked in a breath and chanced another look at the line, he was long gone—and so was Murphy.

Dammit. The bright spot in my day just got covered with a big-ass cloud.

"Hi, Vee. Can we get a couple caramel capps, please? Our usual." Ally Hamilton stepped forward with her sister-in-law Sage at her side.

"Sure thing. How's it going? Where's your cutie babies?"

They exchanged a glance and inwardly, I sighed. Of course the baby-crazy chick asked after their kids. They probably thought I wanted to snatch them at the first opportunity for a long round of snuggles.

They probably weren't wrong. Both Ally and Sage had adorable kids.

"Oh, good. Alex has an ear infection, but it's almost over, thank God."

"Star too. I swear, they get the same things every time. Cousins." Sage smiled and pursed her lips as she eyed the pastry case. "Hmm, should I get one of these eclairs to go? Or better yet, I'll get two eclairs and see if Oliver's been a good boy today."

Ally rolled her eyes. "Is he ever? But yeah, good idea. Seth loves those thumbprint cookies. Can I get a half dozen of those to go, please?"

"Yeah, and three eclairs, please," Sage chimed in. At Ally's look, she shrugged. "Hey, PMS. Which is a good thing these days since it means I'm safe for another month." She kissed her fingers and held them up toward the sky.

Then she started to cough. "Um, from wicked bad cramps. That's what I mean. When I get crazy sugar cravings before, then I usually have milder cramps. Weird, right?" She bit her lip and flashed a *help me* look at her best friend. Ally just sighed.

Right. Because both Ally and Sage had sexy guys—twins no less —who were madly in love with them and had planted babies in them without even being asked. And now Sage was glad not to be knocked up again.

Wicked bad cramps, my keister.

Every little slice of daily life seemed like a personal shot against me and my situation. Which was just silly. They were my friends. Well, kind of. I knew them a little through Rylee, but I wanted to get to know them more.

Not stand here and pout while they looked at each other uncomfortably as the silence between us extended.

"Coming right up," I said brightly, shaking myself out of my stupor.

After I filled their orders, they flashed sympathetic glances at me as they stuffed far more in my tip jar than was necessary.

Number fifty fail-whale moment of the day.

On my next break, I took a chance and looked at the disaster zone that was my inbox. Now up to 202 emails. My box was overflowing, quite literally.

Chewing on the corner of my thumbnail, I scrolled through some one-handed. A bunch went right into the trash. And I do mean right in. Salacious offers were an instant delete, no response necessary. Concerned comments from townsfolk who thought I'd lost my sugar cubes were starred for later replies.

Then I came upon an interesting one indeed.

On the surface, it wasn't that much different than the other worried emails. Just something about it tweaked me in the chest. Dangerously close to my heart.

Vee,

I'm sure you're getting lots of responses to your offer. I wanted to make sure you knew it was posted in the Crescent Cove main group. If it's a mistake, I can help. We can pretend it was just a joke. I'll say I hacked into your account as retribution for you putting peanut butter in my brownies. Peanut butter belongs in many things, but not brownies. Why ruin all that gooey chocolate perfection? But if you were serious, if you meant your request... I guess you can count me in.

SINCERELY, CABIN FORTRESS

THREE

Dear Cabin Fortress:

Your name intrigues me, as does your kind offer. But I was the one who put my post in the wrong group, so I will take the heat. I'm a cuppa half full kind of girl, so maybe it'll widen my net—so to speak—to more prospective baby daddies. Like, say, yourself. Though you said you guess I could count you in. Have you had time to decide if you're still lukewarm about it or have you moved to hot?

YOURS, VEE

I'D ONLY READ HER NOTE ELEVEN TIMES.

Fuck.

I didn't know how to answer her. I'd wanted her to be mine for so damn long even seeing it written to me teasingly had put me in a funk all damn morning. I'd been waiting for an answer for what felt like forever and now I was frozen like a deer on the damn highway. So stupid.

I swiped my forearm across my sweaty brow. Crescent Cove was enjoying an unseasonably warm September. Even the nights were still hot as hell. It was as if August had decided to sit on our little lake town and stay awhile.

And I was dying.

"Moose, are you fading on me?"

"Nah. I'm fine." I took a long swig from my water bottle and wished I hadn't read the forecast before leaving this morning. Then again, I'd been watching my phone like a damn maniac, hoping I'd get a reply from a certain someone. Everything after that had been frying me from the inside out anyway.

Add in the fact that the freaking weatherman lied. It was *not* going to be breezy and cool. And my thermal shirt was not meant for this level of heat.

Everything sucked.

Something soft hit me in the back of the head. "Dude, you're killing me just looking at you."

I turned to find a tank shirt on the grass at my feet. "I'm not wearing your shirt."

Lucky stood with his big-ass booted foot propped up on the stack of lumber we were cutting. He guzzled down a beer, making sure he was giving a maximum show for the young mom inside who had been plastered to the window since we got here. "It's clean. I had it in my bag for the gym later. You need it more than I do. Besides, the ladies don't mind when I strip down for my workouts."

"You strip down to breathe," I muttered and picked up the shirt.

"Was that a crack out of you?" Instead of being insulted, Lucky tipped his head back and howled out a laugh. "Didn't know you had it in you, choir boy."

I sighed and swapped my soaked through shirt for the tank. At least it was black. "Piss off."

"Saucy." Lucky winked at me. "Good for you. And now you don't look like you're going to keel over." He tossed me a beer and I caught it against my chest. At least I hadn't dropped it. "Now if you'd drink that, maybe you'd loosen up a little."

"Leave him alone, Luck."

I didn't need Gideon to handle him. I wasn't a stuck-up type or a choir boy. If he saw the murder and mayhem I designed for games, he'd think twice about the church comments. In fact, I'd just sold my fourth Zombie Chasers game to one of the biggest video game outlets in the country.

And it was twisted as fuck.

Because that was how normal people got their aggressions out. Not by stripping for every woman to stare at them in a five-mile radius. Lucky was barely twenty-four, but he was massive and had enough testosterone for three guys. I might have lost a lot of the computer geek softness of my college and grad school days, but I'd never be the guy taking selfies of their abs.

Ever.

Kind of like Lucky did through his lunch break to get people to hire him as a personal trainer.

If my girl wanted to see me without a shirt in dim light, then well...that would be okay. If I had a girl. Maybe.

Someone like Vee.

I was officially pathetic.

I'd stopped by the café after work yesterday and it had been mobbed. Everyone had been buzzing about Vee and her post on The Cove, our town Facebook group. Wondering what a nice girl like her wanted with a child out of wedlock. Crescent Cove still had a lot of old school people living there.

Others joking about how they'd love to take her up on the offer.

Still others with a far darker level of discussion.

Before I punched someone dead in the face for talking about her like that, I'd had to leave.

And now I had her note burning a hole in my pocket.

I'd had nightmares that she wouldn't reply then there it was. Sweet and cute with a side of flirty. Totally Veronica.

Except it felt even more flirty.

Would she still be that way if she knew it was me?

Lucky came over and snatched the beer. "If you're not going to drink it, I'm taking it back."

"I didn't want it in the first place. It's not even noon."

"Speaking of, it's your day to pick up lunches over at the café." Lucky waggled his eyebrows. "Make sure you let that hot mama barista know you're single and ready to mingle." He cracked open the can and tipped it back. "Nothing better than going bareback in a sweet, willing girl."

I shoved him back a good foot. "Don't fucking talk about her like that."

Lucky flipped his hair back and tucked his can into his pocket. "Well, then. You got the hots for the little baker? She's aching for a baby daddy."

"It's not like that."

He rubbed one of his pecs. "Not what your little shove said. I'll give you a pass because I saw how many bees were swarming around her honey pot."

I curled my fingers into fists.

"Now, now, Moose, I'll give you one pass," he took the beer out of his front pocket, "but only one." He lifted one long finger with a wink, then took a long gulp from the can and finished it before crunching the can and tossing it into our recycle bin. "Man up," he said over his shoulder and sauntered over to the paver cutter, put his glasses on, and flicked the switch on the wet blade.

Christ, the heat must be getting to me.

Or the fact that I had wanted Vee for so long I couldn't even breathe around it. And now the whole damn town was looking at her like she was a big ole ice cream cone and it was ninety-seven-degrees and one hundred percent humidity. Oh, and couldn't forget the talking about her like they were longing for a bite.

I stalked away from the pile of lumber I was supposed to be measuring and pulled out my phone. My fingers flew over the keys before I could stop myself. Anger and frustration leaked into my words, but I was working on too much adrenaline.

And the thought of her messages overflowing with other men.

Men that could replace me so easily.

"Just go over there, for God's sake."

My back straightened at Gideon's voice.

"I don't know what you've been waiting for, but now's definitely not the time to be a pussy."

I swung around to face my oldest friend in town. "Oh, and are you manning up about Macy?"

Gideon stuffed his hands in his front pockets. "Little different there."

"I don't see how."

Gideon rocked back on his heels. "I have a whole different set of problems. You? Not so much. Both of you are unencumbered, both young, and Vee's all about being serious no matter what she says in that ad on The Cove. You? Dude, you were born to be attached to a woman and with a family."

"She wants one part of a man—and not necessarily mine." I rubbed the back of my neck. "She doesn't know I'm alive."

"Because you don't speak."

He wasn't wrong. Every time I tried to open my damn mouth, I went absolutely brain dead. I had three different master's degrees but speaking to this one woman was beyond me.

"Go get our lunches and talk to her." Gideon shook his head when I tried to open my mouth to argue. "Charge it to the company and just go. The natives are getting restless."

I tipped my head back to stare at the cloudless sky. "You suck."

"I'm your fairy fucking godmother. Go get your princess, you idiot. Oh, and ask Macy for a bunch of those caffeine smoothie things she's doing. I'm fucking addicted."

I trudged back to my truck. My pocket exploded with text orders from people on the team. Word got around fast and no one wanted to miss out on café food. Unfortunately, none of the notifications included a reply from Vee.

Our current job was only a few streets over from Main Street, so it was a quick drive. Summer and fall were Gideon's busiest seasons, then it would be me snowed in up at my cabin for most of the winter. I held off on most of my big projects until then.

Like impregnating a particular baker?

Ugh.

I had to park down the damn street because, as usual, Brewed Awakening was hopping. As I passed people enjoying the unusually sunny day, I heard more comments about Vee. Didn't people have other shit to talk about?

Okay, so not everyone was, but it felt like it. And I should have stopped at my damn house to get a real shirt. Lucky was my size, but he liked to wear his shirts a size smaller to show off his freaking body.

I, however, did not.

Maybe I should have put my sweaty thermal back on.

Maybe I should just make a phone order and come in the back entrance? Fuck.

"Murphy."

I turned toward the breathless voice. Only one person called me Murphy. Not even my mama did. My cheeks burned as I looked down at Vee. "Hey, Veronica."

Her eyes drilled into my chest and down to my belt buckle before traveling up to my neck. Instead of looking at my face, she swallowed and took another slow perusal past my buckle this time.

"Wow. I didn't realize all that was under your clothes."

I crossed my arms. Fucking Lucky. Way too damn tight. She was probably horrified. "I had to borrow a shirt." I blew out a breath. "Just a hot day at work. Sorry, I don't usually show off this much of myself."

Her eyes darted to my face finally. "No, you do not."

My gaze drifted to my boots. Stupid. Now I was making it a

thing. And I was officially a loser trying too hard with a tight shirt on a body that definitely should not be accentuated no matter how much rowing I did on the lake.

"Yeah, sorry. I..."

I want to take you to dinner.

I want to impregnate you.

I want to try as many times as possible.

I want you to see me as more than a customer.

I want everything.

"I need to make a lunch order."

"Oh." She tipped her head in that sweet way, where her bottle green eyes sparkled with a touch of some inner joke I was never quite privy to. "Sure, we'll fix you right up. Sorry, I'm not working the counter right now." She lifted the empty dishes in her hand. "We're swamped."

"Right. That's okay. I'll go make an order with Jodi."

"Okay." She paused and her dark lashes fluttered down as she stared at my chest one more time before she bustled away. "Oh, have a good day, Murphy." Her smile was wide and kind.

And I was a chump. "You too."

I fisted my hands at my sides and stalked to the line. I made my order and my gaze kept seeking her out as she wound her way around tables. She talked to everyone with such ease. Except me. When she was near me, she tried to work with my bumbling conversational skills but invariably, she had to give up.

It was always too busy to stay and deal with the social anxiety king of Crescent Cove.

And I wasn't always like this. That's what sucked. My little circle of people, I was fine with. The minute I got within twenty of feet of Vee, I became a freak.

The sharp whistle brought me back into the present.

"Ready to order, hot stuff?" Macy flicked her ponytail behind her shoulder.

I felt the stain on my cheeks again and cursed this damn muscle shirt. I dug out my phone and rattled off the order for me and the rest of the guys. "And put it on Gideon's tab."

"You boys are definitely racking up his tab. Who's drooling over the crew today?" She waggled her eyebrows. "Not like you to show off your guns, Moose."

I rubbed my arm. "Yeah. Hot one today. We're over at the Shannon house."

"More babies. She was in with her son recently." She shook her head. "Ramping up the baby fever that's already raging in here. Next it's going to infect—"

"You?"

"God, no. I was going to say Jodi, but she's still a child. If she gets it too, then I'm moving out into the middle of the freaking lake. Order up," Macy shouted over her shoulder and tucked a paper under the overflowing stack. "You tell Gideon he owes me." She shoved a six-pack of smoothies across the counter.

"Thanks, Macy."

She jerked her head to the side. "Get out of here, Moose."

I gave her a half smile and moved to the next line where we waited for our food. The café was a well-oiled machine, even as busy as it was. But I couldn't concentrate on watching Jodi or one of the three new girls who started working in the café this past week.

No, I couldn't keep my eyes off Vee.

She was laughing her way through a crowd of guys.

My hands fisted again when I heard an off-color comment. Just because she was making it known she wanted to create a child didn't mean she had to listen to that junk.

It wasn't a meat market.

Okay, so maybe she was looking at it like a bit of a market and the meat...

God, now I sounded like the crass idiots cracking jokes at her.

I dug out my phone and still no reply.

Then again, she didn't really have time to answer a message with this place bursting with people. Then she stopped and took her phone out of her hip pocket. Her eyebrows climbed up and she quickly shoved it back away.

Did she see my note?

Did she hate it?

Was she going to push it into her spam box like more than eighty percent of her emails and messages? Because that wouldn't shock me.

Tons of perverts and busybodies had replied to her on the public post, so I couldn't imagine what was said in the privacy of an email or message. And yet at the same time, I didn't give a crap what anyone else said to her.

I just wanted her to notice me.

And that was as pathetic as me staring at my damn boots instead of talking to her.

My name was called at the end of the counter and I grabbed the huge box full of food and drinks. I needed to escape before I saw her again. She was so beautiful with that golden halo of braids on top of her head with little licks of purple peeking through. Her style made her different from any other woman in the room.

But I had her memorized. I didn't need to stare her down again. She didn't need another set of eyes following her every move along with the rest of the town.

I shouldered my way out the door and stalked down the sidewalk to my truck. People avoided me on the street and the usual smiles came with wide eyes as they hurried by me.

She was driving me nuts, and it must be starting to show.

I tucked the box of food on the front seat of my truck and pulled my phone out. Still no answer.

Before I could stop myself, I sent off one more message. I got in and headed back to the job I knew and loved almost as much as my own business. To where numbers and measurements made sense and spring green eyes didn't confuse the hell out of me.

FOUR

Vee,

I'm guessing there are a lot of people vying for your attention at the moment. I'll be brief and to the point. Be careful. I hate the comments I hear while I'm in town. If you were mine, I'd never treat you that way. What you're doing for yourself is beautiful and any baby would be lucky to have you as their mother with or without your male counterpart. I'm more than interested if you're still looking.

YOURS IF YOU'LL HAVE ME, CABIN FORTRESS

THE INSANITY CAUSED BY MY NEED FOR A DOLLOP OF SPERM IN my egg casserole was supposed to die down. I'd figured a day or two, maybe three tops.

It was day four. No stopping yet.

My inbox was still a disaster. I was tempted to ask Jodi or one of the younger café ladies with time on her hands and a sense of humor to do some screening of my messages. I didn't want to overlook my possible soul mate—I mean, sperm mate—but jeez. A girl had to work for a living and couldn't weed through salacious emails day and night.

The bright side was that Macy was making tons of cash. The café had even gotten a feature on the local nightly news last night, and though nothing had been specifically mentioned about my procreation practices, the female anchor had been a little too chatty when it came to "Macy's newsworthy employees."

My boss had taken me aside afterward to make sure I understood we were still cool, and she wasn't pissed about the recent spotlight on her business. She was still counting those dolla-dolla bills, and hey, if I happened to find a worthwhile sperm candidate, yay me.

I was so grateful to her for dealing with this lapse of judgment, as some in the community had called my post. And not only that, for making the most of an, uh, sticky situation.

Tilting my head, I squeezed more frosting on top of the baby head cookies I'd just baked. I'd let them cool and now it was time to add the little curls of frosting hair on each one. The girls had rainbow squiggles and the boys did too, shaped into a mohawk. No traditional pink and blue here. We were an all-inclusive café. To that end, I'd also made a gender-neutral baby cookie. No identifying characteristics at all on that one except ruddy cheeks and bright brown eyes.

I had another tray of cooling cookies on the rack. Those were shaped like children's toys. A wagon, a ball, a kind of creepy doll-looking thing that I'd shaped myself and wouldn't be making again.

At least they'd taste delicious.

Speaking of tasting, I was tasting the flavor of bitter defeat at missing Murphy the last few days.

Not that I was looking for him, exactly. That would be foolish. I had an inbox full of prospects, not to mention my voicemails and in-person offers. I'd probably need an agent soon. Wonder where I'd find one willing to help me on my quest?

Woman of reproductive age seeking representation in screening candidates with ready sperm. Personal traits of sperm-owner negotiable. Willingness to try a few new positions while making transfer a bonus.

I let out a giggle. Yeah, probably wouldn't be finding too many takers for that role anytime soon.

"Seeing a beautiful lady laughing definitely makes my day that much better."

For a second, irrational hope bloomed in my chest that maybe Murphy had changed his voice and his personality and had decided to speak freely for a change.

Not that we never talked. We did. Just not much and not often.

I wasn't sure why I was so determined to hear him string more than a few sentences together in my direction. Maybe it was because I could tell he was the kind of man who read books and thought important things and would never make fun of me for wanting to have a baby on my own.

He'd think my method of trying to find a guy was ridiculous, of course. Because he was classier than that, and maybe a little old-fashioned to boot. He would never have to worry about such a thing even if he had a mind to procreate, since I always caught chicks checking him out when he was busy poring over the muffin selection or probably reading about some vitally crucial trade deal on his phone.

But it wasn't Murphy speaking to me. It was Lucky from Gideon's construction team, and though I'd seen him come in with Murphy a few times, I didn't know if they were friends. Murphy was a solitary sort. I didn't know why that appealed to me too.

He didn't check any of my usual boxes, yet he intrigued me more than anyone had in a very long time.

And Lucky was waiting for a reply.

"Thanks. I'm not beautiful—" I didn't get the sentence out before he leaned forward and placed his finger over my mouth.

"Don't argue with me, beautiful. Now what kind of delectable treats are you making in your secret oven?" Lucky grinned, and I wondered if I'd ever heard anyone use an appliance as a sexual euphemism before. But I was pretty sure he was.

The bell dinged over the door and my gaze cut that way, probably because I was seeking escape. I liked Lucky. He seemed nice enough, if a little cocky. He was good looking, and he knew it, which unfortunately lessened his appeal.

And none of that really mattered right now. Murphy stepped through the door, his eyes narrowing on me and Lucky. He'd focused right in on us as if his vision was a laser and we were his target.

"Vee?" Lucky prompted, glancing over his shoulder toward the door. Then his smile widened. "Should've known. I'll just leave the lovebirds alone." He held up his hands palms out while I frowned at him. "Can't blame a guy for trying, especially when the writing is on the wall." His grin flashed and my frown grew.

Was he the guy I'd been talking to online? Well, the one I'd paid the most attention to. It wasn't as if Cabin Fortress was the only man who'd sent a nice note. There had a been a few. Unfortunately, there were far more of the dirty kind—and not even creatively dirty. Just garden variety unfunny crudeness, mixed with a couple of dick pics.

Even those hadn't been worth my time. I wasn't into looking at penises as a rule, except on the occasional night when my rich fantasy life didn't get the, ah, job done. Still, the ones that had landed in my in-bin had been more snort-worthy than arousing.

"Writing on the wall? What writing is that?"

C'mon, give me another hint it's you I've been talking to.

Though strangely, disappointment churned low in my belly at the possibility. Lucky was a fun guy. Even hot. But he wasn't—

The café door opened again, and I forgot what I'd asked as a familiar blond walked in. I started to smile at Sage until she let out an inhuman squeal and threw herself at Murphy.

I expected him to gently set her back. Murphy didn't do public displays of affection like that, or at least I assumed he didn't. Instead, he picked her up straight off her feet, wrapping her in a giant bear hug that made me curl my toes into my ballerina flats and my hands into fists.

Since I was still gripping my frosting tube in one hand, that was not good.

A stream of baby pink frosting shot out of the tip and made a beeline right for Lucky's deep green shirt.

"Fuck, I'm sorry," I gasped, making a couple of the town biddies look up in shock and irritation from where their book club was discussing their latest choice in the reading nook.

If it was Christian Grey-related as I thought I'd heard as I was refilling their drink orders, they shouldn't have been so dismayed by the word *fuck*.

"Easy there," Lucky said as I grabbed his shirt and attacked the splatter of frosting with a napkin. A dry one. "Think you're gonna rub a hole right through to my six-pack, beautiful."

I kept rubbing, though I paused long enough to turn to the sink for some water before I resumed my fruitless efforts. Now he had a giant wet spot too.

And Murphy was still embracing Sage, who was pressing her hands against his chest and smiling up at him with rapt attention while he spoke.

Unless he was offering her the best deal ever on a new addition for her house—not that she needed a good deal, she'd married a dude made of freaking money—I was probably going to burst a blood vessel.

But since I didn't know what he was offering her, I just kept rubbing Lucky's shirt. Hard enough to rip my napkin and not help the spot at all.

"Hey there, it'll need some kind of cleanser to remove it." Lucky sighed when I didn't pause. "Yeah, okay, you do what makes you happy."

"Vee, I need a coffee and to get back to work," Mrs. Buck said from behind Lucky in line.

"Looks like she's trying to set up that babymaking right here," someone else muttered.

I ignored them all. My attention was focused on destroying the fibers of Lucky's shirt while I watched Sage and Murphy chat like best friends out of the corner of my eye.

Now she was showing him baby pictures, unfolding a long string of them contained in plastic that resembled a fold-out credit card holder. He was smiling and pointing to different ones, listening intently as she rambled on.

I'd always liked Sage. A lot, in fact. Sure, I was a wee bit envious that her big problem in life now was having so much sex with her gorgeous husband that she had to continuously worry about having an unplanned baby, but them's were the breaks. She was a great woman and I was happy for her that she'd found love.

What I wasn't happy about was that she'd also discovered extreme buddydom with Murphy. Mainly because watching the two of them chatting felt as if Sage had been granted the keys to a city I had barely even located on the map, never mind explored.

God, why was I so...well, obsessed with Murphy now? I'd always thought he was a sweet guy, but this was bordering on foolish.

And I was about to tear a hole in Lucky's shirt with my incessant scrubbing with my holey napkin and like three drops of water.

Dear God.

I jumped back and shook my head. Lucky's green shirt now had a huge blot of water on it and little brown pieces of napkin had stuck to the material. "Dammit, I'm so sorry."

"No harm, no foul, beautiful. Wonder what they're talking about, huh?" Lucky leaned on the counter, clearly unconcerned that he looked like he'd just spilled a drink on himself. "My guess is it's about that baby of hers. This town is all about babies. Why do you think that is?"

"Wrong person to ask, Luckmeister." I smiled tightly and tossed the wadded-up napkin into the trash. "Did you forget I'm the town's poster child for wanting a baby? And without a man, no less." I pretended to smack my cheeks. "How dare I?"

Lucky barely blinked. "Well, can't say it's without a man, now can you?" His smile was slow and did not elicit the butterflies in me he was probably hoping for. "I wouldn't be opposed to—"

"Hey there, Vee." Sage popped up beside Lucky at the counter and clasped her hands over her heart. "So sorry to cut the line, but Moose and I are parched, and this guy seems to be hogging all your attention." Sage elbowed Lucky hard enough to make him grunt. And move aside. "Just a couple of tall coffees, pretty please?"

I sent Sage a grateful glance for interrupting whatever Lucky had been about to say, then I made the mistake of looking at Murphy. He was staring at the back of Sage's head as if her bouncy blond curls held the answer to world peace.

"We're out of coffee." I smiled at Sage. When her perfectly cheerful face fell, I let out a forced laugh. "Just kidding. Anything for you and Moose," I enunciated carefully.

Finally, he looked up and met my gaze. For a second, just one, his perceptive hazel eyes burned into mine, and my heartbeat raced. His lips parted, and I swore he was about to say something profound. Like...

I don't care about Sage's baby. I want to make a baby with you. Let's start right here. Right now. Who needs a bearskin rug when there's a rug shaped like a pair of eyeglasses in front of the fireplace in the reading nook?

Instead, he let out a dry cough. "Thank you, Veronica."

Blah. So much for significance.

"No problem," I said brightly, turning to fix their coffees the way I knew they liked them. "I live to serve."

"If so, why don't you serve some of us back here?" Mrs. Buck called out. "Tired of the favoritism, just because he's the size of a redwood tree. They both are. Pushy males."

I looked over my shoulder at Lucky, who wore a shit-eating grin and had tucked his thumbs in the front pockets of his jeans. He was now chatting with Sage, who'd again whipped out her baby pictures. Behind them, Murphy was flushed right up to his eyebrows.

He was so cute. Mrs. Buck? Not so much.

"Pipe down back there, or we might run out of coffee," I called, tacking on a little laugh to show them I was joking.

I was not. There was no call for making comments about Murphy. His redwood size had given me more than a few aroused moments, thank you very much.

Macy swung out of the back with Jodi and cocked a brow at me as she noticed the line. She'd also probably heard my not-so-funny comment. "You doing okay out here?"

"Sure thing. Afternoon lull." I finished making Murphy's and Sage's coffees and slid them across the counter to them.

I needed to make up for my jealous thoughts. I was not that girl. It wasn't Murphy's fault I wanted to scale his bark like a hungry lizard. Nor was it Sage's fault she was naturally friendly and had a gorgeous baby girl and a husband with such an obviously gifted sperm delivery system that she was constantly worried about eluding it.

It was time I settled my karmic debt by doing a good deed.

"On the house," I added.

Macy groaned behind me. "Why, is she pregnant too? Isn't there a waiting period for this crap? At least get one off the teat before you shoot out the next." Macy spoke low enough that only I could hear, then she put on an apron and moved to the counter. Her expression resembled that of a warrior entering battle as she faced the restless coffee-seeking heathens. "Who's next?"

I turned away from the counter and flicked off my apron before grabbing my phone and heading into the break room.

Maybe I'd never have a chance with Murphy, but I had my online mystery man to keep me entertained if nothing else.

If he ended up knocking me up, bully for me.

I didn't need a real relationship or love or a man in my life longer than the hour it took me to mount him—assuming I was blessed enough to manage to get lucky on the first round.

But not *with* Lucky.

I shuddered and opened my inbox. *Please don't let him be my mystery man.*

Though if it was him, he was far sweeter online than he seemed in person. It couldn't be him, not with Cabin Fortress's manners. He had an almost old-fashioned nature mixed with a healthy dose of seductiveness at unexpected times.

I opened Cabin Fortress's latest email and grinned. Nope. This wasn't Lucky.

I was almost possibly maybe sure of it.

FIVE

Cabin Fortress,

I have questions. You said you're interested but I'd like to clarify what lies behind your manners, if I may. Do you mean you'd like to go on a date before we get down to business? Some friendly conversation, some dinner, maybe some dancing first? Or would you prefer right into the sweaty sheets without anything else? I'm fine with either, but I'm curious about your preferences. Hope we talk soon.

VEE

I PACED THE LENGTH OF MY LIVING ROOM, MY TRIPLE SCREEN workstation taunting me from the far side of the room. Moonlight spilled through the wall of windows and the view that usually calmed me left me itchy in my own damn skin.

I'd been staring at the same reply for hours now. On my phone, then on my television-sized monitor that I should be working on. I had my preliminary notes back from Nelson, my contact at GameSoft. Only I couldn't concentrate on the thousands of lines of code.

Nope, it was the seven sentences that had my brain reeling and my body way overheated. Then again it was still fucking hot as hades at eleven in the evening. The vaulted ceilings of my A-frame cabin usually kept things pretty cool. Add in the lazy fans buzzing above me and things should have been copacetic in my life.

Again, that was a big ole nope.

I crossed to my wine fridge and unearthed a Malbec. I needed to chill the fuck out.

This woman was making me nuts and she didn't have a damn clue I existed.

Story of my life.

The slightly flirty tone under a veneer of politeness told me she thought it was a stranger. And okay, so we were near strangers. A few mumbled words between coffee and food orders did not make a friendship.

Because I was a moron and couldn't get up the nerve to actually speak to her.

Where the hell was my electric corkscrew?

"Christ," I muttered as I dug through my drawers. My older brothers had been here for the first football games of the season. The wall projector was too much of a draw when they wanted to go over each and every play with the newest coach for the Giants.

Me? I didn't give a crap. I enjoyed football enough to let my idiot brothers come over, but I'd rather watch a movie all things considered.

But as usual, they'd ransacked my kitchen. And my wine bar since they'd finished off the beer. And I hadn't replenished. At least they'd left me one bottle.

I found my manual corkscrew and frustration notched up with each twist. Too much frustration evidently, since I shredded the cork into the wine.

I poured half the bottle into a wine glass and picked out the shrapnel of cork. I didn't even let it breathe. All the things I'd been taught when I toured the Andreas winery a few months ago went right out the window. But damn if they didn't make a helluva wine.

With two long pulls, the warmth curled up from my empty belly and splashed through my veins. I pressed my hand to the window and tried to center myself with my favorite view. Moonlight shimmering off the lake was exactly why I'd built my house here.

The half-empty glass hung from my fingers as I cooled my forehead on the glass. The alcohol was definitely doing its job. Enough that maybe, just maybe, I could figure out a way to write back to Veronica.

Everyone called her Vee, but to me she fit her full name. Just as she was the only person on this earth who had used my given name since my school days.

But right now, she didn't know the man behind the messages was Murphy Masterson.

I was as nameless and solitary as the handle I'd used for my email.

What I'd named my company.

I didn't hide my name, but I certainly didn't advertise that I was behind the LLC. It was just easier in the gaming world to have a few layers with so much theft of code and dark web sales. I could protect myself well enough without going to felonious levels like some of my compatriots.

I padded on bare feet to the bottle of wine and refilled my glass before heading to my workstation. I set the glass down between my ergonomic split keyboard. There had been some nights when I'd put a thirty-ounce cold brew coffee right there to get work done. To talk to Veronica, I might need the same size wine glass.

"Liquid courage, don't steer me wrong."

I opened my browser and found her email again.

Normally, I used an email program, but I didn't want anything tracking back to me right now. I tapped my lip with my wine glass as I read her letter one more time.

Did I want to keep my manners?

Did I want to slide into that flirty banter she was looking for?

That I saw her use with Lucky today. Well, maybe. I wasn't really sure if she'd flirted with him. But they'd been chatting, and he'd definitely been in *his* flirt mode.

My fingers tightened on the fragile stem of my glass. No, I couldn't go there.

Not tonight. I'd do something I regretted.

I set my glass down. Like follow the rabbit hole of that green light next to her name that meant she was online right now.

That kind of regret.

My finger hovered over my track pad. Who needed to formulate a reply when there was a chat window available as part of this email client?

And she was right there.

CABIN FORTRESS:

Is it too forward to break into your evening with a chat window? Or would you prefer the man with manners?

My cursor slowly blinked at me without a response.

I sat back in my chair, resting my glass on my stomach as I stared a hole into the middle screen of my trio of screens. A line of code was still working on the left screen and the right was a series of different projects I was monitoring.

The center was all for her.

If she'd speak to me.

GOODTOTHELASTDROP:

If that's your segue into a dick pic, pass. I can assure you it doesn't "put me in the mood" for anything but homicide.

I laughed and sat forward to set my wine on my desk. God, this woman.

CABIN FORTRESS:

I'd never be so crass. That's at least fourth chat behavior.

GOODTOTHELASTDROP:

So you're not a 72-year-old? I wasn't sure with the super sweetness of your emails.

Sweet Jesus. No wonder it took a few emails to get her talk to me. She probably thought I was an old man looking to pat her on her head.

My thoughts were far more carnal than that.

CABIN FORTRESS:

Definitely not. I'm the youngest male in my family. Just turned thirty to be exact. My mama taught me to treat ladies with respect.

GOODTOTHELASTDROP:

I appreciate it. Manners are hard to come by these days. What are you doing up so late?

CABIN FORTRESS:

This is my usual time to work. It's quiet. Just me and the night sounds. Unless I turn on the sound system. Nice thing about no neighbors. I can do what I want.

GOODTOTHELASTDROP:

None? Just what kind of fortress are we talking about, buddy? Do you have an unusual number of shovels and tarps in your shed? Stones making little markers?

CABIN FORTRESS:

Let me guess? MFM fan? True Crime?

GOODTOTHELASTDROP:

Are you a Murderino?

CABIN FORTRESS:

God, no. I live in the freaking woods. I don't
need that kind of stuff in my head! Don't
worry, I'm no Ted Bundy.

GOODTOTHELASTDROP:

There's many other kinds of serial killers.
Just like sprinkles and ice cream flavors—
lots of different combinations. People
thought Ted Bundy was super nice,
remember? And hot. Do you fall in any of
those categories? Not that it's a deal
breaker. Well, except for the serial killer
thing. That's definitely a no-fly zone for me.
Not that you'd probably tell me. Haha.

I sat back in my chair. I didn't know how to answer that. Of the
Masterson boys, I definitely wasn't top of the pile. My brothers, Penn
and Christian, were the ones who attracted all the attention from the
female contingency. From football quarterback to second in
command in our sheriff's department, Christian had literally been the
golden boy since he was born.

Penn, who split from Crescent Cove as soon as was humanly
possible, was the dark horse of the family. A graphic novelist, he split
his time in New York City and Los Angeles. But he came in to see
our mom once every other month. Every time he did, the town went a
little crazy in reaction. He was rich, worked with Hollyweird, and
looked like he should be a leading man in the stories he wrote.

Yeah, I couldn't compete with them.

But I did have the guy-next-door look she seemed to prefer, at
least based on her post. Chris Pratt and I could be brothers. He was a
bit more jacked than me thanks to his action star status.

I smoothed my hand down my torso. The rowing kept the cookies
from showing too much though. I did love Vee's cookies.

GOODTOTHELASTDROP:

Still there? Did I scare you away with the
serial killer talk?

CABIN FORTRESS:

No. You didn't scare me away. I just wasn't sure how to reply. I'm okay looking, but no leading man if that's what you mean.

GOODTOTHELASTDROP:

That doesn't matter to me. Kind eyes and manners are way more interesting than a guy prettier than me.

CABIN FORTRESS:

You say that now, but what happens if I look like a guy who escaped from the Alaskan tundra?

GOODTOTHELASTDROP:

A good razor and a shower will fix most anything.

CABIN FORTRESS:

Not into the mountain man look? I thought everyone enjoyed Aquaman.

GOODTOTHELASTDROP:

Haha. Well, if a woman is breathing, they usually enjoy Jason Momoa. I'm not going to say I'd have a hard time if you look like him, but I wouldn't want a man to only be interested in me for my looks.

CABIN FORTRESS:

All women are beautiful.

GOODTOTHELASTDROP:

Now that's a line. Besides, you already know who I am. Do we know each other? Why the secrecy?

My fingers paused on my keys. We knew each other by name, but we didn't know anything beyond that. I wouldn't lie, but would she still be interested if she knew it was me? Painfully shy Moose Masterson? Not that she called me Moose.

Her soft voice dripped with a touch of honey when she said my real name. Same as I used her full name.

There was something sweet and sexy about the full version. I didn't want to be like all the rest who used her initial.

I didn't want to be one of the pack in any way.

CABIN FORTRESS:

I only know you as much as the next guy who goes to the café. That's simply the entire town at this point.

GOODTOTHELASTDROP:

All right. So, I've served you? And not in the biblical way. At least not yet.

Good God. She was going to kill me. Because now all I could think about was her serving me. Servicing me. And that was a black hole I couldn't get into. Not with this much wine in me.

Speaking of wine. I lifted my glass and finished it off.

Probably not a good idea.

CABIN FORTRESS:

Don't tease a guy, Vee. We're simple creatures which is why so many of us have come for you already. Why I was hoping we could talk, and I could prove to you that I'm worthy.

GOODTOTHELASTDROP:

Worthy? Chivalry still, Fortress?

CABIN FORTRESS:

Women hold all the power in what you're asking. We're but a small piece of what you need.

GOODTOTHELASTDROP:

I think I need more wine for this conversation.

CABIN FORTRESS:

I've already drank a bottle to screw up the courage to keep on talking.

. . .

We spoke well into the night. I found out her favorite movies, television shows, music. We swapped concert stories and found out we both loved country and rock. I poured myself another large glass of wine and then things took a turn.

GOODTOTHELASTDROP:

It's easy to talk to you.

CABIN FORTRESS:

I can type really easily. Spitting out words in real life…

GOODTOTHELASTDROP:

Yeah, I get tongue tied too.

CABIN FORTRESS:

You always seem so full of life and bubbly when I see you.

GOODTOTHELASTDROP:

So, you do come in a lot?

CABIN FORTRESS:

I backed into that one. LOL Let's just say you know me far more here in this little chat window than in real life. Through no fault of your own, it's all me.

GOODTOTHELASTDROP:

It's easy to make small talk. Ask a question and most people run with it and are more than happy to talk.

CABIN FORTRESS:

What if you don't want to know it all?

GOODTOTHELASTDROP:

So very much a guy response.

CABIN FORTRESS:

I'm a nice guy. I help my friends and my family. My mama definitely has me wrapped around her finger when she needs a new set of shelves or some project done that she saw on TV.

GOODTOTHELASTDROP:

Much different than my mom. Her idea of a project was up and moving to Fiji for four years then heading to Bali without letting me know her forwarding address.

CABIN FORTRESS:

Wow. Adventuress.

GOODTOTHELASTDROP:

Something like that.

CABIN FORTRESS:

You don't have siblings?

GOODTOTHELASTDROP:

Just me and my mom when she decides she wants to visit.

CABIN FORTRESS:

So that's why you're so independent.

GOODTOTHELASTDROP:

Is that what I am? When I can only think of one thing in my life? A baby.

CABIN FORTRESS:

You know what you want. What's wrong with that? Takes a strong woman to go after what she wants.

GOODTOTHELASTDROP:

I've got everything else.

CABIN FORTRESS:

And you don't want a partner?

The cursor blinked. Her name still had a green light on, but there were no little letters saying *typing*. No response.

Had I pushed her too far?

Wanted to know too much for a nameless man on the internet?

GOODTOTHELASTDROP:

I'm tired of waiting for the traditional order of things. To see if we have the same morals and sexual compatibility. I can usually find one or the other, but not both at the same time.

CABIN FORTRESS:

Which do you want for this project?

GOODTOTHELASTDROP:

Right now, I want a little fun and I want a baby. Making a baby doesn't have to be a dry process—definitely not dry. Haha.

CABIN FORTRESS:

LOL I'd make sure dryness was not a possibility.

GOODTOTHELASTDROP:

Is that right?

CABIN FORTRESS:

A good man makes sure his girl is well satisfied. Anything else is rude and selfish.

GOODTOTHELASTDROP:

Does that include nights where it's just a girl and a guy scratching an itch? When she's not your girlfriend?

CABIN FORTRESS:

Goes double. If I only have one impression, I'm going to make it a lasting one.

GOODTOTHELASTDROP:

Well then. That is a good answer, Fortress.

CABIN FORTRESS:

Good enough to keep talking to me for
more than one night?

GOODTOTHELASTDROP:

I guess we'll see. However, I do need to go
to bed. I'm the baker and that means I have
to get up in a few hours.

CABIN FORTRESS:

I'm sorry I kept you up.

GOODTOTHELASTDROP:

It was worth it. Goodnight, Fortress.

CABIN FORTRESS:

Can we chat again?

GOODTOTHELASTDROP:

Yes.

I pushed back in my chair and spun it around. "Yes!" I quickly
rolled back to my desk.

CABIN FORTRESS:

Looking forward to it.

GOODTOTHELASTDROP:

Me too.

CABIN FORTRESS:

Sweet dreams, Vee.

GOODTOTHELASTDROP:

You too.

I leaned back, my arms dangling off the sides of my chair.
Speaking to a woman on the internet wasn't unusual for me. There
would be few women in my life if I didn't go the online route. I was a
programmer as well, so the computer was my natural habitat.

But this felt different.

A peek into Veronica that I didn't usually get. And yes, it wasn't really fair she didn't know it was me, but in this instance, I needed all the help I could get. There were far too many men interested in her post.

I sat back up and reached for my keyboard. I dashed off a quick note, adding a link to a song I thought she'd enjoy.

Keeping me in her mind with a song was a good first step.

Just before I sent off the note, I noticed that I'd addressed it to Veronica. I quickly corrected it to Vee. She'd never used her full name in the few times we'd written to one another.

I could only hope that one day we would reach the stage where both of her names came into play. For now, I would take all of Vee I could get.

SIX

Vee,

I'm glad we got to chat last night. I haven't enjoyed myself like that in a very long time. However, I'm sorry I kept you up late. I wouldn't want to get in trouble with those who look forward to your perfect little confections at the café. Especially the brookies. They're my fave. Can't wait to chat again. Until then, here's a song by one of my favorite singers.

Link: Baby Be Crazy, Brantley Gilbert.

YOURS, FORTRESS

I SMILED AS I REREAD THE MESSAGE THAT CONTAINED MY NEW favorite song then hit replay for probably the hundredth time over the last week and a half.

If there was such a thing as being addicted to online chatting, I was on my way to finding out.

We were talking so much that it was becoming the favorite part of my day. After I took a shower, I'd bundle into a robe, wrap my hair up in a towel, grab a glass of wine, and sit down to talk to Cabin Fortress.

As the days progressed, we both relaxed. We talked about everything and anything—and sometimes we veered toward crossing the line from polite conversation to making each other moan.

We were so close to going to the next level. Cyber moaning would lead to real life moaning—and hopefully, procreation.

Assuming we could just climb this last little hump of hesitation.

I was all in. Mostly. It was foolish to pin my hopes on one Murphy Masterson ever noticing I was pining for him like a virgin every time he came in and ordered from anyone who was not me.

And I had not been a virgin in a very long time. Going back to feeling that fumbling and clueless was no fun.

Cabin Fortress made me feel the opposite.

"Hey, Vee, can I get a raspberry caramel macchiato, please? Heavy on the whip." Steve smiled. "Changing it up today. Need a little extra sweetness."

I yawned and shuffled to fill Steve's drink order. He was a regular and normally, we chatted easily while I fixed his coffee and bagged his blueberry muffin.

Today? I was so tired I could barely stop yawning long enough to make change.

Last night, I'd talked to my rustic Casanova until almost three a.m. I'd taken a leap and asked if maybe we could talk on the phone this weekend, and he'd diverted me by saying he felt as if we'd learned so much about each other that we might as well have already spoken on the phone. Then he'd mentioned having a weakness for blonds with rainbow streaks in her hair and I'd let it go.

And...sent him a selfie in my hair towel and robe, making sure a little bit of wet cleavage showed.

I wasn't hugely endowed, but I was happy enough with my bounty from nature. From the way he'd sent back a tent emoji and a few eggplant emojis along with a half dozen heart icons, he must've been okay with how I looked too.

He knew who I was after all. I was the only one in the dark here.

Not that I minded the mystery. Much.

Okay, it was bugging me as much as wondering why Murphy had gone one hundred percent mute in my direction. And I knew that was disingenuous, having a thing for two men at one time. But they both intrigued me.

At least I had some kind of chance with Cabin Fortress. With Murphy? Haha, nope.

"Vee? Are you okay? You don't seem like yourself." Steve coughed, his ears turning pink. "How are you doing on your, um, journey to, um, motherhood?"

God, did anyone not know of my Facebook post in this town? I was beginning to think not.

With a weak smile, I passed Steve his bagged muffin and his coffee. "Fine. Great. Thank you. Have a nice day. Please come again. Tomorrow. Bye."

Steve flashed me a quizzical look and left.

I filled orders methodically for a couple of hours until my break. Lucky showed up just before I was about to step into the back to have my lunch, and he convinced me to sit with him at a table in front instead with a cup of cocoa and a pita pocket sandwich stuffed with sprouts and chicken salad, one of the new offerings in Macy's ever-expanding product line.

We'd been talking for a few minutes—while I ignored the far too interested looks of some of the customers seated around us—when I decided to go on a little fishing expedition.

"So, you live alone?"

"Am I supposed to admit now that I have a wife and kids stashed away?"

I shrugged and picked off a corner of bread. "Just making friendly conversation."

"Hmm. Yeah. I live alone."

I set my chin on my fist. "That's nice. I do too. I have an apartment here in town. Right up the street actually. Are you in the town proper?"

"Actually, no, I'm outside a bit."

"Oh, is that so? How far outside? Not all the way to near Syracuse? Surely you wouldn't commute that far?"

"No. Other side of the lake."

My stomach twisted and it wasn't because the chicken salad had gone bad. "By the woods or near the older houses right by the water?"

"Other side of the lake," he repeated, a wrinkle forming between his brows. "Are you angling for an invite to my place? Because if so, you don't have to try that hard, beautiful. You're welcome anytime."

I laughed it off and picked up my pita pocket, taking a big bite so I didn't ask any more probing questions I probably didn't want the answers to anyway.

If my mystery man online was Lucky, then clearly, he had a hidden sweeter side. Besides, it wasn't as if he was a hardship to look at. He'd make a cute baby.

That was all I cared about, right?

Right.

The door opened and I swear, the molecules in the air charged and buzzed. I knew it was Murphy without looking. And I also knew I wasn't going to sit here with Lucky when I could speak to the occupant of most of my thoughts lately.

Take the bull by the horns, Dixon. Or the horn. *You know what to do.*

"Be right back," I muttered to Lucky before rising to rush back behind the counter. I grabbed an apron and slung it on while discreetly nudging the new girl, Clara, out of the way just as Murphy stepped up to the counter.

"Hi there," I said brightly. "Lovely day outside, isn't it?"

He blinked at me, obviously surprised I'd usurped Clara, who was still wearing a bewildered expression. Then he glanced over his shoulder at the big windows. "It's raining."

"Oh. Right. But rain is so...cleansing, don't you agree? Like it falls down and you feel renewed. Refreshed. Or maybe that's just me. I'm like a daisy, soaking up all that...water."

He pressed his lips together. "Uh, sure."

He thinks I'm a moron. Because I am.

Already my excitement at taking command of this situation was dwindling. He was a hard man to maneuver. Probably because he was so large in all the best ways. But he was also serious and completely unsusceptible to flirting. If that was even what I was doing. He probably thought I had a social disease.

Maybe I did.

"You seemed really friendly with Sage. I didn't realize you two knew each other."

Another good one. As if this town wasn't the size of a postage stamp. Almost everyone knew each other it seemed like, which was why my sperm request had been the slingshot heard around the village.

He shocked the hell out of me by smiling. "Oh, sure. We've been friends since high school. Lost touch for a bit but now it's like the old days."

I grabbed a rag and scrubbed the already spotless counter. Better to give my uncharacteristic aggression—read seething jealousy—a place to go. "How nice. What were the old days like, exactly?"

Murphy's smile dimmed. "We were pals. Dated some. Went to the prom together actually." His fond laugh stomped on the left ventricle of my heart.

Hell, it probably squashed the whole thing.

"Wow, so then you must be real good friends, right?" I laughed and leaned across the counter to punch his arm. He stared down at where my fist had made contact—basically it was like a gnat tapping a Sequoia—and then back up at my face as if he was confused at the turn of the conversation.

As am I, Murphy. As am I.

"Not quite sure what you mean, but she's a nice girl. So's her husband. I mean, Oliver's not a girl." Murphy exhaled. "Can I just grab the order for Gideon's crew, please?"

"Her husband is nice. But I bet he'd probably rip off the arm of anyone who tried to make the moves on Sage. Not that you couldn't take him." I punched him again, because that move had worked so well the first time. "You're a big boy, right?"

Oh my God, I was dying inside. Millimeter by millimeter. Any second now, my body would turn to ash and just dissolve to the floor.

"The order," Murphy said, his voice strangled.

"Right." I glanced at Clara, who was wringing her hands and looking stupefied. She wasn't the only one. "Can you snag that, please? I'm still on my break."

Rather than asking me why the hell was I serving customers then —kind of, badly—Clara hurried to comply.

"Yes, better get back to your lunch date." Murphy looked pointedly over his shoulder at Lucky, who was wiggling his fingers at me from our circular table.

Wasn't that a kick? Not only had I fully embarrassed myself, Murphy was now asking me to go away.

I'd just go dunk my head in a puddle now. That way I could soak up more water like a dumb-ass daisy.

"I'm sorry," I said in an undertone. I couldn't look him in the face. "I'm sleep-deprived. And I'm trying to cut back on caffeine."

With that brilliant explanation, I fled.

I did not go back to finish lunch with Lucky, although my stomach was growling. I also didn't make it back on time. I was too busy hanging out on a throne in the john, scrolling on my phone so I didn't think about what a pathetic excuse for a single woman in her twenties I was.

Good thing I'd met Cabin Fortress online. It was clear I needed time to come up with proper responses.

It was also clear it was good I was trying to procreate on my own. The chances of me finding my dream man when I couldn't even make two minutes of pleasant conversation were slim.

The weird thing was, I wasn't really *that* bad normally at social stuff. I mean, I was no dating wizard, but I'd had my share of boyfriends. Some long-term, some short, but none had run away screaming when things had come to their natural end. At least that I was aware of. The last guy I'd dated had even said my blowjob technique was spectacular.

Which was neither here nor there, since he'd said it while I had his dick in my mouth and he'd broken up with me two days later, but whatever. I had to take my wins where I found them.

But something about Murphy made me act...well, ridiculous, especially lately. I wanted to make such a good impression that I just lost all sense.

Or maybe I really needed to return to my regular amount of caffeine. Fast.

The final option was to ask Sage what she had that caused Murphy to act so natural with her. Was it their shared past? Had she rocked his world in a 1989 Pontiac after the prom?

Or before?

Then again, she also wore a summery floral perfume. Perhaps it was that. It couldn't hurt. I smelled like flour and coffee beans. Which weren't bad scents, just not particularly sexy.

I dropped my head in my hands. I was fucked.

Except not.

To try to drag myself out of my tsunami of woe, I looked at my phone again. I reread the end of last night's chat log with my mystery man, smiling a little at how we'd danced around the subject of sex. We were doing that more lately. Veering closer and closer. Last night, I'd told him in an offhand way—ish—that I didn't mind the idea of a little light bondage with a lover.

Not that I'd ever experienced it, but it was on my fucket list. Similar concept to a bucket list, except it referred to sexual experiences I wanted to have. The list was getting longer every day my dry spell extended.

Now I might be on the verge of scaring off Cabin Fortress with all my talk of ropes and ball gags.

Nah, I hadn't gone that far. Thank God.

With a little wine in me though, it was anyone's guess what would pop out of these fingers. Especially when I was horny.

My mystery man was really good at getting me horny.

So was Murphy.

Maybe my libido was just an indiscriminate ho. Because these two guys seriously rang my bell.

It was better than wondering if my loins were so eager because it'd been so long since I'd enjoyed an actual penis that didn't have a jack that said DC power.

Rather than pondering that disturbing thought, I sent off a quick note to Fortress to try to mitigate last night's wine-induced chatter. Sort of. I didn't really know how to make things better, only worse.

Too late now. The message was sent.

Somehow I stumbled back upon my post in the group. It was buried under more recent posts, but it had so many comments that it kept bouncing back up. I read the newest comments with one eye closed, expecting the usual filthy remarks.

I definitely got some of those.

BigTireMan: Goodtothelastdrop, shouldn't I be saying that to you? Maybe I'll put it on my résumé. If you wanna see it, hit me up.

LastRodeoo069: I'm not sure if I can impregnate you, but I'd love to try. How's tomorrow after lunch? My wife is leaving for a business trip. I'd love to have some biz of my own. Har-har.

*Raiders4Lyfe: If you're serious, Vee, I'm game. I've been told I never miss a target, and I have lots of practice with this one. Lots. *winky face**

I sighed. God, men could be seriously gross.

But then I read another kind of comment. A much better one.

PurpleUni: *I just wanted to say thank you for being so brave. I would love to do something like this, but it's scary and hard to know where to turn. You've given me hope that I can be as proactive as you are. Women shouldn't have to wait forever on a dream that may not happen for them. I hope you find your Mr. Right Now.*

Aww, how sweet. And best of all, that wasn't the only one like that. There were several others, and when I checked my Facebook inbox—which I'd avoided for days—there were more messages waiting there. Enough women wanted some direction and support on how to go after the baby they wanted that I decided to make another impulsive move.

One that felt really good.

I added a comment to my post.

Vee: *Thank you so much for your kind words, ladies. I haven't felt particularly brave lately. Mostly foolish, to be honest. But hearing from a few of you has given me renewed confidence. I'd love to chat with some of you in person, if you'd like to meet up. Just message me here and I'll get back to you. Maybe we can all help each other with support at the very least.*

A knock thundered on the bathroom door just as I hit enter on my comment.

"Vee, are you taking up my bathroom so paying customers can't use it? You better have an epic case of the runs. Otherwise get yourself out here and back to work."

"Coming, Mace." I hurried out of the stall and washed my hands and splashed some water on my flushed cheeks. Then I rushed to throw open the door and smiled at my annoyed boss. "Don't suppose you'd mind loaning me your reading nook for an evening, would you? Just for an hour or so. Pretty please."

If I needed it, but I was thinking positively.

I was, dammit.

Macy looked skyward. "Lord, why am I being tested?"

"If I get the turnout I'm thinking I might, you'll have at least five to ten new customers by the end of the night."

"I'm listening. Talk fast before my patience swirls down the bowl like your tips."

I grinned and slid my arm through hers. "Just think. A whole group of women who want to have babies meeting here. Isn't that fabulous?"

"You're fired."

SEVEN

Fortress,

Last night it occurred to me that maybe you were assuming I might want you to tie me up. Not you, per se, but a man I became intimate with. I didn't want you to think I only like bondage games. I'm quite fine with so-called regular forking. Girl on top? Yasss. Man on top? Oh, yeah. Doggy style? Dude, sign me up. I might even be down for some back door backgammon, with lots of prep. I've never done that though, so I'd have to stock up on lube and that warming jelly for that one. Just saying I'm an open-minded sort. Are you an open-minded guy? Please elaborate.

YOURS, VEE

Sweet Jesus, this woman was going to kill me.

I stared at the ceiling of my bedroom. Sun streamed through the floor-to-ceiling window. And I was making a damn good impression of a sundial.

Christ.

I looked down at my poor, lonely dick tenting my quilt. Morning wood was a good bit of the problem, but the other half was definitely one Veronica Dixon and her message.

We'd been dancing around the topic of sex in our chats and last night she'd put the scarves and silk rope ideas in my brain. I still hadn't recovered from that, but the rest?

My phone buzzed in my hand and I groaned. I wasn't sure I could take another email from her. I'd be in a cold shower again.

I was getting damn tired of them.

Not to mention they weren't working. I looked down to see Gideon's name and relief helped a few of my problems.

One, that I'd originally had a long day of nothing on tap.

If Gideon needed me, at least I could stop obsessing about this woman. At least for five minutes.

I swung my legs off the side of my bed and read the text. A single day job a few towns over sounded like the perfect way to get my head straight.

Because I really didn't know how to answer that message.

I replied back that I'd meet him on site and set my music to filter into my bathroom from my phone. I liked a rustic look to my cabin, but I was a proud geek. I'd created my own smart house and was looking into maybe adding it as a project I could work on with Gideon.

In the winter months, the construction business was a lot slower. While I had my company Cabin Fortress for gaming and apps, I still liked to come up with new ways to challenge my brain. Installing smart homes could be a way to keep me busy in the off months.

I was still picking over ideas as The Brothers Osborne rocked me through a shower and shave. I had a little time to work on one of the outsourced projects I should have done three days ago.

Veronica was a distraction I wasn't used to.

Compartmentalizing my life had been easy until that damn message on The Cove group. Now I was juggling two jobs and a secret identity. Cabin Fortress Man, I was not.

Unfortunately, Brewed Awakening was way out of the way for this job, so I made my own substandard coffee. The grounds were fresh from the café, but Macy had some magic in her machine. It never tasted the same.

I filled my thermos and pulled on my Carhartt jacket. Finally, there was a snap in the air. Fall was my favorite season. The air was different. Crisp with a hint of the winter to come, but there was still enough sun to make the outdoor work bearable.

I pulled in behind Gideon's truck on a huge circular drive. It was so freshly paved I expected my boots to stick on the blacktop. I heard the telltale headbanger music in the backyard. Fucking awesome. Lucky would be on the crew today.

He generally was, but occasionally Gideon had multiple jobs going at once, so he spread out his people. Just my luck—pardon the pun—that I got to work with the guy who was making it his mission in life to flirt with the woman of my goddamn dreams.

And she flirted back.

The huge fucker practically had Darwinism tattooed on his shoulder. Followed by, "I make awesome swimmers and was born to breed."

Fuck.

My fingertips went white with the grip on my thermos as I stalked around the house. At least the music was loud enough that I didn't need to make small talk with him.

Gideon waved me over to the edge of the property. "We're pulling down this old tree house and building something a little sturdier for the little man who lives here."

I tipped my head back to look at the very crooked, very precarious lines of lumber. "Dad tried to do it himself with YouTube again?"

"Yep." Gideon put his hands on his hips. "Macy's coffee?"

I held out my thermos. "Kind of. Her blend, my coffeemaker."

Gideon made a face but filled his to-go mug anyway. "Thanks."

Lucky came up. "Is that Macy's coffee I smell?"

I opened my mouth to tell him to fuck off, but of course I didn't. He took my thermos and dumped most of it in his tumbler made for giants.

"Oh, sorry. Did you have some?" he asked over the mouth of his cup, waggling his eyebrows. "Damn good stuff. And she's hot as fuck. Not to mention that cute little sprite that works with her. I'd bang the lot of them."

"Jesus, Lucky." Gideon shot him a look. "Did your mama hand out any manners?"

"That would require having a mama." Lucky turned away with his mug, whistling in his off-tune way.

I couldn't imagine not having a mom. And that meant he was a lot more like Veronica than I was. Another point in his goddamn pro list. Shit.

"Don't let him get to you."

"I'm not."

"You're a shitty liar, son." Gideon took another swig from his cup. "Let's get this done. I don't want to charge them for another day of labor."

"You sure we can get this done in a day?"

"Why you and Lucky are here. If anyone can do it, it's the three of us."

I sighed. That was the truth. We were the quickest and most precise ones on the team. The good thing about a time limit was that meant Lucky didn't have time to make a lot of smart-ass comments.

I jumped up on the wide, sturdy branch and climbed the tree to start ripping down the plywood nailed to an inch of its life.

Slowly, I smoothed my hand down the bark. "Dad didn't know what he was doing," I whispered to the tree. "We'll fix you up and you can give their little boy years of fun."

"Are you talking to the tree?"

I flushed at Lucky's voice. "No."

"I think you are. You're made to be one of the famed dads of Crescent Cove. What the hell is taking you so long to talk to the current baby mama chaser?"

My molars clicked together. "Can't we just work?"

"Well, you've been dancing around the cute baker for weeks— hell, for over a year now. What the hell is taking you so long?"

"Why do you care? You're flirting enough for the both of us."

"I mean, I'll take her up on the offer to bang one out for a chance to get a few of my swimmers to hit the bullseye. Hell, I probably have a few kids out there anyway. Not like it's a big thing to me."

"Keep your unwrapped shit away from her."

"Aww, Moose. You keep giving me the death glare like you've got laser beam superpowers, but don't do anything about it. Besides, I'm clean as hell, young Jedi. I just know my light saber has some extra strength prowess."

Way to mix your metaphors, douche.

"So, get in the ring," he continued. "She says she's not into the whole family values part, but just look at her. She's already got the baking part down. Bun in the oven and she's on her way to going for housewife of the year."

I jumped down to the grass, my boots crunching through the first leaves that had come off the trees. I crowded into him. "First of all, have you even heard of the word feminism? Do you even know what you're saying? And second, keep talking about Veronica like that and we're going to have a problem."

"What are you going to do, Boy Scout? Have your big brother arrest me?"

I pushed him back three steps. "I grew up with three brothers. I can take care of myself, son."

"Hey!" Gideon's voice cut through the crackling air. "Take a corner, guys. What the hell?"

I stepped back, but my hands were still fisted at my sides.

Lucky grinned and shook out his mane of hair. "Man, it is easy to push your buttons, Moose."

"You think it's funny?"

"Look, I might not have a mama, but I'm not a bastard." He shrugged and tugged a water bottle out of his front pocket where he kept one at all times. "Just trying to get you to move shit along. Someone's going to snap her up."

"You?"

He laughed and took a sip. "I mean, I could, but I wouldn't. We're friends-ish. I wouldn't be that much of a dick. I'm an asshole, but I don't poach."

"What do you call the last few weeks?"

"Operation Torture Moose." He lifted the bottle in salute, then chugged the entire contents before he tucked it back in his jeans. "Ready to get this done?"

I took a step forward and Gideon slapped a hand on my chest. "All right. He's just messing with you. He's mostly harmless."

"Mostly," I grumbled.

We stayed out of each other's way for the rest of the day. I detangled the tree from the weird hodge-podge treehouse pieces. A floor that didn't know the meaning of level and a roof that actually did. Which was stupid, because you needed a pitch to the roof, or you'd end up with rot.

It was a hot mess, but at least the man had been willing to try to make something for his kid. I had to give him points there. Unfortunately, a lot of people thought YouTube and a book was enough to get them into weekend warrior status. At least he'd called in for help before the kid climbed up the tree.

As we were working through the day, the kids came home. School was in full swing now that the end of September was in sight. Two boys came racing out to ask a million and one questions as we built the skeleton of a far simpler structure. The big difference was that this one was actually structurally sound.

But unfortunately, because it was September, the days were getting shorter. The mother called the kids in for dinner, but two pairs of fascinated eyeballs were forever in the back window while we worked.

Lucky clowned around with them a bit. Gideon was busting his ass to get the wood cut as fast as me and Lucky could screw and nail it in place. The sun was setting, and we had the flood lights out to try to get it completed.

We worked past seven and finally managed to get it mostly done.

"I'll stop by and do some finishing flourishes tomorrow."

"I told her we'd get it done tonight."

"No charge, Gideon."

He frowned at me. "You don't have to do that."

I shrugged at the wide-eyed kids dancing around the bottom of the tree. "It's for kids, man."

"Yeah. If I didn't have a job lined up tomorrow, I would have done the same."

"Well, it's my day off."

"Are you sure?"

"Yeah, definitely." I waved at the older boy, Max. "How can you say no to them?"

"Why do you think Dani gets away with murder?"

I laughed. "I figured she'd be back already. Didn't school start?"

"Yeah, she's being tutored while her mother is on set in Spain."

I crouched down to put a few more bolts in the floorboard. "Spain? Wow."

"Yeah." Gideon shook his head. "The movie schedule got extended. How could I make my kid come home from that?"

"For school?"

"Yeah, then I'm the bad guy. It's bad enough I'm the hardass through the school year who actually gives her stability. Jess gets to be the cool mom who's a famous actress and takes her to fucking Spain. I'm just a carpenter in a small town."

No bitterness there. I winced. "Sorry, man." Gideon rarely mentioned his ex-wife, so I left it open ended for him to say more if he wanted.

He shoved his hammer back into his holster. "Sorry to be a whiner." He stood up. "But hey, I think we're done."

I raked my fingers through my hair to get the worst of the sawdust out. "This thing is awesome. Think we should let the kids come on up?" I asked loud enough for them to squeal in excitement.

"Asking for trouble, man," Gideon said out of the side of his mouth.

Max scrambled up the ladder with his little brother hot on his heels. The best part of a job like this was the kid aspect. Someday I'd make one for my kid. I had the perfect tree behind my cabin.

Veronica's kid?

Our kid.

Jesus, I had to stop thinking that way. She wasn't looking for her forever guy, just a milkman delivery. And while I wanted to play her milkman, I wasn't so sure I could walk away if she was carrying my kid.

Not just wanting to be in his or her life, but their mom's. Their mom was my focus right now and the nebulous idea of a child was like a flash out of the corner of my eye. Just out of my eye line, but I knew something else was over there.

Something that could be amazing.

I shut it down as the kids pushed by me to check out the clubhouse area we'd set up. Their parents already had furniture from the original blueprints of the treehouse. We'd followed the plans and simplified some of it to get it done in a day.

I was pretty sure the kids wouldn't care about the octagon windows and other fussy things on the original plans. They just wanted the big window to push open and talk down to their parents. They wanted the big cable spool we'd taken from another job and used as the table. They were more than happy with the boxes of games they could play.

It was the perfect hideout for a pair of boys.

I peered down to see the father looking up at us longingly. I tapped Gideon on the shoulder. "Want to let the dad up?"

"Oh, yeah. Hard to look away when they're having so much fun. You were right about that big old spool. It made the perfect table."

"And now we don't have to look for a way to get rid of the beast."

"Thanks to that pulley system you made up on the fly."

I shrugged. "Will be perfect for their mom to send up food." I laughed and flipped open the secret door, wrapped my foot in the rope, and lowered myself to the ground.

"Cool!" I heard from above me.

I waved up at them and turned to their mother. "Sorry about that. They're probably going to want to do that."

She waved me off. "Oh, that's okay. I'll make sure it's Max and Taylor-proofed by tomorrow. I do love it though. I can send up food or homework." She threw her arms around me. "You made them so happy. And my husband is thrilled."

I patted her back. "Glad we could help. I'll stop back tomorrow to do a few finishing things, but it's pretty much all done."

"I can't believe you guys did all this." She stepped back, her eyes shining in the limited light. "Thank goodness it's a warm night. I think I'll go find their sleeping bags and let the three of them sleep up there."

"That sounds really nice, Mrs. Bridgers."

"Thank you so much."

"You're very welcome." I stretched my back out with a few exercises I used for working at my desk all day. Being a guy well over six feet, I had to do a lot of crouching to make a treehouse. I was sore, hungry, and beat.

The laughter from above was worth it though.

A squeak and a whimper dented the laughter. "Gideon?" I shouted up.

"Yeah?" He peeked out.

"Everything cool?"

"Yeah, can't you hear them freaking out in here?"

"Yeah. I just thought I heard something else." I looked around and when the sound came again, I headed deeper into the edges of the brush near the Bridgers' property. The closer I got to an overgrown lilac tree, the louder the sounds got.

Little distress-filled squeaks.

Crap, I hoped I wasn't disturbing a wild animal den. A family of foxes wouldn't be out of the realm in this area. There was just enough brush and trees to make a perfect home for them.

I peeked around the bush and found a cardboard box. "Son of a bitch." I quickly pulled my jacket off as the squeaks became clearer. Puppies. A freaking litter of them, just left.

People were the fucking worst.

"Hey, little guys." I crouched down beside the box and they all scampered toward my voice. They were cold and so freaking tiny. I immediately stripped off my chambray shirt and put it in the box and they burrowed into the material still warm from my body.

I lifted the box and met Gideon at the bed of his truck. He'd backed it into their yard to pick up all the tools.

"I wondered where you'd gotten off to. What the hell did you find?"

"Puppies."

"Oh, no. No, we don't do puppies on jobs."

"I know, man. I can't leave them to die though."

"Well, shit."

"It's all right. I'll take them back to my place for the night."

"Are you sure? Who knows what they have?" Carefully, Gideon tipped the box his way and one of the more enterprising little bundles of fur tried to leap up for his hand. "Holy crap, they're tiny."

"And cold. I can't believe someone just dumped a box of puppies."

"Probably had a knocked-up dog and didn't want to deal with the aftermath."

"It's cruel. Good thing it wasn't colder tonight."

Gideon shook his head. "Softie."

"Yeah, well, I just can't leave them."

"No, I guess you can't. Don't let those kids see them. Their mother will kill me. They already have three cats."

I laughed. "All right. You good?" I glanced over at the last of the tools.

"Yeah. Lucky will help me pack up."

"Whatcha got, Moose?" Lucky came over and whistled. "Oh, man. A box of pups? Damn, that sucks."

I rolled my eyes. "Understatement. I'm assuming the shelter is closed since it's after eight."

"Yeah, there's a 24-hour vet in Laurel."

"I'll just take them home for the night. Give them some food and bring them to the shelter in the morning."

"Boy Scout," Lucky coughed into his hand.

I took my box of precious cargo and walked away before I did something stupid. "C'mon, little guys. We'll turn the heater up and get you guys warm."

The drive back to my house, with a quick pitstop at a pet store for supplies and advice, was relatively uneventful. Once they were warm, the puppies drifted to sleep.

I rushed around to feed them and get them cleaned up before I had my cyber date with Veronica. No, Vee. I couldn't keep calling her Veronica out loud or I was going to fuck up one of these times.

But she was so stubbornly Veronica in my head.

Even when the in-person Veronica was being a little crazy lately. I chalked it up to the insane level of fame she'd cultivated with her baby daddy hunt. But no matter how we interacted at the café, when the night came...it was just us.

CF and Vee and the insanely intimate conversations we had about life, food, parents, and the all-important baby she longed for. God, I wanted to give that to her.

And more.

So much more.

The little chat chime had me sprinting for the computer. One of the puppies didn't like the sound and made a sad howl.

"Shoot. Oh, little guy, no." I glanced at the computer then back to the little caramel-colored pup. I scooped him up. He was trembling and trying to burrow into my skin. I didn't know what else to do, so I tucked him into my shirt. He settled down instantly. "Well, hell."

I shrugged. At least he was quieting down.

GOODTOTHELASTDROP:

Are you there?

CABIN FORTRESS:

Yes, sorry. It's been one of those days. Most of it good, then my evening took on a crazy left turn.

GOODTOTHELASTDROP:

Good left? Like with whipped cream?

I groaned. She was determined to kill me. I was still reeling from her earlier message and today had been insane.

GOODTOTHELASTDROP:

Or did I scare you with my email? You didn't write back.

CABIN FORTRESS:

No. Believe me, that was a no. That letter was perfect. And I've been thinking about it all day.

GOODTOTHELASTDROP:

But you didn't reply.

CABIN FORTRESS:

There was a work emergency today. I ended up wrapped in meetings all day until just a little bit ago. Then the left hand turn.

GOODTOTHELASTDROP:

Do I get a hint?

I peered down at the little bundle of tan fur snoozing against my chest. How on earth was I supposed to explain this? Real life was encroaching on our little bubble way too much lately.

From Lucky's wrecking ball style jackassery to a six pack of puppies, things had been crazy this week.

CABIN FORTRESS:

A certain beautiful rainbow-haired woman asked me how open-minded I was. It got a guy thinking many less than pure thoughts. And I don't want to scare you away.

GOODTOTHELASTDROP:

How impure?

CABIN FORTRESS:

I have a fireplace in my room, and I've been picturing you spread out on my reading chair. It's one of those long chairs you can nap in. All that firelight on your skin and me, tracing every inch of you with my lips. It might not be daring, but I'd be so fucking thorough, Vee. You'd be worshipped.

GOODTOTHELASTDROP:

Oh, that's impure enough. I am so onboard with that kind of impure.

I sat back with a puppy burrowed into my chest and I've got the hottest girl on the damn planet wanting to talk sexy with me. Maybe even cyber.

Why was this my life?

I looked down at my little charge and sighed. He was way too content. There was no way I could put him down. This particular little guy was almost always trying to get into my sleeve or jacket.

CABIN FORTRESS:

If I go any more impure, I'm going to need some alone time, Vee.

GOODTOTHELASTDROP:

Well, we don't want to waste that particular piece of you. It's a very precious commodity.

Of course it was. I was fighting off an epic boner and she only wanted what was in my balls. I kept forgetting that part.

GOODTOTHELASTDROP:

Not that I don't mind sampling the goods a few times prior to any type of plan we might have about making a baby. If you were serious about that firelight situation.

CABIN FORTRESS:

Oh, I was serious.

GOODTOTHELASTDROP:

And yet you won't let me talk to you on the phone.

I sighed. How was I supposed to get around this? If she heard my voice, it was game over. Not that I could keep this going on forever. It was either end it or let her know who I really was.

I got up and grabbed my phone to take a picture of my windows and the darkness of the lake in the distance. I manipulated the photo a little to show my broad shoulders and a little of my profile in the reflection. Not enough to really show her anything of value. But enough so she might be appeased a little while longer.

CABIN FORTRESS:

How about a tease for now?

GOODTOTHELASTDROP:

Goodness, you weren't kidding about that view. I'm liking the guy in the picture too. You have nothing to worry about with me. I hope you know that, Fortress. It's about the real you, not a face, a body, or a voice. I like what I'm learning about you. But I'll wait a little longer for you.

CABIN FORTRESS:

Not much longer. A computer just isn't
enough the more I get to know you.

GOODTOTHELASTDROP:

Me either.

CABIN FORTRESS:

I have something to do really early
tomorrow. Can we talk tomorrow?

GOODTOTHELASTDROP:

Definitely. It was a long one for me today
too. Sweet dreams.

CABIN FORTRESS:

Same to you, Vee.

I looked down at the sweet puppy curled into me. At least one thing made sense in my life. "C'mon, pal. Let's get you back with your brothers and sisters. Big day tomorrow."

Maybe not only for the puppies.

EIGHT

Vee,

I have to admit your note put me in one helluva state. One that required a long-ass shower of the chilly variety. I love a woman who is willing to ask for what she wants. For us guys, it's a lot of fumbling around hoping we don't take stuff too far. Me? I'm very good with my hands and my tongue. Enough to keep up with you and then some. Did I mention I have many sturdy surfaces in my cabin? If not, I do. We can get as creative as you want. I'm so very up for anything you're into.

YOURS, CF

CABIN FORTRESS LIVED IN MY BRAIN PRETTY MUCH continuously, especially after I'd read that note. Though we'd chatted every night for the last few days after he'd said he was up for creativity, those particular words were on repeat in my mind.

I just wasn't sure what I wanted to do about them quite yet. And right now, I had other fish to fry than those involving my libido.

"Ladies, quiet, please. Let's grab everyone's drink orders and then we'll get down to...chatting," I finished weakly, clasping my hands as I faced the assembled ladies who were piled up in the reading nook.

That wasn't much of an exaggeration. The women were lumped together on the tidy circle of couches and chairs in the café like a bunch of exuberant puppies. I had vastly underestimated the number of women who would show up.

Like...vastly.

I'd considered moving the meeting to the new movie area we had out back on the patio, but it was a chilly and raw night, not at all suited to outdoor activities.

Thanks so much, central New York.

Fall could be lovely, or it could turn into monsoon season on a dime. I really hoped the rain wasn't here to stay yet, because that meant cold and snow were right behind.

The natives were restless at this early turn in the weather, asking for hot cocoa, fancy coffee drinks, and chocolate pastries in copious quantities. Macy had taken one look at the crowd, arched a brow at me over my "little" gathering, and called in more help.

The cash register would be ringing tonight for sure.

"Forget just drinks. I caught sight of those petit fours over there. I've never seen so many flavors."

I flushed. "Thanks. I do those. We'll be sure to get orders for baked goods too, just as soon as Clara and Jodi and—"

"Could I get a sandwich instead, please? I missed lunch. I worked a double today." A woman who I recognized as a waitress at the diner leaned down to rub her foot. She'd kicked off her shoes the second she'd taken a seat.

Since I knew all too well what long hours on my feet were like, I winced in sympathy. "Sure thing. We'll get dinner orders too for anyone who wants something more substantial."

"Well, I think we all want something more substantial, right?" A woman with a high red ponytail glanced at the brunette woman beside her and laughed. "At least for a couple of hours. Then bye."

I laughed awkwardly, though inside I wasn't all that amused. Sure, I'd made jokes like that too. It was natural when you were on the search for some extra seasoning in your egg salad. I just didn't think it was necessarily right to treat the guys we were talking to as a commodity. We wouldn't appreciate such treatment ourselves.

But I'd leave that discussion for later. Right now, I was pretty sure we had attracted some gawkers and drive-by types, so a few minutes of discussion about the realities of searching for a man to have a child with should weed out the ones who weren't serious.

I turned toward Jodi as she and Clara approached, pads in hand. "Thanks, ladies. I really appreciate your help with this."

"No problem." Jodi bit her lip and glanced around. "These are all your friends?"

"Not exactly. We're just working together on a common problem."

I didn't really want to advertise what we were doing, since this was a place of business and people in town tended to gossip early and often. Though it would come out soon enough if this meeting took off. Everything seemed to rapidly become common knowledge.

Jodi nodded, her pencil poised over her pad. "What would you like to eat and drink?"

I pressed a hand to my jumpy belly. "Oh, I couldn't eat a thing. I'm all—"

"Oh my God, you're pregnant already?" Jodi's voice carried far more than I wished. "Wow, girl, you work fast. Go you!"

Before I knew what had happened, seventeen women and a good segment of the café patrons swarmed around me, talking and laughing excitedly. More than one of them groped my not flat belly as if they were probing for aliens.

It wasn't fun.

"Hey now, personal space, please." I tried to laugh and found it got caught in my throat. "I hate to break it to all of you, but I'm not pregnant yet. The only thing in my belly right now is what's left of a quesadilla bowl I had at lunch."

I should've been surprised Murphy picked that moment to stroll in. I mean, why not? It had only happened multiple times at the worst possible instant. That this was later than he normally showed up didn't seem to matter. Somehow when I said awkward things, he got the message to arrive.

This time, he didn't even pretend not to stare at me across the café. And at the women still clustered around me, focused on my belly as if they didn't quite believe what I'd said.

For God's sake, it had only been a little more than two weeks since I'd posted on Facebook. How fast did they think I worked?

"Just a second," I muttered, breaking free of the crowd to run to Murphy like he was a lifeline.

It didn't make sense. I'd practically driven him out of here a few days ago and he'd been scarce since. Why should I think he'd help save me in this situation? And what did I have to be saved from anyway, except the weight of everyone's expectations? Ones I'd helped put in place.

That of course I'd find someone who wanted to knock me up.

That of course we'd have good chemistry and sex would happen easily and naturally.

That of course I'd get pregnant first try.

As if it was all that easy. And maybe I'd been naïve enough to not really think it all through and think something similar.

I was getting schooled in reality now.

"Save me," I said in an undertone as I reached Murphy and grabbed his arm. Such a solid, sturdy arm. One that would make the woman lucky enough to have them around her feel so safe and protected.

And possibly more than a little turned on, if that woman was me.

"You're pregnant." His voice was utterly flat. "Congratulations."

"No. God, no." The laugh that left me was dazed and on the verge of hysteria. "I haven't even been with any—there's no one—holy corn!" I let out a yelp as something furry poked out of Murphy's hoodie pocket and swiped his tongue over my wrist, right above my tattoo of two crossed whisks.

It might've been the insanity of the moment, but those big brown eyes locked onto mine and I fell deeply, irrevocably in love.

"You were supposed to stay hidden while we were in here, bud."

The puppy paid Murphy no mind. Right then, I didn't either. All my focus was for the tiny ball of excited fur.

"Who are you?" I cooed, shifting to hold out my hands to the little brown darling in Murphy's pocket. His *pocket,* for heaven's sake. "Oh, you're just a baby. A wee one. Aww, come here." The puppy was already trying to do just that, his little legs pumping as he scrambled into my hands.

"Guess all men find you irresistible," Murphy said in a voice almost too low for me to hear.

Almost.

"Where did you find him? Ah, he's so sweet." I tried to hold on to the squirmy puppy while he climbed up my chest and burrowed into the space between my neck and shoulder.

"Picked up him and his siblings on a construction site. I took the others to the shelter—"

"What? Oh, no, no. We can't give him to no stinkin' shelter. Right, Latte?"

"Latte?" Murphy smiled. "Did you just name my dog?"

"I'm sorry, I kind of did, didn't I?" I let out a little self-conscious laugh. "He's just the perfect color of one, and he's so warm." I shifted the puppy so that we were nose-to-nose. He licked mine and I laughed again, the panicky feeling from being fondled by a bunch of strangers fading as if it had never existed.

Thank God.

Thank Latte.

My gaze connected with Murphy as he watched me cuddle with his dog.

Thank Murphy.

"Hey there, Vee, can we get this meeting going, please? Some of us have places to be," the ponytailed redhead from the group called out.

"Right. Lord. I have to go back over there." Reluctantly, I started to hand the puppy back to Murphy, then had the brightest idea of my life.

Maybe.

Possibly.

"Hey, do you have anywhere to be?"

Murphy's expression got a little cagey as he eyed the cluster of restless women behind me. "Depends."

"On what?"

"If you need me or not."

Oh, God. It was a damn miracle I didn't melt into a puddle right there on his boots. This man didn't say much, but when he did speak, I swore every one of my girly parts did a freaking cheer.

"I do. I do need you." Desperately. I wasn't even sure how much and all the reasons why, but right then? I was positive I vitally needed Murphy Masterson in my life.

His hazel eyes softened. "Really?"

"Absolutely. I ran to you, didn't I?"

He smiled and I wanted to grab his arm again, except this time I'd slide a little south and slip my fingers between his.

My gaze dropped. He had such big hands.

Such big feet.

Did that mean...?

Sweet mercy, I'd been thinking about babies too much. Now I was strictly focused on the process.

With him. Just with him.

"These women contacted me because they want to have babies too."

Murphy frowned. "So, what, you're like their spokesperson now?"

It made me laugh. "No. Well, not exactly. More like they want to get up the nerve to have a baby by themselves too. Or they want help finding someone to have a baby with. Or someone to talk to who understands."

"Hmm. Like a matchmaking service for women and men willing to share their sperm."

"No, not that—" I pursed my lips and shifted the now snoozing puppy to my other side. "Huh, maybe. That's an idea. I mean, there's sperm donors of course, but that's even more impersonal and expensive to boot."

"You wouldn't charge that much."

"No." Wait, what was I charging for, exactly? I couldn't keep up with this conversation along with the hormonal ping-pong match going on below my waist. "But it would've helped me a lot if I could've used something like that, rather than embarrassing myself in front of my whole town. If it was a private site, that would've been a lot more convenient." My mind was starting to buzz.

"Let's go talk to them, see what they're really looking for. Some may be just attention seekers. Or nosy."

I tried not to gawk at him. This was officially the longest conversation we'd ever had. "You'd be willing to do that with me?"

"Sure." He shifted from foot to foot. "Plus, you've stolen my dog."

I smiled and buried my face in Latte's downy soft fur. "Are you sure he didn't already have a name?"

"Yeah, he did."

I couldn't help feeling a little dismayed. Silly. The puppy wasn't even mine. "Oh, yeah? What is it?"

Murphy nudged me back toward the reading nook. "Latte."

I slid him a sidelong glance and grinned like a besotted idiot as we rejoined the group. Oh, yeah, I was totally in a spot to be calm and cool and help these women. It wasn't as if I wanted to lay down in front of the fire and point my toes to the ceiling and tell him to take me.

Nah. Definitely not.

I knew someone else who'd offered to make my dreams come true in front of a fireplace. Actually, that was wrong. Cabin Fortress might be the real deal and Murphy was just a nice guy I had a hopeless crush on. He didn't want to give me a baby. Until tonight, he hadn't even wanted to be in a conversation with me.

So, what had changed?

I stopped dead beside my chair—which was now taken.

"Vee?" He patted the arm of the chair he'd snagged. Some of the women must've moved aside to make room for him. Maybe they figured he was here to do a public service?

I let out a giggle and Latte licked my cheek.

"Thanks." I'd no sooner perched on the arm—nice and close to him—that he rose and gently pushed me onto the seat. "Cheater."

"Sorry about before. We got the wrong idea." The brunette with the redheaded friend grimaced and sipped from her mug. At least they'd been served while Murphy and I were chatting. "I guess we were so excited for you that we got ahead of ourselves."

"That's okay." I smiled at everyone and stroked the contentedly sleeping puppy.

He wasn't the only one who wanted to snuggle up and snooze, though I would do that *after* intimate acts with Murphy, not before. I imagined he was a nice supportive surface to curl up against.

Ugh, supportive surfaces made me think of Fortress again. I had to send him a note. I didn't even know what I'd say. I liked him a lot. But I liked Murphy too.

Maybe I should try to find out how much Fortress liked *me* before I made any firm decisions. That seemed proper.

Properly cowardly, but whatever.

"We should discuss why we all met up tonight and what we each hope to get out of this," I began, somehow bolstered by the presence of the puppy—and the puppy's owner. "But first, I think we should do introductions and share a little about ourselves. I'll start. I'm Vee Dixon and I'm an Aquarius."

That earned me some laughter.

"I live here in town and I'm the main baker for Brewed

Awakening. I also do some of the artsy things, like the sandwich board out front."

"And she makes the best coffee of anyone in this place," Murphy added as I flashed him a grateful smile.

"I heard that," Macy called from behind the counter while she waited on a customer.

We all laughed.

One by one, everyone volunteered whatever they felt comfortable putting out there. It took a while, as there were close to twenty women present and one Murphy. When the circle reached him, I expected him to back out.

Instead, he said he was a lifetime resident of Crescent Cove and had a couple different jobs.

"And I'm a Taurus."

I reached over to smack his thigh at that, and he surprised me by smiling. Though there was a bit of pink on the tips of his ears, he was being far more relaxed than I'd expected.

Maybe my flirting skills were improving. Or perhaps the improvement in his reaction to me came from the fact I wasn't intentionally flirting at all. I was just being me. The real me, not the weirdo who seemed to appear whenever Murphy showed up.

Thankfully, she seemed to have taken the night off.

"That's great. So, you all contacted me in one way or another after seeing my post about searching for a man to have a baby with, potentially with no strings. Do all of you want to have babies on your own or are you just exploring your options?" I looked around the group.

Almost half of them indicated they wanted to have a kid without necessarily needing a partner. A few mentioned wanting to hear more or that they might be interested in the future if not now. The rest didn't answer one way or the other.

I shifted the still sleeping puppy on my lap and he rolled over and kicked out his paws, garnering more than his share of puppy appreciation. He was too blitzed to realize it.

"What were most of you hoping to get out of this? Some others to talk to and commiserate with?" I thought of Murphy's comments before we'd rejoined the group. "Or are you hoping to figure out a way to make the process easier?"

"I can't speak for everyone," the redhead's brunette buddy said, "but I know me and Andi here would like to do what you did."

"Oh, no." I had to laugh. "No, you definitely do not want to do what I did. I caused a spectacle, even if I didn't mean to."

"I gotta know, did you really post in the Facebook group on purpose?"

"No." I tucked one of my braids back as it slipped free. "I'd meant to post it in a local singles group, which wasn't the ideal place either."

"Because you weren't looking for a hookup, just the baby part," the waitress from the diner prompted. Ivy, I think she'd said her name was.

"Don't get me wrong. If I met someone cool, that would be a bonus. I'm not against the idea of romance. I just don't want to wait forever for a Mr. Right who might not be driving up my lane anytime soon." I shot a look at Murphy under my lashes, only to find him watching me intently. Not with amusement. Not with disgust. Just open curiosity.

As if he wanted to understand my motivations.

He wasn't the only one. The longer this had gone on, the more I'd questioned myself. Did I really fully understand what I'd undertaken? Babies grew up. You had to support them for a full eighteen years, and I'd pledged to do that all on my own on a baker's salary.

Examining it from all angles made it easier to see why some people had thought I was nuts. Perhaps I was.

But I still wanted a baby. Probably more than ever.

Even after all of this. Even if it didn't happen quickly. Even if it was hard.

"It's not a quick process or a simple one," I continued. "I'll admit I was a bit too hasty in putting up my post. I hadn't considered all the steps. How difficult finding a guy I can get intimate with for this purpose would be, even if he was agreeable."

"So, why not just have some fun banging random dudes?" Andi asked, nudging her friend who threw back her head and laughed. "Why make it some big thing and invite the whole world into your business?"

"She didn't do that." Murphy's voice was like steel. "It was the town's choice to wade into something that didn't have to do with them."

In shock, I gazed at my surprising defender. Was this really happening?

And here I'd believed he'd think I was ridiculous to undertake this. If he did, he sure was hiding it.

"Oh, yeah, and why are you here anyway?" Andi smirked. "Did she reel in a big fish already?"

I wanted to crawl under the chair, but I couldn't move fast enough with the sleepy puppy on my lap.

Murphy wasn't bothered in the slightest. "I'm a friend. All you need to know."

Damn, Murphy with the comebacks. Hidden sides for the win.

I licked my lips and studied his profile out of the corner of my eye. What other hidden aspects did he have to his personality?

I tried to get the group back on task. "Returning to your original question, Andi, I'd never take advantage of a man and sleep with him to try to get pregnant without his knowledge. That's hugely unfair."

"But if they aren't going to be part of the kid's life anyway, what difference does it make? Didn't you ever see the video for that old Heart song?" Andi's brunette friend—I'd already forgotten her name —snapped her fingers. "You know, the one where they plant a tree in the garden after a hookup on a rainy night and the kid has his eyes, but her husband couldn't get the job done?"

Though that flood of words barely made sense, some of the others were nodding.

"Speaking as a guy," Murphy said, "which may not be an opinion you want, but I agree with Veronica—Vee—that doing that to someone is cruel. You should always give a person the choice. If they decide they're fine with being hands off ahead of time, that's one thing."

"You're male. You don't know what it's like." One of the other ladies flicked her fingers in dismissal. "Try being a woman nearing middle age with no prospects in sight and tell me what you think then, okay, Romeo?"

Murphy's ears reddened, but his voice remained steady. "I'm sorry if my valid opinion tweaks your conscience. Maybe you should think about that."

Before she could respond, he rolled on smoothly. "Again, as an outsider with a possibly unwanted opinion, it seems to me you all need a list. A way of keeping track of who wants what and where you're at in the process before you decide what to do about it."

"So, the present male is taking charge of our vaginas yet again." Andi's friend rolled her eyes. "Typical."

I cleared my throat. "No, I think he's got a point. Unless we all just want to sit around and drink wine—"

"Coffee," Macy corrected as she polished the counter.

I had to smile. She never missed a trick, that one.

"We need some kind of way of keeping track in an orderly fashion. Like maybe something in Excel or hell, I don't know. Anyone have any experience with that?"

"A database." Murphy nodded. "Sure do. Easy enough to put together."

My palms grew sweaty as I stroked Latte's silky fur. *Now or never, Dixon.* "Maybe we can get together and work on it."

Some of the women started to rise.

"No, no, not all of you, not yet. Murphy and I." I cleared my throat again and sneaked a look at the man in question. "I could come over tonight?"

Whoa, bold. I was either a genius or a fool. Possibly both concurrently.

"Sure." His lips twitched. "But don't we need some info to compile first?"

Huh. Good point. I was obviously focused on the front end of this proposition and not so much on the back.

Unless it involved me lying on mine.

Hastily, I grabbed the notepad I'd set aside for this very task and gently nudged the dog aside so I could write. Latte slid into the space between my thigh and the chair arm and didn't wake up, making me laugh and all the others *ooh* and *ahh*.

He was a cutie, all right. Almost as much as his owner.

I wrote my contact number on top of the notepad along with a few headings for needed information to get started with. We'd add on as we went.

Look at that, I was already thinking of this project as a *we* kind of thing—specifically a me and Murphy kind of thing.

"Fill out what you're comfortable with and give it to the next person, please." I passed the pad to the woman closest to me. "Murphy and I will set up a database and get in contact with you for our next meeting. Hopefully, we can split into smaller groups based on interest. Exploration vs. needing help finding a prospect vs. just gathering information for the future. It would be nice if there was a way that we could match people with interested guys, assuming there are any."

"Pretty sure we have one right in our midst." One of the women in back laughed behind her hand.

"Murphy's just here to help. Practice on someone else." I flashed a quick smile. "But that's down the line. First, we'll try to set up a few smaller groups. Leave your email addresses and I'll contact everyone when we have another date to get together."

"And possibly somewhere else you will be meeting." Macy delivered refills to a couple of people and shot me a smile of her own. It was as sincere as mine had been. "Just saying."

That was a worry for another day.

I tucked Latte against my hip as he started to stir and rose to my feet. "Thanks for coming, everyone. Maybe we can find a way for this to be beneficial for all of us." I glanced at Murphy and my smile grew. "Thanks for your help."

"Anytime." He nodded at Latte. "Looks like you have a friend for life."

"We're buds." I lifted him to my face and kissed his wet little nose, laughing as he lapped at my face. "Best buds, right?"

Murphy slipped his hands in his pockets. "I better take him with me. Since food and all."

"Oh, I can watch him for a while. We'll be meeting in a—"

"Vee."

I sighed as Macy's voice intruded into my happy puppy bubble. Reluctantly, I handed the puppy back to Murphy. Latte looked at me forlornly, but he quickly scrabbled up Murphy's sweatshirt to snuggle up in the hood scrunched behind his neck.

Murphy let out a wry laugh as he tried to crane his neck to look at the puppy, and I swear, my already compromised ovaries made themselves known.

And how.

This guy was father material. Forget that, he was excellent boyfriend material. One of the good ones. I'd stake my blueberry tarts on it.

And I didn't want to wait for someone else to figure that out before I'd had my chance.

"Thanks again. Truly. You don't know how much you helped."

"No problem." He slid a glance at the chattering women. "It was fun."

I laughed. "Sure it was. I'll see you in a couple hours? I want to help out here for a bit since I created some chaos with this meeting."

"No problem. I'll make dinner. So, bring your appetite."

I watched him walk out with the puppy snuggled in the folds of his hood. No problem there. No sirree.

"He didn't even buy anything," Macy said with disgust as she crossed through the passthrough to head into the back room. "Am I running a business or a damn charity here? Sometimes I don't know."

A minute later, she poked her head back out. "Vee? We're low on petit fours again."

Because the women I'd met with had cleared her out. It had been a good night for Macy too, no matter how she groused.

"Coming." I said some quick goodbyes to the women and grabbed an apron so I could get to work.

If luck was on my side, maybe coming was in my sorta near future after all, and not from cyber—

Oh, fuck. I dropped my apron and fumbled out the phone I hadn't touched in forever. I owed Cabin Fortress a note.

And an apology.

But I couldn't tell him about Murphy. Not yet. Nothing had happened, not really. I liked them both.

So much.

As an idea formed, my thumbs blurred over the keys. Perhaps after this note, Cabin Fortress would make my decision for me. This would prove how committed he was to getting to know me.

Let the baby daddies fall where they may.

NINE

Dearest Fortress,

I have to say your note was very stimulating. I also like sturdy surfaces. But I forgot to tell you I also really like beds. My bed is piled high with stuffed animals and pillows. I can't have sexy times without lots of pillows around me and under me. I'm petite, and I think it's a security thing. Also, I always have to bring my bear with me. Sir Mix A Lot has been with me since childhood. You don't mind if I bring him along the first time we get freaky, do you? He won't be participating. Unless that's your kink. Haha.

STILL YOURS, VEE

"What in the hell?"

The dog barked as if answering me.

I shoved my phone back into my pocket before I scooped my new charge off his current favorite perch. When we were in the truck, he liked to sit on my shoulder and watch the world go by out the window. I couldn't say I hated it. And I was getting used to him a little too easily.

I gathered all my purchases and muscled my way into the cabin with a dog trying to burrow into my shoulder, enough bags to cut off my circulation, and two different Veronica personalities swimming in my head. I was officially going insane.

And what the hell was I supposed to do with this new note from Veronica?

I mean, what in the hell? A bear?

I dumped the bags on my table and retrieved my phone again. I reread it, making sure I hadn't misconstrued anything.

Nope. She'd actually said she liked to bring a security bear with her.

And freaky? She hadn't spoken like that in all the nights we'd talked online.

I mean, yeah, we were getting hotter around the edges with each conversation, but for fuck's sake. That was some weird shit. And nearly a Jekyll and Hyde situation compared to how she talked to me at the café.

On the last few visits for my daily caffeine intake, she'd been almost manic. That was partly why I'd skipped visiting the café for a couple days.

Today? That was more like how we used to act around one another. Polite with a hint of maybe more than polite.

But she'd looked up at me with those bright green eyes with excitement about her little project while cuddling the freaking dog— Latte, his name was Latte now—and how could I tell her no?

To anything.

I was doomed. And still had ended up with a dog somehow. It had broken my heart to drop off the rest of them at the shelter, but since they were tiny and the hypoallergenic kind, they had a waiting list for them. I knew they were all going to a good home.

And thankfully, they were all healthy regardless of the asshat who'd put them in a box and left them to die. Fucking heartless humans. Why I liked spending as little time with them as possible. I got most of the peopling I needed out of working with Gideon.

I was perfectly happy to be a freaking hermit. Especially if a certain baker might want to hermit with me. Maybe.

If I didn't totally fuck everything up.

At least I'd cut down on Veronica's trouble factor with Macy. Macy had been at the end of her rope with the group of women taking over half the café. Adding in a dog to the melee wasn't happening beyond the meeting. Even that had been pushing it. Though I figured Veronica could work around that easily enough.

"But for now, it's just you and me, bud." I tucked him into the hood of my sweatshirt as I did a quick and dirty clean-up of my house.

I lived alone and kept pretty tidy, but I forgot to do things like dust and vacuum.

Latte snoozed behind me, occasionally licking the back of my neck for me to reach around and give him a scratch. Other than that, he was content to just chill out while I took care of the domestic shit I'd neglected.

I set my pressure cooker up with a warm and hearty chicken stew. It was probably a little unfair to use my online Vee knowledge to impress her today. And dangerous because what the hell would I do if I screwed up and said something Fortress would know, but not me?

Lies, Masterson. All of it was lies, no matter how you sliced it.

Oh, speaking of slice. I rushed over to the bag of groceries I'd picked up on the way home. I took out the fresh loaf of French bread and sliced it, wrapped it, and put it in the oven to warm up.

I tucked the four-pack of mini cheesecakes I'd bought into the fridge—I should've gotten some of Veronica's creations instead—then whipped up some fresh whipped cream while the pressure cooker did its thing.

One of the few things I could do was make a decent meal, thanks to my mama. She wouldn't allow her boys to be useless in the kitchen.

And having a cabin on the lake meant going to get fast food all the time was close to impossible.

So, I could cook. Passably anyway. I didn't have Vee's grace with the sugary end of the spectrum, but I could make a damn good whipped cream to add to some fruit toppings.

A little head peeked over my shoulder. "Like strawberries, Latte?"

I frowned. Was a dog allowed to have strawberries?

I Googled and fell down a rabbit hole of dog owner woes and scare tactics as Latte and I shared half a dozen strawberries. They were on the okay list for dogs, thank you.

Grapes, however, that was a hell no. Especially with the size of my dog.

Our dog? Huh. I didn't know how to work that.

Pretty much like a baby would work with her current plan of attack. Joint custody if both of us were in agreement. Christ.

I didn't want joint anything. Well, okay, that was a lie. I wanted us joined at the hip as much as humanly possible. What I didn't want was just to be her babymaker. I already wanted more.

And that was where things were getting really murky.

I liked her too much and she didn't even know who the hell I really was.

I collapsed into my desk chair with Latte burrowing back into his hood bed now that his insanely tiny belly was full. Man, should I have even gone with strawberries? The vet at the shelter wasn't even sure how old the puppies were.

Barely weaned off their mama was all he could guess.

I guess I'd find out when he shits seeds like a machine gun or projectile vomited before digestion happened.

Fun.

I did a few more searches about what puppies should and shouldn't eat between trying to formulate a response to my Sir Mix A Lot problem.

We all had our kinks, but that seemed especially precious for

Veronica. She had a sense of whimsy to her, considering the multi-color hair she had going on. But a teddy bear that had to accompany her on date night?

Or whatever we wanted to call a hookup?

Hmm.

I started to reply, then wandered off when the pressure cooker beeped that it was ready and finished decompressing. I turned on some music while I made gravy and made sure the veggies weren't mush.

My alarm buzzed on my watch reminding me I had fifteen minutes before she was due to arrive.

"Ready for some food, pal?"

My hood wiggled with Latte's furious tail wag. I laughed and scooped him out of the hood to set him down with his puppy-prescribed food. Which was precisely a thimbleful for such a little guy.

He wolfed it down and whined for me to settle him back into my hood.

My doorbell rang and I swore. "She's early, dammit."

I rushed around to make sure nothing would burn and cursed because I hadn't gotten to wash up yet. My online search down the puppy-problems-and-feeding rabbit hole had officially eaten way too much of my time.

I washed my hands, dried them, and tucked my towel into my belt on my way to the door. I swung it open and smiled, swallowing down my nerves. "Hey."

"This is your place? It's incredible. I thought I was going to drive forever to get up your driveway." She didn't wait for me to move out of the way, simply marched in with the scent of vanilla and sugar in her wake.

"You're early."

"Oh, right. Sorry about that. I'm perpetually early. Better than being late though, right?"

Latte perked up at the sound of her voice and tried to climb off me to get to her. "Okay, okay. Hang on a second, bud. You're going to hurt yourself."

She turned back to me with her eyes shining again just as they did a few hours ago. "Oh, he missed me." She rushed over and laid a hand gently on my chest as she went onto her toes, then plucked the puppy out of my hands. "I'll take him."

That was a totally unnecessary touch and now I was even more confused. She was just here for database help, right?

Though she had volunteered to stop by tonight. Was she sending signals I was just too thick to get?

"Aren't you just the cutest little boy in all the world?" she crooned to him as she wandered into my living room. "My goodness, Murphy. This is quite the house. When you said you had a cabin by the lake, I was expecting something a lot more rustic."

I looked around at my space, taking in the vaulted A-line ceiling and nearly floor to ceiling windows that looked out on the lake. "It is a cabin."

"This is a luxury cabin at best. It's incredible. And you built it your— Oh my God, that kitchen." She cradled the dog against her chest and twirled around my large farmhouse kitchen. She set the dog down and swiped her hand along the floor. "Cork," she said reverently.

Right then, I was very glad I'd hit it with a mop after I vacuumed.

The dog trotted after her with adoration hearts popping out of his eyeballs. Considering I knew that look, I didn't blame him. I probably wore the same expression on my face most of the time. She quickly moved to the big sink and washed her hands then trailed her fingertips along the granite counters and over my small appliances.

"You have everything."

I shrugged and crossed my arms before leaning my hip on the kitchen island. "I like to cook."

"And it smells amazing." She turned to the pressure cooker, which was now on its slow cooker setting. The steam rose up and floated around her. She closed her eyes and drew in the aromas. "Wow. May I?" She lifted the spoon on the rest.

"Sure."

She dipped it in and took a taste before twirling around to me again, cupping her hand under the spoon as she held it up for me. "You gotta taste this."

"I cooked it." But I grinned down at her.

"That's true. But I bet it tastes even better now." She blew on the spoon. "Come on."

I leaned down and sampled it, watching her face the entire time. I dribbled a bit and she laughed.

She didn't even hesitate, just swiped her thumb over my chin and brought the bit of gravy to her lips. "So good." A little wrinkle formed between her eyes. "So, you build stuff, and you can make a database? And you cook?"

I rolled my lower lip behind my teeth. I shrugged.

Be cool.

Don't start to sweat.

"I'm trying to get into smart houses. Takes a little bit of everything to do that."

"Oh." Her forehead smoothed. "Well, that's a little bit more than the average handyman." She looked up at the vaulted ceilings of my cabin. "I guess you'd have to be to afford all this."

I shrugged. "I do okay."

"I'll say."

I needed to veer her away from this line of conversation. "Speaking of dinner, I even have fresh bread from the market bakery too. I didn't have time to bake some myself."

"You do *not* bake bread."

"I like the rustic kind that you eat with stew or soup, but yeah."

"We're totally doing that one snowy night."

I swallowed. She was thinking about more than today. More than me just helping her out.

I wasn't great with signals, but even I was starting to pick up some now.

"I can't believe you did all this anyway. Especially after I'm asking you for a favor. That doesn't seem right."

"I don't mind. I don't get to cook for people too often." I looked down at my feet before I did something stupid like lower my lips to hers.

"Well, all I do is cook—well, bake—for people. So, this is really nice. Thank you."

"You're welcome."

She took a step back and washed the spoon before laying it back down next to my Ninja Pot. Latte decided he'd been ignored long enough and started dancing around in circles.

"Uh oh. Does someone need to go outside?" She crouched down and scratched along his ears. "I think he does."

"I'll take him. Too many predators out there for this little guy." I scooped him up and prayed he didn't pee on me before I got him outside, then noticed my damn computer was still on.

Shit.

My logo was bouncing around the screen. Way to go, idiot.

"Speaking of...it was a long ride."

"Huh?" I blinked back in at her voice.

"Bathroom?"

"Oh, sure." I pointed to the wall just beyond the kitchen. "There's a little water closet just there."

She tilted her head at me. "In the wall? Oh, is that a hidden door?" She pressed against the little seam and the door popped open. "How cool is that?"

"I didn't want to ruin the flow of the house, so I hid it."

"Well, I love it." She smiled and slipped inside, closing the door.

I rushed over to the computer and clicked on the mail and chat window. Damn, I'd only written half a letter back to her. No time to figure that out right now. I'd just do it later.

I heard the toilet flush, then the water running.

Move faster.

I tried to close the email window, but Latte gave a little distress bark and the quick whoosh of the *email sent* sound told me I had not hit the right thing at all.

"Shit," I whispered.

I didn't have time to unsend it, and that option didn't work half the time anyway with web email clients. I'd have to do some triage later. Maybe I'd just keep her busy, so she didn't look at her phone until we were apart.

Not that I'd be saving CF any trouble. But he could fast talk his way out of situations better than I could.

I could practically hear my best friend now.

Talking about yourself in the third person, son? Slippery slope there.

Something else I could worry about later.

I flicked off the screen and hustled out the back door before she could come out and find me.

I'd have to face the music before long, but maybe we could have dinner and some pleasant conversation first.

Tomorrow would come soon enough.

TEN

Vee,

I have a very nice king-sized bed we can make super comfortable for you. I'm not quite sure on the bear though. Could we turn him away from us? I'm not sure I could...perform under those circumstances without a few practice rounds. At least I'd hope you'd feel secure enough to try it without Sir Mix A Lot. Besides, I wouldn't want to compromise your bear. I plan on—

THE NOTE STOPPED. JUST STOPPED. JUST LIKE MY HEART AS I stared back and forth between the unfinished note I'd just received and the spotless mirror.

I was standing in Murphy Masterson's hidden away bathroom—or water closet as he'd called it, which I found old-fashioned and sweet—in his hidden away cabin.

Did I somehow have a fetish for the sort of man who isolated himself in the forest? Did this mean I was doomed to end up on *Forensic Files?*

Maybe I should be looking for a plunger or long-handled brush I could use as a weapon if necessary, instead of trying to figure out if coming back out braless was sending too strong a message.

Please fuck me—if you aren't a serial killer.

Though that really wasn't the kind of question it was easy to segue into before fucking. And I'd never be able to live with myself if I found out after.

But it'd be easier to die with a few orgasms under my belt. It had been so long I expected cobwebs to grow over my girly rhododendron any day now.

It was always the quiet ones and Murphy definitely qualified. But I was reasonably sure he wasn't homicidal. The only reason my brain had gone there was because I liked two guys who lived tucked away from society. They weren't the only people who preferred such a lifestyle, but it did seem odd that I'd happened to start talking to a guy with the same setup as Murphy.

Either I had a dangerous fixation on rustic types without even realizing it or something was…suspicious.

A cabin.

Murphy.

Could it be?

Could it not be?

When I'd first entered the bathroom, I'd been dazed and happy that I was actually in private with Murphy. In his inner sanctum so to speak. Then I'd realized I was far too revved up to just work on a database with him, and if it wasn't right to screw someone before a first date, it definitely wasn't right to screw them before dinner.

Maybe? I didn't have a handbook for this sort of thing. Nor did I know when I'd gone from liking Murphy from afar to wanting to get naked with him, but I supposed once you started embracing your needs, they stood up and shouted for relief.

Or maybe that was the battery pack on my vibrator.

I glanced at my phone again. When my email had chimed, I'd finished up and washed my hands, then discovered Cabin Fortress had abruptly ended his message.

As if he'd been in a hurry.

Like he might be if he'd been interrupted by a dinner guest.

I narrowed my eyes at the mirror as emotions warred inside me. Elation and anger, worry and joy, relief and confusion. Beneath all of them was the feeling of being a total idiot.

Not the first time I'd felt that way recently, and I didn't like it one bit.

I needed to find out the truth.

Before I lost my nerve, I hurried to open the bathroom door and rushed out, looking right and left. That the place was a big open concept helped. You didn't really need a tour when everything was wide open.

I hurried through the kitchen and into the living room, my ears pricked for any sound. Murphy and Latte would be back any minute.

And look at that, there was his desk. Three monitors. Big fancy setup. Was that where he sat every night when he talked to me?

If. Still a big if. There was no proof yet. Just my interest in both men. Just the fact that both lived in cabins. Both did stuff with computers.

Could I already feel so comfortable with Murphy because down deep, I already felt like I knew him?

Or that could be my conscience trying to explain away why I wanted to have sex with a man I barely knew. I wasn't one to care about conventions much—obviously, judging from my baby proclivities—but this was sudden even for me.

Or was it?

Bypassing the view out the gorgeous floor to ceiling windows, I zeroed in on my target. His desk was unreasonably tidy. Figured. If I'd had to guess if Murphy was a Felix or Oscar from *The Odd Couple,* I would've gone with Felix. Everything had a place, rather than my organized chaos.

I sat in his big chair and swiveled between the screens, finding the monitors turned off. Once I turned them on, they were all locked down with passwords. Naturally. He wouldn't take any chances.

So, I'd just open the drawers.

Guilt niggled at me, but not much. I'd become Officer Vee. It wasn't snooping if you had probable cause.

Time to serve the warrant.

The first drawer was so tidy I had to roll my eyes. Not in disgust. Sheer jealousy. Could I hire him to help me get my life in order? It was probably hopeless.

Perhaps I wouldn't find anything lying around. It wasn't as if I even knew what I was looking for. A notepad with Vee and Cabin Fortress doodled in a heart? Not likely.

I went through two more drawers and nada. Nothing. Just paperwork that was too dry for me to sort through and tidy stacks of office supplies. He had enough black pens to survive a few shortages and the same number of reams of paper.

I liked a man who was prepared, except when he was thwarting me from proving my case.

If there was any case to prove. Just because my nose was wiggling like a damn bunny's didn't mean much.

The back door slammed, and I jerked to my feet. Belatedly, I realized that when he stepped inside, he could see me quite clearly.

Where I'd been rifling through his desk.

Maybe I was the budding serial killer. Or a fraud alert waiting to happen.

We stared at each other across the space without saying a word. I was barely even breathing. Then Latte let out a yelp and Murphy set him down, only for the dog to beeline straight for me on his wobbly little legs.

I scooped him up and buried my face in his damp fur, buying myself another moment.

Until Murphy spoke.

"You figured it out."

I went still. My breath stuttered to a halt. But I lifted my head and met his eyes squarely. "Figured what out?"

Finally, he looked away. "You were digging through my desk."

"Maybe I needed a pen. Or a condom, so you could lay me down by the fireplace and trace my body with your tongue. You know, give or take a verb and adjective or two."

I waited for him to duck his head or to look chagrined or *something*. The kind of cowardly thing most men I'd been acquainted with would've done after being nailed to the wall.

Not Murphy. He was the exception to every rule.

He just met my gaze head on. "I still want that. I want it even more now."

"Oh, really? Oh, really?"

Yeah, my comebacks needed some work. But who could blame me? I was clutching the dog and trying to stay standing on watery knees while my pulse thundered out of control.

Murphy's head was basically just a giant pulsing tomato at this point, throbbing in time with my heartbeat.

"Yes, really." He set down Latte's leash and stepped farther into the room, until I threw out a hand to ward him off.

He stopped immediately, but Latte decided to try to scramble up my arm. I tucked him firmly against my side and sucked in a breath. "Did you have fun with this?"

"Fun with what, exactly?" His voice was so even that it seriously pissed me off. "If you mean talking to you every night, absolutely. Speaking to you was the best part of my day. But if you are referring to—"

"Conning me? Lying to me? Making me fa—" I cut myself off and shook my head. I couldn't scream with the puppy in my arms, and I couldn't put him down or else I was going to scream.

Right now, Latte was a safety measure for Murphy. I hoped he realized that.

Murphy raked a hand through his hair. "I didn't mean to lie to you. And I definitely wasn't conning you."

When I let out a screech that made Latte turn panicked eyes my way and start to pump his legs, Murphy moved forward again.

"Give me the dog, Veronica."

Back to Veronica. I hated how much I loved when he called me my full name. But he'd called me Vee at the café. Something I'd only just now realized.

His two roles blurring.

Two personalities, halves of the same whole. Which one was the truth?

Or were both of them really Murphy?

Stubbornly, I held onto Latte, shifting him onto my chest. He snuggled right in, clearly not holding my histrionics against me. "No. He's mine."

For a second, I thought Murphy was going to laugh. The bastard. But he sobered and held out a hand, saying nothing.

I glanced at the lamp on his desk and pictured him sitting there, talking to me all night while I felt guilty for wanting both Fortress and Murphy at the same time. While I was certain I didn't have a snowball's chance in Miami of actually dating Murphy.

And while I'd been tormented, he'd held all the cards.

"If I give you this dog, I'm probably going to throw this lamp at your head. Tomorrow, I'll feel bad I did it. Tonight? It will feel like sweet justice."

"Okay. Still give me the dog. Please."

I narrowed my eyes at him. "I just threatened you with bodily harm and you're more worried about the dog—which I would never, ever hurt, by the way—than your own physical safety."

This was why I knew this man would make a good father. He was so utterly calm and reasonable.

I wanted to kick his ass. Couldn't he at least get pissed back at me, so my anger didn't flame out before it barely got started?

"I know you wouldn't hurt Latte. I also know you wouldn't want to scare him. He's just a baby, Vee."

I let out a broken laugh. "One minute I'm Veronica. One minute

I'm Vee. Which am I to you? Or am I just a big joke, the laughingstock of the town you couldn't resist toying with for sport?" Even as I asked the question, I knew it wasn't true.

Could never be true about Murphy. After talking to him these past weeks as Cabin Fortress, I was even more sure of that. He couldn't have faked everything.

Maybe he hadn't faked any of it, except the part about us not being that familiar to each other. If we hadn't been before, we sure were now.

"No." His voice was almost violently steady. "You aren't a joke. The farthest thing from it." He took an unsteady breath and tipped back his head before meeting my gaze squarely once again. "You asked if you're Veronica or Vee to me? You're both. You're beautiful and impetuous and strong and brave and smart. You're going to be a wonderful mother someday, and any man would be lucky enough to—"

"Wait. You want to have a baby with me? That was true too?"

He swallowed hard, his Adam's apple moving up and down. "It took me a few days to get there, but yeah, I guess I do."

I sank to his chair, clutching the puppy carefully to my chest while I tried to make sense of what I was hearing.

"You barely know me."

"Maybe that was true a couple of weeks ago, but it's not true any longer. Everything we talked about was all true. I didn't lie about any of it, just hid a few details that would allow you to identify me."

"But why didn't you want me to know it was you? And how the hell were you going to knock me up if I never saw you in person? Newsflash, online ejaculation doesn't count."

"Thank God, or you'd have been pregnant a few times over by now."

I blinked. And blinked again. "You're saying you...while we...on the computer...while I was...what?"

"No, but it was a close thing."

"I aroused you that much?"

He never looked away. "Oh, girl, you have no idea."

Slowly, I stood and walked over to the couch to set Latte on the thick blanket tucked there. He stared up at me, his little tail wagging, while I spoke softly to him and urged him to lay down. Once he complied, still watching me, I pivoted toward Murphy.

"Do you realize what I've gone through these past weeks? First, I put up that crazy post in the wrong place. I didn't know who would respond. Meanwhile, there's this guy who comes in the café who never speaks to me no matter how I try to flirt."

His brow furrowed. "When did you try to flirt?"

I buried my face in my hands and laughed. I wasn't near to tears, thank God. Because beneath the now fading feelings of hurt and confusion was a thick layer of relief.

My two men were one. I didn't have to choose. Amen to that.

"You never spoke to me, but you talked so easily to Sage. Yet you were online trying to get me naked every night."

Not able to have this conversation in front of a child—who just happened to have fur—I rushed into the kitchen, as far away from Latte in the cabin as I could get.

"I was not trying to get you naked," he shot back as he followed me, his tone rife with indignation. "But if I had been, so what? Wasn't that what you wanted from this whole thing in the first place?"

I stopped near the counter and whirled around to shove him. I had to get my aggression out or that lamp was going to be in peril anyway. "I don't know what I want anymore. Yes, at first, I wanted a freaking baby."

"But now you don't?"

God, did I hear disappointment in his voice?

This man. I didn't know what I was going to do with him.

Okay, that was a lie. I had a pretty good idea. But he was gonna grovel first, dammit.

"Of course I do. But I was hoping to meet a decent guy. And I didn't."

He reeled back as if I'd sucker-punched him. "You didn't?"

"No. I met two of them. Goddammit. And I wanted both, and I didn't know how to choose, and I thought that made me some kind of horny ho, when in truth you were driving me crazy—"

"Shut up. Just shut up and listen to me. I didn't tell you because I didn't know how."

"What? Why? Why couldn't you just open your mouth and come clean?"

"Because I'm me and you're you."

"What?" I shoved him again, half for the pleasure of feeling my hands against his firm pecs. So firm. Jesus. "Talk sense."

"Here's some sense." He gripped me by the shoulders and lifted me up on the counter, so we were eye level. "You're my dream girl. You're everything. And I couldn't find the words to tell you. So, shut up already."

Our chests were so close, but our faces were even closer. He was out of breath, and so was I. But that didn't stop me from cocking my head. "Why don't you make me?"

"Why don't I?"

His mouth came down hard on mine, his lips warm and soft and oh so hungry, and all I could think was finally.

Fucking *finally*.

ELEVEN

Cabin Fortress: Dream Girl Alert! Flatline imminent. I may not survive.

I CUPPED HER FACE, MY ENTIRE SYSTEM HUMMING AND crashing at the same time.

This woman was everything. I wasn't lying about that. And I was terrified that she was going to disappear now that she knew I was Cabin Fortress. The rage in her eyes was nothing next to the hurt.

Things had just gotten even more crazy and convoluted, but I wanted to be her baby daddy and her lover. I wanted even more than that if I was truly being honest. But she wasn't ready for that level of honesty.

I was way ahead of her. Had been for well over a year.

But I had right now to convince her that we were worth the chance. Worth a gamble.

Her legs rose to hook around my hips and I knew I had one chance to get this right.

Bring every A-game you ever had in your life, son.

I lightly wove my fingers into her hair. It was soft as cornsilk and just as fine. A rainbow explosion of colors twisted and flowed over my wrists as I pushed through the little clips and twists she had had going on. She was forever braiding and pinning her hair back because of the work she did.

I'd always wondered just how soft it would be and it was even better than I could have imagined.

She groaned into my mouth and I deepened the kiss, turning her lightly so I could taste every last inch of her. I wanted to know everything about her. Every nuance, every breath, every gasp. I wanted to swallow her whole and let her know just how much she was wanted.

Before I could pull her closer, she wrapped her arms around my neck and hoisted herself up, so we were eye-to-eye.

"Nice guys don't kiss like that."

I squinted at her. "First of all, did you just quote a movie at me?"

She licked her lips with a devilish smile. "Maybe. And because you're Mr. Sneaky, you should know what movie it's from. I told Fortress on one of the first nights we chatted."

I smiled and shifted her tighter against me. *Bridget Jones' Diary.* I didn't know the exact line, but I figured I was damn close. "Who told you I was a nice guy?" I asked against her mouth before I went in for a second round.

She laughed into the kiss and then we were both sunk. We kissed like we'd known one another for years, not weeks. And while Murphy had known Veronica for a damn long time, it was the deeper, quieter connections between Vee and Fortress that had finally pushed both of us beyond our shyness.

Beyond the social barriers that wouldn't let us get past the polite pleasantries of customer and barista.

There were no awkward glances and fumbling touches now.

I cupped her perfect ass and fit her against my very hard, very happy cock. Finally, he was going to get a little bit of heaven. Well, if I totally didn't screw everything up.

It felt like I'd been waiting for her forever.

Probably because I had been.

"Off," she said against my mouth. "Too many clothes."

I leaned back enough to drag my hoodie over my head. I had a chambray shirt under it, but she was already worming her way under it to get to my chest.

"Goodness."

"Veronica," I said with a laugh as she got tangled in the shirt. Then there was no more laughter when she ripped the shirt open and buttons rained down around us. "Holy shit."

She raked her nails through my chest hair. "Nope, that's my line. Look at all this gloriousness you've been hiding under your layers. For shame." She peered up at me with lust and excitement in her gaze.

"I..." And then I was a goner when she shimmied downward and her mouth buzzed along my pecs down to my belly. I tried to suck it in, and she gripped me harder.

"So strong and big."

I wasn't sure what to say to that one. I wanted to preen, but that wasn't me. That was my brothers and others I knew. I wasn't the guy who got naked in the middle of the kitchen with all the fucking lights on.

But right now, I felt amazing. And strong and sexy. At least that was how she saw me and that was enough.

My belly quaked as she ran her nails down the arrow of hair that led to the snap of my work pants. "Programmers don't have bodies like this," she said and jerked the snap open.

"They do if they're part time carpenters."

"I'll have questions about that later, right now?" She pushed me back a step and slid off the counter to reach into my pants. "Right now, I want to see all the goods."

I swallowed and groaned as she tightened her super fucking

strong fingers around my very hard dick. Of course, she wanted me for this. I was a tool to reach her very clear goal.

A baby.

She drew me out of my boxer briefs and licked her lips. "Tell me you have a condom."

I blinked before my hands came back up to rest on her hips. "Condom?"

"Yeah. We haven't had the baby daddy talk and tests and all that other stuff. Right now, I just want this." She squeezed me firmly and coasted her thumb over the sensitive ridge of my head. "Inside me. It's been a damn long time, Fort–Murphy. It's been a long time since I wanted to do this with anyone. Added to the fact that it's been a crazy few weeks where I wanted to do it with *two* men."

I lowered my forehead to hers with a groan as she found the little drop of precum her words had caused. "It's been a fair bit of time for me too, Veronica."

She closed her eyes for a moment before her endless lashes fluttered back open. They weren't caked with makeup either. Soft and natural with a little bit of something to make her green eyes glow.

But it was all her.

No artifice.

Just the girl of my freaking dreams.

"The way you say my name makes me crazy. No one ever uses my full name. Heck, they even call me a million different ones, but never pick the right one. No one but you."

"Ditto, girl. Not even my mama calls me Murphy."

She wrinkled her nose. "I don't like Moose. Not that they aren't perfectly majestic creatures, but it has a whole different meaning the way people say it. And you're not a moose. You're Murphy. My Murphy," she said and pulled me back down to her mouth.

I growled out her name into the kiss as she stroked me, making me even more insane. I'd wanted her for too long to have her going at me like this without some serious repercussions. I would not be coming in her hand like an untried teenager.

No fucking way.

I tore my mouth away and whipped her soft shirt over her head. All her hair was down, and the colorful waves danced around her shoulders and down her back. "I don't think I've ever seen you with your hair down."

She shook it back and her surprisingly full breasts pushed at the lacy cups of her bra. I traced the back of my knuckles down the slope of one before lowering my mouth to the tight tip pushing against the fabric.

She slipped her fingers into my hair and held me tight as I sucked her through the stretchy cup. I curled my arm around her waist and hauled her up so she could wrap her legs around my middle.

I shifted her higher and nudged her bra away from one nipple and groaned around the soft skin before I circled the taut peak. She held onto my shoulders and arched to give me better access.

"God, yes." Her voice broke through the silence of the room and urged me to do more, cover every inch of her chest and neck.

She giggled at the rough scratch of my heavy two-day's growth. I flicked open her bra and it hit the kitchen floor.

Latte yelped and raced for the lace. He immediately tangled himself in the straps.

"Oh, no." She held onto me but was hanging down to try and help the puppy.

Me? I was still trying to get around the fact that Veronica was naked in my arms. And her unbelievably perfect breasts were dragging across my chest.

"Murphy. Help him."

"Right."

I set her on the kitchen island and scooped the dog up with her lacy strappy bra thing. He was trying to gnaw on the straps. "Okay, okay. No, sir. That's not yours."

I brought him into the living room and set him on the couch with the blanket he'd commandeered. Evidently, he liked the Sherpa-like underside of my cozy plaid blanket.

"Give a guy a break, huh?" I squeezed one of his half dozen toys and the pup attacked the little pink elephant.

"That's right. Kill it." I looked over at Veronica with a smile and held up the bra I'd saved. "I don't think he hurt it."

She waved it off and swung her legs where she sat on the edge of the breakfast bar. She leaned forward enough that her breasts swayed lightly, and my damn tongue went bone dry.

Don't say bone, man.

I turned back to her, my pants bunched around my hips, my dick tenting my boxer briefs. "Tell me the moment wasn't ruined."

She crooked her finger at me, and I returned to her as casually as my bunched pants allowed. "No way. Unless we have to run into town for a condom because I so don't have one in my purse."

I dug my wallet out of my pocket. "Would you think less of me if I admitted I'd purchased a fresh pack after you started talking dirty to me on the internet?"

Her smile widened. "Even when you knew I might not be cool with knowing Cabin Fortress's alter ego?"

"Gotta say that my dick really wasn't thinking it all the way through. And I was hoping you wouldn't hate me when you found out. If we ever got there." I fished out the condom and set my wallet on the counter.

She hooked me closer with her ankle and plucked the condom out of my hand. "I like a man who knows what he wants."

"This man wants you. So very much."

She swallowed and I wondered if I had gone too far, too fast.

This definitely wasn't going exactly the way I'd planned, but it was perfect for me. "I can put the food on warm and take you back to my room. I'll show you just how much I want you."

She reached between us, down to where I was still as hard as a damn tire iron. "I'd like that." Then she bit her lower lip. "For the second round."

"Girl, you're killing me."

Her smile widened. "I kinda like when you call me that. It's always Veronica."

"Veronica," I said softly as I traced my fingertip around her nipple.

She closed her eyes and sighed, then her eyes popped wide when I tugged not-so-gently on the tip. I didn't want her to think I couldn't play.

That this couldn't be wild and intense.

I wanted to be careful with her, but if I could get her riled up, maybe she wouldn't notice that I'd probably only last marginally longer than a first timer.

I lifted her butt and dumped her flat on her back. I took the condom from her and set it to the side. She made a little *yip* and laughed as she struggled to get up on her elbows. "You can watch," I murmured, "but right now, I'm just glad I don't have any neighbors that are close."

Her eyes widened. "I knew it, you *are* going to murder me."

Murder her pussy maybe, but I didn't think that would come out right. I tugged at her tight jeans as I arched a brow. "Murder? You came out here thinking I might not be safe?"

"Well, it's always the quiet ones. And now that you can fess up to knowing about our Murderino discussions, you know why I'd think so, pal."

Her jeans slid free once I got them past her delectable ass. I tugged off her tennis shoes, then tossed her jeans over my shoulder onto the nearby dining room chair. "Now, now. Don't get all worked up again. I thought I was forgiven."

"You kissed me quiet." She tapped her pink unicorn-socked foot against my shoulder. "Big difference."

I curved my hand along her calf. Freaking knee socks. Only this woman could make striped pink unicorn socks sexy. And they were, dammit.

I was so leaving them on.

I kissed my way along her ankle to her knee and flicked my

tongue along the skin there before easing her knee over my shoulder. "Well, then let me beg for forgiveness."

"On a kitchen island?"

I dragged my nose along the soft skin of her inner thigh. "Yep. All clean even. Well, until I'm done with you."

"Where did this cocky guy come from?"

I grinned against her skin, then nipped the fragile flesh at the top of her thigh. "I've got the girl I've liked for a damn long time here with me. I'm going to make the most of it." I lowered my mouth to the cotton panel covering my target and blew lightly against the fabric. "If you're okay with that?"

She swallowed but didn't stop watching. "Can I have that towel to cushion my elbows? I'd like to watch."

"Damn, girl." I reached for the fresh towel beside the tiny prep sink I'd built into the island.

Keep it light.

Keep it light.

Jesus, I wanted to devour her.

I tossed the towel on her belly, then covered the little wet spot on her panties with my mouth. I would damn well make it a larger one.

One step at a time.

My cock was a fucking flagpole under the counter I was leaning on. But this was about her right now. And I wanted her screaming my name. If there was one thing I was good at, it was pleasuring a girl.

When you were a guy with a less than desirable body—at least back in the day if not now—you made sure your techniques were top of the line. And I'd never had a girl complain. Thank Jesus.

Though it was a little disconcerting that she was watching so intently.

Was it because she wanted to soak it all in just like me?

Or was she testing me?

She sat up a little and cupped my cheek, then trailed her finger down my jaw. "My serious Murphy is coming back. I'm not sure if I missed him or want him to go back into hiding." She rubbed her heel along my back like a cat. "Whatever you do, I'm going to like it."

"Is that right?" I traced my tongue along the elastic edge of her panties.

She licked her lips. "Oh, yes."

"Because it's been awhile?"

She tipped her head to the side. "Because it's you."

"Fuck, that is not helping."

Her smile came back. She opened her legs a little wider. "Does that help?"

Leaning back a little, I dragged her closer to the edge of the counter to get my hands under her ass. I peeled her panties away and she yelped.

"Cold."

I splayed her open with my shoulders. "You'll be warm in a second." Then I put my lips where I'd been dreaming of placing them. I licked her as if she was a popsicle on a hot summer day. Not a damn drop wasted.

She arched up under me and I held her down, clasping my fingers together over her narrow waist as I learned every corner of her. From the little places that made her shake, to the singular combination of suction and tongue that made her curl up around me and scream my name.

I focused on my directive.

My goal.

And the number of times I could get her to yell my name.

Her flavor became part of me, like a brand-new strand of DNA in my bloodstream. Nothing had ever tasted as sweet and spicy as this woman. Her thighs shook around my head, and I swore I was probably missing a handful of hair, but damn, it was worth it.

I finally looked up from her swollen pussy to find her eyes still on me. Her chest was rising and falling as if she'd just run a marathon and her cute pastel rainbow-tipped hair stuck to the light sheen of sweat on her chest.

I couldn't help myself, I rolled up to my full height and pulled her up to meet me. I groaned into her mouth as her slightly chilled skin met my chest.

She reached between us to find me still hard as hell. "Are you done?" she asked between pants and kisses. Then she pulled me even tighter and kissed me harder. "Because I don't think any man has ever done such a complete job before." She scraped her teeth down my chin. "Ever."

I licked the last bit of her off my lower lip. "I could go for days, Veronica."

She let my erection go and laced her hands behind my head. "Normally, I'd call your bluff, but I think I believe you. And I'm not sure I like it."

I frowned down at her. "Why not?"

"Because you're far too controlled. I was losing my freaking mind, and you're as cool as a cucumber—pardon the pun."

"Oh, there's nothing cool about me." I hooked her tighter around me and fumbled along the granite for the condom I'd pulled out before. "I just wanted to make sure you knew I was worth it."

She shifted back to study me. "Worth it? Because your mouth is more talented than my entire repertoire of baking skills?"

"I doubt that."

She curled her nails into my shoulders. "Seriously, Murphy. I don't need you to impress me with your oral prowess. I just want to have fun with you."

I frowned and touched my forehead to hers. "And you're not?"

"Of course I am, but it's not all about me." She laid her hand on my chest. "It's about us. Together."

I clutched the condom. "It had to be about you, or I'd go off in a hot second." I closed my eyes and pressed my lips into her shoulder. "I want you too bad."

"Then show me."

I thought I had been. I'd just have to work harder.

She pulled my hand between us and pried my fingers open to get to the condom. She ripped it open and slipped it free. "Even ribbed for her pleasure," she said with a laugh.

"It's all about you."

"Us."

I stared into her eyes. I wasn't sure there had ever been a woman quite like Veronica in the whole of my life. "Us," I agreed.

As she rolled the latex on me, I tipped back my head at the pressure of her touch and the stupid latex. But I was also so glad it wasn't about creating a baby.

Yet.

I knew it would be coming, but right now, it was about *this*. About mutual pleasure and feeling so goddamn good.

"Murphy," she whispered.

I stared at her and moved in until the tip of my cock found her heat. I reached down to make sure she was ready for me, but she grabbed my hand.

"Just you," she breathed, inching closer to the edge of the counter.

Then she drew me inside.

It felt so good that I wanted to close my eyes and savor it. To lock the memory away in the night, but that would make it only about me. Not about us.

So, I watched her face as I stretched her open with my hips. As I gripped her thighs and held her still while I buried every single inch in her welcoming body.

"God, yes," she hissed out on a long, slow breath.

And I matched that breath, because she literally felt like heaven.

My personal version of it.

I slowly drew out and fit myself back into the sweet clasp of her body. When she hooked her legs around me again, I gripped the edge of the granite and cushioned her from the hard edge as I thrust into her again and again.

She curled herself around me like a vine and met me stroke for stroke, groan for groan, and my name was the sweetest chant from her lips.

I lost it. Every chivalrous and polite stone that had built me crumbled in her arms. I drove into her and chased a pleasure so profound I couldn't possibly come out on the other side as the same man I'd once been.

She found my mouth. The kiss was messy, wild, and imperfect, brought with biting lips and crashing teeth.

It was *us*.

Too fast—too soon—she threw back her head and shook around me. I followed her so quickly, it could've been nearly at the same time.

I came so hard that my cabin faded from my periphery and there was only Veronica and her wild, colorful hair with her bottle green eyes.

My heaven.

TWELVE

I LIFTED HER LIMP NOODLE BODY OFF THE KITCHEN COUNTER. I wasn't doing much better, but oddly, I was starting to feel reinvigorated after our little interlude. Very unusual for me. I had to admit I usually was ready for a nap.

"You're not the napping bear kind of guy?" She curled into me, her face in my neck as her breath tickled my ear.

I secured her tight against my chest. "Normally, yes. Right now? I'm just going to take care of you, all right?"

"If you take care of me any further, I'm going to have to be hospitalized for dehydration."

I brushed a quick kiss along her temple. "You'll like this."

"Oh, I liked the last one just fine, Fortress."

"Fortress, huh?"

She linked her fingers around my neck. "Well, you are built like one. Very fitting name."

I grinned. "This man is built to shelter you, girl."

"He so is." She kicked up her now bare foot. "Onward. I could get used to this carrying thing."

"You fit in my damn pocket."

"I'm not that small."

"You are."

"I'm not six...what?"

"Three."

"Mercy."

I laughed. "You should see my brothers."

"The famed Masterson brothers."

"Yeah, my older brothers. Me? Not so much." I walked down the hall to my master suite at the back of the cabin.

"Oh. You weren't kidding about the fireplace."

"No, ma'am." I'd had the option to do a gas fireplace, but I was more of a crackling wood guy. Even if it was messy as hell.

"And the chaise is real too." She met my gaze. "You're the real deal, huh?"

I shrugged and veered off from my king-sized bed to my bathroom. "I'm just a guy, Veronica."

"I doubt that very sincerely."

"Lights."

She gasped. "Did you just talk to your bathroom?"

"I have a smart house."

"Like one of those sci-fi kinds? You know, where the shower attacks you with scalding water?"

I laughed. "Not quite that AI, thanks."

"Sure, until the robots attack."

I turned us so I could get the large glass door open and set her on her feet inside my steam shower. I was a big guy and required a lot of room. "So, you don't want a nice hot shower?"

"Didn't say that." She nibbled her lip. "Maybe turn it on manually?"

I laughed and pressed my palm to the plate on the wall to override the voice functions. "Do you like a hot shower or..."

"Blistering."

I stroked the back of my hand down her back and she shivered. "On this soft skin?"

"Like a lobster," she said with a grin over her shoulder.

"Fucking dream girl." I reached back and programmed it to 102°. Three jets and an overhead rain shower started. "Good?"

"Oh, sweet mercy." She tipped her head back toward the gentle rain and held out her arms to feel the spray from the other jets. "I'm never leaving."

I'm never letting you go.

I wasn't stupid enough to say that part aloud. But I grinned down at her as she twirled once before dragging me under the hood with her. She turned her nose up, eyelashes starred with water and happiness.

This particular mental snapshot would follow me to my grave.

I lowered my mouth to hers and couldn't help but smile into the kiss as she went up onto her toes to meet me. She hooked her arms under mine to grip my shoulders as we softly swayed under the rain hood. Lazy kisses led to lazy touches.

"Alexa, play 'Into the Mystic'."

She ran her nails lightly down my back to grip my ass. I definitely rose to attention, though I'd been halfway there anyway. She rubbed her middle along my shaft as I rained suds down on us. Her rainbow hair coated her skin, leaving her tight pink nipples to peek out and drag against my chest as we slowly circled with the song.

There were no words, just Van Morrison's serenade and the water dancing at our feet. Suds teased between us and foamed around my aching cock. She brought her hand between us and stroked me lightly, then more firmly until I was the one tipping my head back to the rain coming down.

"Veronica."

She stroked harder before stepping back for the water to sluice down between us, washing the soap away. Before I could stop her, she crouched down and took me between her lips. She moved us a step away from the rushing water, and I had to slap my hand against the tiled wall as she took more than half of me into her mouth.

Between her hold and suction, I was so far gone. I couldn't do anything but watch and pray I didn't embarrass myself. I tried to urge her to her feet, but she wouldn't be deterred. With hot jets of water stinging my back, I tried to protect her from the deluge of water. I didn't have the brain power to turn off some of the shower heads since she'd told me to turn it to manual.

All I could do was take it.

She held me captive with her witchy green eyes and a mouth made for sin.

I tucked her hair behind her ear, trying desperately to let her know she needed to pull away, but she wouldn't hear of it, just doubled her efforts and I growled her name as the steam and her touch blurred my vision. I widened my stance and simply held on as the orgasm reduced me to rubble once again.

She was destroying me stone by stone and I only hoped I could rebuild myself if she marched away from me with my heart and possibly a baby.

I pulled her up, curling my arms around her shaking body. It was steamy and warm, but the water wasn't reaching her anymore.

I did all I could do. I pulled her back under the hood and warmed her through. Both of us were weaving like drunks. Me because I was fairly sure my rainbow siren had tried to kill me with her wicked mouth, and her because of the steam. We chuckled as we shared my fluffy washing scrubber.

There really weren't any words I could come up with, but the silence wasn't uncomfortable. No, it was intense and comforting at the same time. Finally, I turned off the water and pulled her out to wrap her in a fluffy towel.

She shivered and I pulled out a second towel for her hair. The gray towel swallowed her with enough room for two more people. "Sorry. I only have me sized towels.

"How handy, I like you sized towels." She blotted her hair dry as she crossed to the huge window.

She looked good in my space. Too good. Especially for the number of times I'd imagined her right there. Firelight turned her rainbow hair gold and the room felt right for the first time in a long time.

Dangerous thoughts, son.

"Hungry?"

She turned around, her lips quirking as she lowered her towel to show her fire-kissed shoulders.

I cleared my throat. "For food."

"I could eat." Her gaze flicked down my chest to my waist.

I gripped my towel at my hip and glanced down. Was she checking me out?

No.

That was crazy. I moved to my large armoire and pulled out clothes. I turned and swallowed hard. She was right next to me. I handed her one of my Henleys.

"I don't need my clothes?"

"Oh, you're not going home."

She took the shirt and let her towel drop to the floor. "Is that right?"

Dear God, she was going to kill me.

She pulled the shirt on, then sat on the edge of my bed and tugged back on her unicorn socks.

I stepped into a pair of sweats, trying my damnedest to ignore the fact that she was nude. I needed to feed her and as much as I wanted to keep her naked, I needed to get my head on straight.

I was already so far gone over this woman. She was going to see it and run back to town on foot.

Play it cool, man.

I took her hand. "I'm not done with you yet. Chaise and fireplace, remember?"

She clasped my wrist with her other hand and trotted after me. "I do. But if you feed me, I'm going to snuggle into that king-sized bed and sleep."

I paused before we got to the door. "I'm willing to take a chance."

"So, you don't just want me for sex?"

"Do you?"

She tipped her head in that ridiculously cute, inquisitive manner that pretty much did me in the first day I met her. Everyone else called me Moose and she tipped her head and asked for my real name. Never called me Moose. Ever.

Was it any wonder I'd been interested? Even though it had been my name since high school, hell...junior high, to be honest. She didn't seem to see me as the big, clumsy, shy guy. And around her, I wasn't. Well, I was shy, but I'd managed to grow out of the clumsiness, even if the name had already stuck.

"We both know I have plans, Murphy. But no, sex and your swimmers are not the only thing I'm interested in."

"Good." I drew her down the hall into the wide open plan of my house. "Why don't you serve up some of that stew and I'll stoke the fire?"

She sighed. "The fact that you have more than one fireplace is unfair."

I checked on Latte and found him snuggled down in his blanket, dreaming puppy dreams. "Well, when I built this place—"

"Wait, you really built it?" She opened cabinets and found the large bowls and ladled out a hearty portion for each of us.

"Yep. I mean, not only me. But I worked with an architect and designed it with him. I knew what I wanted. After I sold my third game to a pretty large company, I had enough to do what I wanted." I tossed a few logs on the embers of the fire from before she came and got it moving with a few well-placed newspapers.

"Wow. What kind of games?" She set the bowls on the table and went back for the bread. "Butter?"

"Fridge."

She twirled and made a little strangled sound as she saw my restaurant-sized fridge. "Wow." She swung open both doors. "You have all the toys."

"Fridge is smart too," I said as I came up behind her and slipped my hand along her hip.

"Oh?" She stilled with the fridge still open.

I traced lazy circles on her thigh. "Camera inside so I can check when I need milk."

"God, that's so hot."

Laughing, I twirled her back around to face me and shut the doors. "I worked up a powerful appetite." I toyed with the hem of my shirt and cupped her ass to drag her in closer.

She rested her hands on my chest, grinning up at me. "Then stop distracting me."

"It's a fridge."

"I'm a baker. Do you know how many supplies I could hold in there? I could climb in there."

"Let's not test that theory. But my kitchen is yours."

"Don't offer up things like that, sir. I will take advantage."

Take advantage. Please. "I cook for you, you bake for me. I think this is a win-win."

"Deal." She laughed and slipped away to perch on the edge of a chair at the dining room table. "I gotta say, I've never eaten half naked at the table."

"The table part is the exclusion?" I sat next to her and unwrapped the bread. Thankfully, it was just a little extra crispy, not burned.

"Who hasn't raided the fridge in the middle of the night?"

I choked on the spoonful of food. "Naked raiding?"

She ripped a piece of bread and dunked it into her bowl. "Gets hot in my apartment in the summer."

I groaned. "Cruel, cruel woman."

She took a bite of bread and gave me an answering groan. "Did I mention I'll be sleeping?" She looked around suddenly. "Where's Latte?"

"Burrowed in his blanket."

"Aww. I can't believe you kept him. That's so sweet."

"I didn't really have a choice. He climbed up my arm like a damn monkey. Then climbed in my coat and wouldn't leave me."

"So gruff, but you know you love him."

I shrugged. "He's all right. My brothers will give me hell for having a little dog."

She picked up her spoon and tried to cut up the huge cubed meat.

"Sorry. I tend to make a pretty big bite."

"Works for me. You should see what I put away." She grinned around a spoonful. She chewed and swallowed before giving me the head tilt again.

"What?"

"Your brothers give you a hard time?"

"I'm the baby, besides my sister. I think they believe it's their job to toughen me up. Doesn't matter that I'm thirty-damn-years-old now."

"Sounds nice."

"If nice means getting the crap beat out of me on the rink, the field, and any other place they can find me, then sure."

"Really?"

I laughed. "It's not that bad." Lies. My brothers were hell on earth. I loved them to death and would die for them—even probably kill for them—but they were not easy to live with.

"I'm not even sure where my mom is right now. She checks in every few weeks, so I know she's alive. Last check in, she was in Bali."

"Wow."

"Yeah. My mother's last name should be wanderlust. She loves to travel. Doesn't have a plan, just a stamp in her passport for every port, country, and map dot she can find out there in the world."

"And you didn't want to travel with her?"

She shook her head. "I'd had enough of that as a kid. I never knew which school I'd be transferring to. We zigzagged all over the US before I was eighteen. Once she was legally free of me, she was gone. I've pretty much been on my own ever since." She stood and took our bowls.

I hooked my arm around her waist. "Hey. Don't do that."

"Do what?" She wiggled away. "Cleaning up is what I do."

I followed her into the kitchen. "Not here you don't."

She went to the sink and turned on the faucet. "You cooked, I clean. That's the rules."

"Who's rules?"

She narrowed her eyes at me. "Always the rules."

I turned off the water and drew her over to me. "They'll keep."

"I can't leave dishes."

I lowered my mouth to hers. "You can, and you will."

She tried to brush me aside. "It'll just take…"

I twirled her out to make her laugh.

"Murphy…"

"Veronica." I drew her in closer then bent down enough to toss her over my shoulder. "I have other plans."

She squeaked and hung her arms down my back. "You're a closet caveman."

"Not so closet." I strode down the hall to my room. "I told you I have plans for you."

She smacked my ass.

"Is that mosquito bite supposed to hurt?" I lowered her to the floor in front of the fire, then gently eased her onto the chaise.

She flipped her hair out of her face. "Animal."

But I could tell she wasn't mad. From the state of her nipples, I'd say she liked it. Before I could talk myself out of it, or backtrack and play it safe, I flipped her borrowed shirt off and crowded her farther back onto the huge chair.

"I'll show you what kind of animal I can really be." I inched down a little and dragged my scruffy chin down her skin. It pinked up in the golden light, but she arched into my touch. I didn't want her to ever think she had to be alone again.

But again, it was way too early to say that aloud.

Seeing her sad about killed me. My family may be a pain in my ass, but I wouldn't trade them for anything. So, I wouldn't allow her to be upset. That one thing, I could take care of with the ultimate distraction.

I drew her tight little nipple into my mouth and watched as she tipped her head back in pleasure. I mapped out all the spots that made her writhe under me, and the ones that tickled. Veronica Dixon didn't skimp on anything in her life, let alone showing me just how much she enjoyed my touch.

But this time, I let her do an equal amount of touching.

We kissed like we had all the time in the world. Until our lips were swollen and laughter drifted into broken groans. I drew her hands above her head. "Keep them there."

She looked up at me, her green eyes flickering with gold from the fire. A light sheen of sweat dotted her chest and her need slickened her thighs. I opened her wider and found a trio of freckles on her belly just above her pussy.

I licked them and slowly connected the dots again and again as I feathered my fingers through the light strip of curls over her slit.

One of her hands dropped to my hair.

"Un-uh. You're going to need something to hold onto."

She lifted one brow. "Is that right?"

I nipped her inner thigh. "I didn't have dessert."

"You had your dessert before dinner, pal."

"Appetizer."

"Didn't we go over this? I like touching you too."

"And you will. In one hundred seconds."

"What?"

"Count back from one hundred." I lowered my mouth to her pussy. "If you can."

"Of course I can."

I nodded. "Sure you can."

"One-hundred, ninety-nine, ninety-eight..."

I licked her gently, then a little rougher, my tongue lingering inside her warm flesh. Her words stuttered around the eighties as I gently sank two fingers inside her and brought my thumb up to circle her clit.

I risked a glance up at her and pressed my aching cock into the chaise as she arched and gripped the cushion.

"What number are you on, Veronica?"

"Seventy, sixty-nine. God, what kind of witchcraft is this countdown thing?"

I grinned against her leg before crawling up her to catch her mouth in a hot, hard kiss. "Sixty-eight, was it?"

Her eyes blazed and she gritted her teeth through the sixties as I pumped my fingers inside of her lightly, then harder, then back again, searching for the right combination for this woman. The only woman I wanted to know inside and out.

She wrapped her legs tighter around my hand when she hit the forties. I followed her until she was crowded up at the head of the long chair. I stepped off to get a better angle and flipped her around onto her knees.

"Murphy," she groaned. "God, just fuck me."

"Keep counting."

"Thirty, twenty-nine, twenty-eight." She gripped the chair and pushed back on my hand. I cupped her and growled out her name when her thigh shook, and she soaked me. I lowered to lick her from behind.

She arched and I pushed at my sweatpants. I needed to be inside of her. Fuck, this woman would end me tonight.

I stood and couldn't get over just how gorgeous she was spread out for me, waiting for me.

Mine.

Lightly, I tapped her ass. "Lost the ability to count?"

"If you don't get inside me in the final ten seconds, I'm going to kill you."

I laughed and moved to the end table by my bed. I came back with a condom before she got to five. I straightened her on the couch and slammed home when she hit one.

"God, yes."

We said it together and I pulled her hair to get her closer. She turned to me with another layer of excitement living in her eyes. I was afraid I'd gone too far, but she ground back against me and I had to bite down another oath.

"Harder," she said with barely a breath.

I gripped her hips and let go. I pounded myself inside her oh so willing body. The frustrations of weeks of talking with her couldn't be slaked. On top of almost a year of thinking about her, trying to get up the freaking balls to talk to her.

Wanting *this* and someone like her in my life.

Just wanting her, period.

I reached around to rub her clit, to drag her with me into the yawning stretch of clawing release.

She shook under me, curling herself around my hand, and I still couldn't stop. I emptied myself into the condom until my spine fucking burned. I was out of breath as the room roared back into focus.

I lowered myself to surround her. "Veronica?"

She pulled my hand from between her legs.

"I'm sorry." God, I shouldn't have let go like that. She just made me feel too many things.

"Don't be sorry." Her voice was shaky and her skin warm to the touch. She turned in my arms and crawled up my chest. "It's never been like that." She cupped my face. "Ever."

"I didn't hurt you?"

"No. You made me feel so good. Too good."

"No such thing as too good."

"Tell that to my ruined girl parts."

"Ruined?" I winced.

"In the very best way."

"Oh." I tried not to puff out my chest. But her giggle told me I had royally screwed up there.

"So proud of yourself."

"Maybe a little." I stretched out as much as I could. The chaise was made for bigger men, but not exactly intended for what we'd used it for. "That's it." I rolled off and took her with me.

"You really like carting me around."

"Yeah, I kinda do."

I strode with her to the bed and set her down, then took care of the condom and shut out the lights. She was already under the covers and I followed her in. She settled back into me in a perfect little spoon.

Perfect in far too many ways for me.

I wrapped around her with a sigh. "Staying?"

"As if I had any intention of leaving now? My bones are caramel."

I tucked her hair aside and laughed into her neck. "Good."

"That my bones are semi-liquid?"

"That you're staying."

"Oh…" She laced our fingers, settling them around her middle. "Yeah, I kinda like that part too."

THIRTEEN

CABIN FORTRESS:

I'm not sure how I'm supposed to work today with your smell still on my skin. It's distracting as hell. And yes, it's a good distraction. Make that a great one.

GETTING THAT TEXT WHILE I WAS RELUCTANTLY DRESSING IN Murphy's bathroom the next morning was the best kind of surreal.

Sending back a winky smile was too.

We quarantined Latte in the small bathroom with a toy, his favorite blanket, food, and water so we could go out for a little while. He was all set, but that didn't stop him from whining the minute we shut the bathroom door.

My heart broke as we headed out to Murphy's truck.

"He'll be fine," he assured me.

"He will."

"I'll take a half day at work today so I can keep an eye on him. Don't worry."

I nodded and smiled. Good daddy material indeed.

Walking into the diner a short time later with him securely holding my hand was a few different things.

Amazing.

Incredible.

A moment I'd probably note in my Humane Association pocket calendar with an assortment of stars and a plethora of hearts.

What it *wasn't*, however, was casual.

It probably would've been if Ivy from the baby support group meeting last night hadn't been the one to take our orders. If she hadn't noted the time—four-fifteen, since I had to be at Brewed Awakening by five—with a wide smile and a wink.

"Did y'all have a good night? I'm guessing you did based on your general cheerfulness at a truly heinous time of day." She winced. "I am so not a morning person."

I shot Murphy a glance and fiddled with my coffee-stained menu. "We did, but we're also used to being early risers. Murphy works construction, and as I mentioned before, I'm the baker at Brewed Awakening. Sleeping in is a rarity in my world."

Even after getting my brains banged out. And how.

Who said that the quiet guys were the ones to watch? Because holy truth bomb, right in the center of my rhododendron.

Later, I'd go back to calling it a pussy, even in my own head. Hard not to be so thoroughly debauched and still retain a layer of mental shyness. But I'd have some coffee and eggs first.

"Sadly, me too, but that's as much because my neighbor in 3C likes to entertain her 'gentlemen callers'," Ivy tucked her pad under her arm and did air quotes, "at all hours." Sighing, she grabbed her pad again. "Okay, so coffee and eggs over easy for you, Vee, and Murphy, same?"

Murphy's ears were tinged pink, but just barely. "Yes, please, ma'am. With an extra side of sausage."

"Look at the manners on this one. No wonder you were holding his hand when you came in here. Hold on tight." Ivy noted the orders on her pad and walked off, still smiling a little wistfully.

I didn't blame her. If I hadn't been sitting with Murphy, I would've been wistful too.

Instead, I reached across the table and gripped his hand tight. He smiled at me, and I swear, I lit up like a damn sparkler from my heart to...the *other* heart between my thighs.

"It turns out I kinda have jealousy issues when it comes to you." I rubbed my thumb over his knuckles to avoid meeting his gaze. "It's a new thing for me. But when any female looks at you with that look, I want to squash them like a spider. And I don't squash spiders. All living creatures have value, yadda yadda."

"I like that you get jealous." Even without looking up, I could hear the smile in his voice. And that made the sparklers inside me go off another dozen times. "I get jealous too. I wanted to rip off Lucky's arms and feed them to him when he was talking to you so much."

"I was afraid he was Cabin Fortress."

"Afraid?"

"I didn't want it to be him." I frowned, realizing how true that was. I hadn't even allowed myself to hope my online mystery man was Murphy, because he'd never be into the whole babymaking... thing.

I was so glad to be wrong.

"No?"

"No." I took a deep breath. "I wanted it to be you."

"Really?" His voice warmed even more. "You're not just saying that?"

"No. I've had inappropriate feelings for you for a while, Mr. Masterson."

"Normally, I'd say keep your voice down. In this case? Could you shout it a few times? And I'll record it, just in case you change your mind later."

I had to laugh. "I won't be changing my mind." Maybe ever. And that scared me as much as it thrilled me.

Was it possible to fall for a guy in the course of one night? If I was being honest, I'd been falling for some time now. Getting to know him online had only sped it up and deepened my affection. He was a truly decent guy. Odds were I'd chase him away with my crazy moods or inappropriate timing or complete lack of skill at keeping a relationship of any sort going.

My own mother barely bothered to call. Postcards were about the extent of our communications these days. I'd come to terms with our different personalities years ago.

Probably around when she'd started calling my girly bits by the name of a flowering bush when trying to explain the boys and the bees to me at the horrifying age of seven.

"You weren't looking for this sort of thing."

"How do you know that?" I let out a windy sigh and rubbed his fingers again to keep myself centered. It was too easy to drift on my thoughts and not focus on the reality happening between us. "Oh, yeah, my stupid post."

I didn't truly think of it that way, but it was hard to not still be embarrassed. Especially when sitting with a man who might make me think about the process of making babies, but not just for the purpose of procreation.

"It wasn't stupid. Without it, would we be here?"

"I don't know."

"Me either, but I don't want to find out. I have to think it was all just...meant." He squeezed my fingers and lifted my hand to his mouth, leaning forward to kiss it while his hazel eyes remained intent on mine.

My heart fluttered and for a second—just one—I wondered who was watching us. What they might say. I'd been the center of attention for weeks now, and I didn't want that for Murphy. He deserved so much better.

Maybe even better than me.

"Penny for your thoughts, Veronica."

The rumble of his voice pulled out the truth. "You're such a good guy, Murphy."

He let out an awkward little laugh and sat back, his hold

loosening on my hand. "Let me guess. Next, you're going to say it was fun, but we should go slow." He jerked a shoulder. "I'm okay with that. You can call the shots on how fast we go. Or if we go at all."

I shook my head and reaffirmed the link of our hands. Already, I wasn't sure how I'd go through my day without his strong fingers holding mine. "No, God, no, you think I'm trying to brush you off?"

He shrugged again, saying nothing.

"Were you not there last night when I was screaming?"

"Veronica." His flush was the absolute best. "You weren't screaming." He cleared his throat. "Exactly."

"Bub, I know when I'm screaming, and trust me, I'm still hoarse today. You'll believe it when I stick my face in this water pitcher here."

He didn't respond, just detangled our hands long enough to refill my glass from the pitcher. Making me smile all over again.

"No need for that. Water is free."

I gulped it down before fumbling for his hand again. *Pathetic, Dixon.* "I don't know how to do this."

"What?"

"How we met, what happened last night, it was all so wonderful, but God, we haven't even gone on a date. I've never done—all that before a date before. Hell, even before we ate dinner."

"Me either." He stared down at our joined hands before looking up at me again. "I have to think with the weeks online, we were building up to it. We didn't need all the usual rituals because we'd skipped some steps."

"Yeah. That's logical."

What wasn't logical was that I wanted every step with him. Every half step, every quarter step. I didn't want to miss a single thing when it came to my Murphy.

And see, there was another problem. Screaming for a guy didn't make him yours.

Even if both of your hearts—the emotional one and the horny as hell one—were saying *oh, yes, it does.*

Ivy returned with the coffeepot and some chatter about the kitchen being backed up because the senior club had come in early and were being extra demanding today, since Mr. Ferly's dentures were giving him trouble and he'd returned two breakfasts so far. We commiserated with her and chuckled as we sipped our steaming mugs of coffee once she'd left.

"I'm sorry this isn't going very fast." Murphy glanced at his watch. That he even still wore one charmed me as much as so many other things about him. "I don't want you to start work without a good breakfast. Maybe we should—"

"Don't worry about it." I waved off his concern. "Lulu is working the early shift today too and she'll get some stuff started. I'm never late. Besides, once I tell Macy I got lucky last night, she'll give me the morning off."

Okay, probably not, but at least she'd be cool about an extra half hour since I always pre-baked enough for the coming apocalypse. None of our customers would starve, that was for sure.

Murphy coughed into his hand. "You have that kind of relationship?"

"Sure. Women gotta stick together, man. Any night that doesn't end in a battery-operated party is a victory for all of us."

He grinned and shook his head. "I mean, to talk about such personal things."

"Oh, yeah. She's probably the closest thing I have to a bestie. I have lots of friends, just not a ton of close ones."

"Because you're easy to be friends with. Everyone wants to get to know you."

I tilted my head. "You think so?"

"Of course. You're like Sage—"

I sort of growl-coughed into my fist and his brows lifted. I set down my coffee and waved my other hand. "Wrong pipe. Carry on."

Instead, he leaned forward, his expression intent. "Before Ivy comes back, I want you to know I'm still on board."

My pulse started hammering hard enough that I had to take a few calming breaths.

Good luck, Dixon. You ain't got enough lung capacity for that one.

"When you say on board," I began carefully, "can you clarify, please?"

"In the whole making a kid thing. I want to do it. With you, I mean." He grabbed a napkin and blotted at the puddle beneath his coffee mug. He'd bumped it with his large arm several times already. "I can't say I ever thought about it before your post, but once I worked my way around to it, I...yes. I'd be honored to make a baby with you."

Breathe. It's a simple task. You've been doing it for two and a half decades plus now.

"Okay."

"But it's not enough for me to just inseminate you."

"After last night, I'd say not. You're a thorough sort, Murphy." I had to tease him. Seeing that pink tinge to his ears could've sustained me for a week.

"Not just that, though yes." He took a quick breath and his Adam's apple bobbed. "Yes, I want more of that. If you want that too."

"Yes." I started to say more, but my words vanished. *Yes* was all I could manage.

"But I want to do it the right way. Not just about sex. I want to get to know you better. I want to fall asleep to your laughter. And if we're lucky enough to make a baby... I want to be the man he or she calls Daddy." His gaze never wavered from mine. "I don't want you to raise the child alone. Even if we aren't—if we don't continue, I want to be a part of my kid's life. I have to be, or I'm afraid I can't do this." His chest rose and fell with his rapid breaths. "Even though I really want to be the one for you." His voice dropped. "So fucking much."

My eyes grew so hot that when Ivy approached the table with our tray of food, I turned my head away. I could barely reply to her questions.

· · ·

Does this look okay?

Sorry, can't see right now. It's probably fine.

Is your coffee hot enough? Do you want me to pour?

Throat's too tight to drink, thanks.

You'll let me know if you need something?

What I need is Murphy. I'm scared shitless that everything I've ever wanted lives inside the man sitting across from me, and I don't know how I got so lucky. And if he ever regrets getting on this train with me, I'm not sure if I'll ever recover.

You know, typical light morning after fare. Except not even close.

Ivy finally left and I stared at my plate of food without the first clue how to pick up my fork and eat. My stomach was growling, but it didn't seem to matter.

I was so churned up by what Murphy had said, I wasn't sure I'd be able to chew.

"Veronica."

Wordlessly, I looked up at him.

"If you don't want to go forward, we can stop right here. We're still friends. We'll always be friends."

Oh, God, my throat was so thick, I could barely swallow.

"I don't want you to cry. Dammit, that's the last thing I would ever want." He raked a hand through his hair. "Okay, fine, never mind. If you don't want the rest, for you, I'll do it. We can try to make a—"

I reared up and leaned across the table, fisting a handful of his T-shirt to pull him closer. His eyes widened about ten seconds before my boobs dragged through the eggs he'd soaked in ketchup and Jesus, Mary, and Joseph, I so didn't give a shit. I hauled him closer and kissed him hard enough to probably break his nose to go along with the foot his sweet Sage had injured at the prom.

Difference was? I didn't stop kissing him, even as my left nipple grew hard from the coldness of the ketchup and the warm, firm lips responding to mine.

Sweet, shy Murphy was kissing me back, right in the middle of the diner. Reaching up to fist his hands in my hair as his tongue swept over mine and drove me absolutely batshit crazy.

We broke apart, breathing hard, laughing a little, and our gazes dropped to the explosion of red across my chest.

Fitting, since my heart might as well have projectile leaped right from my body.

"Is that a yes?" His voice was low and deep.

"So much a yes."

"First one yes? Or second one yes?"

"There was a second one?" I rubbed my finger over the smear of lipstick on his chin. "Sorry, you're wearing me."

His eyes lit in a carnal way that spoke to every one of the same dirty thoughts living inside me. "Leave it there."

I glanced down at my shirt and groaned. "Yeah, my impulsive moves never work out well."

"Says who? I think it worked out fine." With a wry smile, he jerked a thumb over his shoulder at all the interested faces at the other tables around us. "Pretty sure they'd agree."

"Whoa. I didn't even notice they were watching." I smiled sheepishly and dropped back down into my seat. And picked off a blob or two of scrambled eggs.

At least he hadn't gone for over easy like I had.

I glanced farther down my shirt. More eggs down there. Those were mine. Lovely. It didn't matter who'd gotten what, I was a buffet of all of it.

"I didn't notice either until they started to clap."

Giggling, I bowed my head to avoid the curious glances—so much for keeping us kind of on the down low, copious handholding aside—and focused on dabbing my shirt with the napkin. "I so missed that."

"Yeah, we were pretty occupied. I'll take you home to change."

"Nah, I followed you here in my car, remember?"

"Maybe I just want to extend our date."

Giving up my shirt as hopeless, I tossed aside the napkin and grinned. "Is that what we're calling this now?"

"Yeah, I guess so. But I'd like to take you on a real one."

Yep, that kicked my fluttering heart back into gear. "What does that consist of?"

"Well, depends what you're up for." He picked up his fork and dug into his eggs, making me laugh. "What?"

"I probably dropped fifty dog hairs in your food." I pushed my own plate away. As hungry as I was, wearing half my meal killed some of the desire for it.

But I didn't regret kissing Murphy in front of the world. My only regret was we'd taken so long to get to this place. Not that it didn't feel damn worth it right now. Maybe all the steps had been necessary to reach where we were.

For it to matter this much.

"Still delicious." He frowned at my plate. "You don't want yours?"

"Not to worry, Ivy Beck to the rescue." Our waitress hurried to the table and tugged our plates away, leaving Murphy holding his fork in mid-air. She presented new breakfasts for both of us, going so far as to set down a new coffeepot and take the perfectly fine old one away. "Don't say I don't believe in romance," she added with a wink before heading into the back with what she'd cleared away.

But only an astute sort like me could see the heaviness in her eyes despite her cheerful demeanor. Not to mention she'd been at the support group meeting, indicating her dating life had probably not been awesome thus far.

"We'll leave her an extra big tip." I dug into my piping hot eggs. Delicious.

And it turned out romance made a girl hungry.

Murphy shrugged and reached for the ketchup bottle, saturating his eggs one more time. "The old ones were great."

"Latte hair and all," I teased.

He shrugged again, forking up eggs at a speed that impressed and fascinated me. Big guy like him had a huge appetite in more ways than one apparently.

I pressed my thighs together at the sudden ache between them.

Settle down, down there. Not the time or place. You already practically mounted him for all to see.

"You know, I wonder if August is aware his little sister is looking for a baby."

I tucked into my eggs for another minute or so until the worst of my hunger was slaked, then tilted my head. "The guy who owns the furniture place?"

"Yeah. Aug's a good guy. Just imagining how I'd feel if my baby sister Maddie was on the lookout for a baby daddy. Of course she's only seventeen, so that's unlikely, but still."

"Perhaps he should feel like it's none of his business?" I suggested sweetly, refilling my coffee mug and taking a sip.

The coffee burned my tongue, which probably served me right for putting that wounded expression on Murphy's face.

"I didn't mean there was anything wrong with it."

"No." I sighed. "I'm sure you didn't. It's just a sensitive subject. Especially when I can't help feeling like some people equate baby daddy with sugar daddy, and that's so off base, it's silly."

"Yeah, considering you wanted takeout on that score, it definitely doesn't make sense."

I smiled despite the lingering flare of annoyance. Saying that methods of procreation were a touchy topic for me didn't begin to cover it.

Then again, it was probably good Murphy wasn't one hundred percent perfect in everything he did and said, though he was damn close. I didn't want to fall in love with him.

I didn't, right? That wasn't part of the plan.

For him or me.

"Takeout is the last resort for a lot of us, trust me. If the option for a healthy, loving relationship presented itself, most of us would happily go for it. But it's hard out there for a pimp, man."

Murphy's lips twisted. "Yeah. Tell me about it."

"Most of us still want the fairy tale, Murphy." I looked down at my plate. "What you offered me a few minutes ago was more than I ever expected. Considering my past, it just wasn't something I thought was a possibility, and I didn't want to regret not trying to have a child when I have so much love to give. Sure, it might happen for me later. But what if it doesn't?"

"What if," he echoed, setting down his fork to take my hand again across the table. That firm grip centered me faster than any amount of pretty words ever could. "As for that date I want to take you on, I'd like for us to have a fancy dinner. Maybe do some dancing, though I suck at it. Then I want to take you home and make love to you." He didn't blush. Didn't look away. "I want very much to give you those things."

My lips trembled into a smile. Maybe I preferred his touch to pretty words, but he had a way with those as well. "I want them too. When?"

"Saturday night?"

I squeezed his hand and took a shaky breath. "You have yourself a date."

FOURTEEN

MURPHY:

I can't get you off my mind.

VEE:

Ditto. What are you wearing tonight?

MURPHY:

Um...pants and a shirt?

VEE:

Can you be more descriptive, pls? I'm
planning my outfit.

MURPHY:

I haven't thought about it yet. I guess a nice
vest, shirt, and pants. We're going to a nice
place.

VEE:

Okay, that leaves out my belly shirt & mini
skirt.

MURPHY:

Belly shirt? I don't know what that is, but I
think I love it.

> VEE:
>
> Oh, you would. It exposes my midriff almost up to my tits.

MURPHY:

...

> VEE:
>
> You okay, Fortress?

MURPHY:

Just considering a longer shirt for the evening. Maybe a roomy sweater.

> VEE:
>
> Not too roomy. I want easy access. Maybe you could skip the boxers, just for me?

MURPHY:

Jesus, I can't work now.

> VEE:
>
> *giggle* Save up your energy for later. And yeah, skip the boxers.

"Do I look okay?"

"Veronica Dixon, if you do not skedaddle on out of my coffee shop with your questions and adorable nerves, I'm probably going to get jealous of your new love or something. And I do *not* do that shit."

I grinned at Macy as she kneaded bread dough. That wasn't her usual department, but her numero uno baker had the night off and my boss claimed she enjoyed expending her aggressions on the bread. From how she was working that sourdough, I could believe it.

"We're just going on a date. Doesn't mean new love."

"Right. That's why you've been flittering around here all week like a lightning bug on speed."

"I'm well rested."

"That is a goddamn lie, because I could go deep sea diving in the bags under your eyes."

"Hey." I tugged out my compact from my tiny purse and frowned as I touched the slight puffiness beneath my eyes. "Don't give me a complex."

"You look amazing. I'm just jealous. Just saying you're so not well rested, because you're spending all your spare time trying to create a whole flock of little Mastersons."

"Nah, we're just practicing at this point. He's been fully wrapped every time."

Macy arched a brow. "So, tell me again how this isn't new love blossoming? His whole purpose was to fertilize your stamen."

I shook my head. Macy knew coffee like nobody's business, but her knowledge of flowers needed work. "My *pistil* is doing just fine, thank you, and we aren't on any timetable."

"You're glowing. And it's not because you're knocked up."

"No. I'm just happy." I let out a sigh and leaned against the counter where Macy was needlessly punishing her sourdough starter. "You're going to ruin that bread."

"It'll be delicious. You think he's gonna propose tonight?"

I choked on air. "Excuse me? Don't you think it's a little soon for that?"

Macy flipped over her dough and pummeled merrily away. "He's a traditional dude. If he's still wrapped, the minute the raincoat hits the floor, he'll probably hit his knees."

"It's been like...no time."

"Yet you're going to try for a baby."

"Not yet."

"But soon?"

I bit my lip. "What does one have to do with the other? Besides, who's to say he even views me that way?"

Macy snorted. "Girl, if he's cool with dropping some fertilizer on your garden, he's thinking long-term." She shifted and gave me a serious look. "Part of serving coffee every day is learning what people want. He might be quiet, but I would bet a tasty slice of sourdough he's looking for home, hearth, and a sweet wife to make him those sticky buns he likes so much."

"Petit fours," I immediately corrected, though he enjoyed sticky buns too. I knew a lot about his wants when it came to food and drink.

Now I was learning what he liked outside of the café too. Outside of the bedroom even, despite the many hours we'd spent there already.

He'd been chomping at the bit for our "real" date, but I'd put it off a bit longer than originally planned because I liked the anticipation. Besides, every day with Murphy felt like a date.

A dream.

It hadn't taken long for us to fall into a routine. He took me to work. He picked me up from work. When he could, he'd visit for lunch and we'd grab the most sequestered table to laugh over our days and tease each other as much as possible.

And after work, we'd eat dinner and fall into bed—and on the chaise and on the counter and wherever else struck our fancy—until neither of us could speak. Cuddling together in the afterglow led to a few precious hours sleeping tangled together. He was a furnace and I'd awakened a few times from hot flashes, but he didn't bitch that I was a cover hog and had a tendency to whack him in the face when I turned over.

Everything was perfect. Even the non-perfect things like Latte watching us have sex, his tiny head tilted, or jumping around yipping when we were making too much noise, was perfect.

All this perfection was scary as fuck for a girl like me.

Because Macy was right. Murphy was a traditional guy. He called his mother every week, for God's sake. I saw it noted in his datebook like an appointment he would never break. And my mother didn't even send back Christmas cards some years.

Did we really make sense beyond the thrill of a new sexual relationship? Especially when what I wanted was probably so different from what he was looking for?

Assuming we hadn't come together in such an unorthodox way, that is.

I pressed a hand to my dancing belly. I truly didn't know. I didn't know much except he made me feel so good.

So happy.

And Macy was still talking, and I had not been listening to her while I was off in my Murphy-related reverie. That was happening more and more lately.

Clearly, I was dealing with the onset of some kind of mental flu.

Like lovesickness squared.

"Can you believe she still hasn't popped? I swear, I half wonder if they got the knocked-up date wrong, or else she's giving birth to an elephant and not a human child. They want to induce her soon, but she's being stubborn as two cats about her baby taking her own time and to leave her the hell alone." Macy pounded the starter with the finesse of a boxer preparing for a prize fight. Poor defeated bread. "Honestly, the woman deserves a medal for sainthood. If my ankles looked like hers, I'd probably excavate the kid myself with Vaseline and strong rope."

Horrified, I stared at the side of Macy's head. She was so lovely, and even more beautiful when she took the time to fuss with her hair and makeup—which was rare—but she had a streak inside her I could not comprehend. "We're talking about Rylee, right?"

"No, we're talking about the Virgin Mary. Do you know any other preggos about to pop?" She rolled her eyes and flipped her dough. "Oh, sorry, I forgot we live beside Sperm River."

I laughed. "You're too much."

"Have you seen her? The poor woman." Macy shook her head. "If Gage came near me with his baseball bat again, I'd probably lock him in his tool shed."

We were still giggling about all manner of metaphors for dicks and male captivity when a loud cry sounded from the front of the café—and it wasn't a displeased customer.

Macy and I exchanged a look as she wiped her flour-laden hands on a towel. "Baby," she muttered.

I grinned. "Yay. Let's go see which one."

"You're a sadist." But she was already pushing me out of the main part of the kitchen into the café.

Rylee and Kelsey Kramer were holding court near the doors, proffering a small male child swaddled in a bright yellow blanket and matching hat. Rylee was not smiling. In fact, she was rubbing the side of her massive belly and rocking from side to side.

No one appeared to notice. The café patrons' attention was focused squarely on one Sean Kramer, barely a few months old and already winning ladies' hearts en masse.

"Can you handle this?" Macy asked out of the side of her mouth. "I want to get Ry to sit down. She looks peaked."

I glanced at my purse. "Murphy will be here soon to pick—"

"If you make nice for me with Kelsey and the kid, I'll give you two extra hours off to fuck your man."

We had an unusual relationship, but it worked for us. "Deal. Thanks."

"No problem." She was already moving toward Rylee. "We have that awesome bread proofing for the morning anyway."

I winced. Yeah, I'd be starting over tomorrow. That bread was toast—and not the edible kind.

But hey, hanging out with Kelsey and the baby wasn't any hardship. Especially since little Sean was so pink and adorable and kept sucking on his lips while I bounced him up and down. Kelsey was full of newborn stories, and she wasn't shy about telling me the realities of being a new mom.

I was both fascinated and terrified.

Maybe Murphy and I didn't need to rush to board the baby train. I wanted a child, but I was also enjoying the practice. Besides, once we reached our objective—assuming we did—then what?

Did the practice end? Or would Murphy prove himself to be the guy I already believed he was?

Not just good father material. Good lover material. Good man material.

Good *husband* material.

I tried not to grimace as I listened to Kelsey. Dear God, I hoped I wasn't going to puke from nerves before our date.

Then the door opened again, and I shifted that way out of habit, a ready smile on my face even as the baby clutched at my hair.

And my gaze connected with Murphy's.

He was clad in a dark vest and pants with a crisp white shirt. Looking so buff and sexy that I forgot how to breathe for so long that Kelsey thumped me on the back when I sputtered.

"You okay?" Her gaze followed mine to the door and she smiled knowingly. "Ahh. Your baby daddy has arrived."

As soon as the words were out, her blue eyes widened in almost comical horror. "Oh my God, I can't believe I said that. He could just be a friend. A hookup. Shoot, I need gum glue."

Laughing felt easy. Natural. It helped that my gaze was locked on Murphy's as if neither of us could bear to look away. "He's a friend. A very good friend."

I didn't know if he'd heard me, but either way, he'd understand, right? We weren't about labels.

And I was all about pretending I wasn't in deep enough to drown.

Murphy approached our small table and leaned down to brush a quick kiss over the top of my head. "Hi there. Sorry I'm late."

"You're late?" I blinked. "I think you're early."

His gaze lingered on my face before shifting to my wrap dress. "You look incredible."

"Thanks. So do you."

His attention shifted to Sean. "Hey, little buddy. Haven't seen you around town too much."

"He makes all the ladies fall in love with him, so I keep him under lock and key." Kelsey laughed as I proved her point by adjusting Sean's blanket, stealing a tickle while I was it.

"He's a charmer already, aren't you, cutie pie?" Sean gave me a drooly smile and I grinned up at Murphy, who was now watching me with a wrinkle between his eyes. I shifted on my seat and offered him the baby. "Want to hold him?"

Kelsey sighed. "Oh, no, did he fill his diaper again already?"

"No, just spreading the baby love."

But Murphy wasn't taking him. He just shook his head and tucked his hands in his pockets. "He looks good in your arms."

"Does he?" I glanced down at Sean and smiled, rubbing my fingers over his pink cheek. "He's a sweetheart."

"Trust me, he's usually bawling his head off by now. You have a way with the little ones, Vee."

Smiling, I rocked him and basked in the moment.

Holding him felt so natural and perfect. I hadn't grown up with siblings or young cousins, so I hadn't experienced holding babies until friends had given birth. But cradling a baby might as well have been something I'd done a million times before. No awkwardness or worry. Just joy that this one thing was something I was meant to do. Even more than baking and preparing food and coffee for others to enjoy.

I was meant to be a mother.

"Would you mind watching him while I run to the ladies' room? I never get a moment to myself anymore. I'd love to put toilet paper down and commune with my thoughts in privacy. If you don't mind?" Kelsey was already on the move. "Be right back," she called over her shoulder.

Murphy dropped into Kelsey's vacated seat and leaned forward to smile at me across the table. "She's right, you know. You're a natural."

"I guess I like making people happy. Big people with their hit of java and a scone, little people with their sticky fists." I chuckled as Sean grabbed a chunk of the hair I'd left down and gave it a surprisingly strong tug.

"You're good at it."

"Yeah?" I cocked my head at him. "You're good at making people happy too, Mr. Masterson. Since my boss has been teasing me for the last half hour about how I'm glowing."

His smile as he reached over to poke Sean's chubby belly made me smile back. And offer him the baby again.

This time, he didn't hesitate. Watching him carefully tuck the little boy into his big, strong arms made my stomach swim in the best possible way.

"You're a natural too." God, I hoped my voice wasn't wobbling.

He didn't seem to notice as he grinned down at Kelsey's son. "Lots of practice with my niece. My brother Travis's girl."

Murphy had such a big family. He was forever naming people and I was beginning to think I needed a chart to keep up.

My own world was so empty. Oh, sure, in the center of it was my job and my friends and lots of reasons to keep busy. On the edges though there was nothing but the horizon.

No ports in the storm, metaphorical or otherwise.

I'd thought I was fine living alone. On my own in most ways. No family dinners to be had, no annoying squabbles with siblings, no teasing arguments—and even not-so-teasing ones—with parents. But hearing all that he had in his life made me wonder what it was like.

God, I wanted family. *My* family. And maybe I wanted to share his too.

If there was room for me.

"What's that look for?"

I made myself smile. "Just thinking about what might never be."

He nodded at Sean. "You mean one of these?"

Because it was easier, I nodded. "Big piece of the puzzle."

"You can't think that way. If it's meant to be, it'll happen. And God, Veronica, you deserve the world." The fierceness of his tone made my eyes fill.

I whisked away the tear that sneaked down my face with the side of my fist. Classy to the end, that was me. "Thanks. I guess we'll see."

"Oh, for fuck's sake, leave me the hell alone."

Murphy's eyes widened as he moved to cover Sean's ears while I shifted to follow the irritated voice I recognized as Rylee's. She was surrounded by Macy and a few other customers and was staring up at them with pure fire in her eyes from where she sat.

On the floor.

"How did you even get down there?" Macy demanded. "You were just sitting up here, now you're down there."

"I can move, okay? How do you think I got knocked up in the first place? Back up." Rylee pointed at Mrs. Gunderson, who was trying to close Rylee's rather indiscreetly splayed legs. "Childbirth is fucking natural, all right?"

I slid a glance at Murphy. "Sometimes I wonder if Macy influences her or it's the other way around."

His lips quirked as he nodded at Rylee. "She's about to go into labor if she isn't already. You should go sit with her. You're the voice of reason."

"How the hell do you know that?" At his raised brows, I hung my head. "I hang out with Macy too."

"She's got that look about her. Your calmness will help."

"Okay, if you say so." I'd no sooner risen that Rylee let out a wail.

"I want Gage here. Not any of you people. Just Gage and my sister. Where is my sister?" Rylee gripped Macy's arm and twisted her neck to try to see around the growing crowd. "Did she leave me to the wolves?"

Macy heaved out a breath and tried to move away from Rylee. "If I'm a wolf, can you stop breaking my damn arm?"

"No. I need you. I love you." Rylee turned her head and sobbed into Macy's shoulder. "There's a wild animal in my uterus and it. Is. Going. To. Kill. Me."

I cleared my throat and glanced at Murphy, who appeared surprisingly smug. "Is the universe trying to tell me to back away while my womb is still blinking its neon No Available Rooms sign?"

"More like maybe you shouldn't turn down the drugs if they're offered to you."

I let out a laugh, earning Rylee's narrowed-eyed wrath. She was quite fearsomely beautiful, like a warrior princess with a swollen belly. "You stole my sister's baby and left her for dead."

Macy patted Rylee's head as if she was a cranky toddler. "Ignore her. Her husband is on his—"

The café door swung open hard enough to nearly fly off the hinges. "Rylee." Gage's panicked shout echoed off the walls as his gaze swung to and fro until he located his now weeping wife on the floor in the reading nook. "There you are. Are you okay, baby? Baby, are you okay?" He rushed toward her with all the drama of a soap opera entrance right before the camera panned away.

Rylee sobbed and reached for him, holding on tight as he swung her up into his arms.

Which was sweet enough to have a few people dabbing their eyes —even me—until Rylee grabbed him by his ears and pressed her forehead to his, speaking loudly enough that Gage's brother Dare could probably hear her next door at the auto shop.

"If this baby kills me, I'm going to haunt you for the rest of your natural born life."

Dare picked that moment to step into the café and motioned to Gage, who hadn't so much as paused while his wife was hurling death threats.

He had to be used to it by now, I was figuring.

"Truck's at the curb. We'll—" Dare paused at the sight of Murphy holding his son without his wife anywhere in sight. "Hi, who the hell are you?"

Well, that proved that everyone in Crescent Cove *didn't* actually know everyone else. I'd wondered.

"I'm Murphy Masterson. I work on Gideon's crew among other things." Smoothly, Murphy rose and held out a hand without losing his grip on the now restless baby. "You must be Dare. I've come into the auto body shop a time or two but usually dealt with Gage or one of the other guys."

Dare shook his hand and took possession of his baby with the confidence of a man with two sons. "Pleasure. Where's my wife?"

"I'll go get her," I said quickly. "She's in the john. I mean, ladies' room. Be right back."

Dare nodded and turned to Gage, who was muscling Rylee out the door with Macy right behind him. Rylee had gone strangely silent, which probably had something to do with the stain on her pretty light blue pants.

The baby would be here soon. Murphy had been right.

I gave him a brief smile and squeezed his arm before hurrying to the bathroom. I knocked on the door and only heard the hand dryer blowing from inside. I knocked again. "Kelsey? It's Vee. Your sister needs you and your husband's here."

Nothing.

I knocked again. "Kelsey? Are you okay?"

I finally chanced turning the doorknob and tentatively stepped inside. "Kel—" The question died on my tongue as I saw Kelsey sitting cross-legged on the counter with a pair of air pods in and her phone in her lap.

What the heck?

Kelsey glanced up and nearly slipped off the counter. "Oh, God. Oh, crap. I took too long. How long was I gone? Oh, fuck." She slid off the counter and tucked her headphones and phone into her big purse. "Where's Sean? I didn't even leave you his diaper bag. I'm such a failure. Jesus."

Her eyes welled up and I rushed forward, unwilling to face another crying Kramer woman this afternoon.

It was bad enough I'd cried myself, and that so wasn't my thing. Usually. Must've been all the hormones in the air or something.

Or bitter reality crushing you like a hundred-pound anvil.

Yeah, whichever.

I gripped Kelsey's shoulders and lightly shook her. "Your husband is here, and he has Sean. And your sister is in labor, and the truck's waiting outside, and you better hurry if you want to ride with them."

"What? The baby? Oh. God, she said her back hurt. I knew it'd be soon, but you know Rylee can be a little temperamental." Kelsey fisted both hands in her flame-red hair. "I have to be supportive. I can't be a frazzled crazy lady who hides in café bathrooms to listen to dirty audiobooks so I feel like I have a semblance of my life back. I can't listen at home, because what if I miss Sean's cries—"

"Kelsey. Your sister. In labor. All the rest can wait."

"Right. Right. You're so wise. Thank you. I'll go now. Thanks for watching my baby. If it turns out I'm incompetent at raising him, maybe you'd want to adopt him? His farts are horribly stinky, but he smells really good after a bath—" She waved a hand at her flushed face. "Okay, I'm going now. I can do this. I can do all of this, right?"

I gave her a wide supportive smile. "You absolutely can do all of this. Go be a supportive big sister to Rylee and help her have that beautiful baby."

"I will. I so will. Thank you so much, Vee." She gave me a quick hug and rushed out the bathroom door.

I let out a long breath and stepped out to find Murphy waiting for me, leaning against the wall. He straightened immediately. "Everything okay? I saw Kelsey run for the hills."

"Yeah, she's fine. Just a frazzled new mom." I took his arm, squeezing it gratefully. "Since I think they have plenty of people with them at the hospital, want to go on that date now?"

"Absolutely." He grinned. "I think we both could use a drink."

"Or seven," I agreed.

FIFTEEN

MURPHY:

Does texting you while you're in the bathroom with Kelsey show I'm whipped already?

VEE:

Nah. It shows you're sexy AF.

MURPHY:

...

VEE:

giggle

MURPHY DIDN'T TELL ME WHERE WE WERE GOING FOR DINNER. I was hoping for the Sherman Inn, just because it was super fabulous and a girl with a baker/barista's salary didn't get to eat at swanky places like that too often. My usual dates didn't often visit establishments like that either. Typically, we'd hit some chain restaurant at best or McDonald's after the movies at worst.

I didn't mind. I didn't have fancy tastes, and besides, I could make a lot of things I enjoyed myself despite being more skilled at baking than cooking.

So, I should've been excited when Murphy pulled up down the street from The Hummingbird's Nest. The bed and breakfast had a lovely restaurant, or so I'd been told. I'd never eaten there.

"This is the surprise?" I tried to sound enthusiastic as Murphy turned off the car.

"Yes. Sage moved our reservations back a few minutes due to the baby hijinks. She'll be heading to the hospital soon."

"Oh, good." I cleared my throat. The green-eyed monster inside me that reared up every time I heard Sage's name in relation to Murphy could leave anytime now, thanks. "I mean, what a shame we won't be seeing her."

"Actually, she's sticking around to say hi before she heads to the hospital."

"Yay. How nice." I picked up my purse and climbed out of the truck before I said something I'd regret later.

Hopefully, I'd regret it later. I truly didn't know what my problem was. Okay, I knew. I was ridiculously jealous of Sage's past with Murphy. I wanted to know details I had no business knowing. Especially if I was acting this irrational without knowing much, imagine if I had a little information to torment myself with?

And it didn't make sense. Before all this, I'd really liked Sage. I still did. She was happily married to someone else, and Murphy and I were doing just fine as...well, whatever we were.

I wasn't normally the sort of chick to worry about other women. I believed in female empowerment and one for all.

Except when it came to Murphy Masterson apparently, who caused me to act more bloodthirsty than *Jaws*.

As I stepped out of the car, Murphy frowned and stopped beside my door. "I was coming around to open it for you."

Who was this man? Although I'd gotten to know him much better, I still couldn't believe his manners. "Was your mother June Cleaver?"

"No, JoAnn Cleaver." He held out his arm for me and I couldn't help laughing as I accepted it.

"Have you ever eaten here before?" I asked as we ascended the wide steps to the bed and breakfast's separate side entrance for the restaurant.

"No, never. I cook for myself a lot."

"Me too. I work my budget like a street corner."

He laughed and opened the front door for me. "Well, no budget tonight."

The foyer was crowded and there was already a line moving toward the stand for the maître'd. We joined the back of the line and made small talk as it inched forward.

Until loud feminine laughter made my ears prickle.

No.

Couldn't be.

There was no way she could be in town. Not without letting me know.

Just the same, I gripped Murphy's arm as I craned my neck to try to see around the people milling about in the entrance area. Then I caught a glimpse of familiar jet-black hair, wound up in her usual mile-high bun with colorful sticks, and my empty stomach fisted.

"So, how do you feel about meeting my mother tonight?"

Murphy frowned. "Here?"

"Apparently." I narrowed my eyes at the suited man she was cozied up to, tucked into his side as if he was a lifelong friend.

Make that a lover.

She leaned up to kiss him and he palmed her ass with his left hand. Where he wore a wedding ring.

My mother was a lot of things, but messing with a married guy? Really?

Of course if you came to town for the first time in forever and didn't bother to let your only child know first, probably anything went.

Murphy reached down to rub my hand where it clenched his arm. I was probably cutting off his circulation. "Point her out to me."

But that turned out to be unnecessary, since she turned her head and let out a gasp. "VeeBee! Oh my God. You're here!" She rushed toward us, her face wreathed with a huge smile. The colorful silk scarves wrapped around her waist like a belt fluttered through the air as she reached for me, pulling me into a hard hug. "You look amazing. A little skinny," she pinched my hip, "but amazing." She made a show of lifting her own boobs and grinning before shifting her attention to a dazed Murphy.

Or maybe I was the dazed one. My mother was a whirlwind.

And I was lying on the shore, broken from the wreckage. As always.

"Who's this handsome fella?" She smiled up at Murphy.

"Mom, this is Murphy Masterson. Murphy, this is my mom, Andrea."

"Pleased to meet you, Mrs. Dixon." He held out a hand.

My mom laughed gaily and shook his hand. "So polite. Where did you find this one, VeeBee?"

"On the internet, when I made a request for a baby daddy."

She didn't seem to have heard me, but the couple ahead of us in line sure did. I flashed them a cheeky smile.

"Oh, and by the way, my last name isn't Dixon anymore. It's Newman." She dangled her hand in my face. "I just got hitched. I didn't know how to tell you, so I sent a postcard letting you know we were swinging through town before we head to Australia. That's where Burke lives. Hey, Burke, honeybun, c'mere and meet my baby girl." She waved to her new husband.

I let out a long, slow breath. I was used to her changing boyfriends like she changed her hair color, but this was a new one. And to let me know via postcard?

Nice one, Mom.

Guess I should've been grateful she sent word at all, even if I hadn't received the postcard yet.

"Hi there, nice to meet you." The tall, sandy-haired man my mother was surgically attached to smile widely and held out a hand first to me, then to Murphy. "Drea said her daughter was a knockout, and she wasn't lying. I've heard so much about you over the last few weeks."

"*Weeks?* And you're married now?"

My mother tightly gripped her new husband's hand. "When you know, you know. The first time we met, Burke said he only had eyes for me, and I felt the same."

The line moved forward, and so did we. Though my legs felt as if they were mired in mud.

"And did I hear you say your name was Murphy?" Burke asked, glancing at my date.

"Yes, sir. Nice to meet you." Murphy slid his arm around my waist, and I found myself leaning into his embrace.

Maybe I was more like my mother than I'd realized. Both of us cleaving to men we barely knew.

Emotionally needy, anyone?

We finally gave our names to the maître'd and my mother and new daddy tagged along with us to our table. It was a secluded one for two by the window, but my mother and Burke pulled over chairs.

"We won't interrupt for long, we promise. We're just going to have a quick bite and head back up to our suite." My mom giggled and patted Burke's thigh. "Honeymoon period, you know?" Before I could reply to that, she smiled at me and Murphy. "I have to say I'm glad to see you dating again. I've been so worried about you, VeeBee, since that last boyfriend left you sobbing on the couch with repeats of *The Notebook.*"

I rolled my eyes. "So worried you sent a postcard to tell me you were married? And that 'last boyfriend' was when I was twenty-two. Years ago."

"Is it my fault you don't tell me much about your personal life?" She motioned to the waitress at the next table. "I'd love a wine spritzer, please. Sorry to bother you."

"Sure thing. Here's some menus while I'm at it." She passed them around and apologized for how busy it was in the restaurant tonight, then took our drink orders.

She'd no sooner left that Sage strolled over to the table, looking absolutely gorgeous in a coral top and short black skirt. "Hi, Moose. Hi, Vee. It's a zoo tonight."

"A lot of business is a good thing, right?" Murphy smiled at her and motioned to my parents. "Mr. and Mrs. Newman, this is our friend Sage Hamilton. She owns this bed and breakfast with her husband. Sage, this is—these are Veronica's parents. I mean, this is her mother, and her mother's new husband." Murphy cleared his throat.

"Oh, yes, we met Sage when we checked in. Such a sweet girl." My mom beamed with more warmth at Sage than she'd smiled at me.

Or maybe that was jealousy talking again. Maybe I was going through PMS. Or JIMS?

A jealousy-induced mental spiral.

"Yes, it was great to meet you, Mrs. Newman. I didn't realize you were Vee's mom though."

"Indeed. This is my baby girl." My mom poked my shoulder in case I'd forgotten our familial link. "So, you two girls are friends? Are you BFFs? It seems like you should be. Although you have a baby, don't you, Sage? Along with that sexy husband." She laughed and glanced at her own spouse. "Not as sexy as my Burke though."

"I do have a baby and a sexy husband, and yes, Vee and I are friends." Sage smiled so warmly at me that I felt guilty for my uncharitable thoughts.

They'd partially dissipated in her direction anyway, since they'd rerouted to my mother.

For fuck's sake, this night was supposed to be for me and Murphy. Not to serve as an opportunity for my mom to recount everything Sage had that I did not.

My mom who hadn't even bothered to make me her first stop in town when she was visiting.

Why would she?

Flashing a huge smile, my mother chose that moment to regale us all with how she'd met Burke in a tiki bar in some country, the name of which I'd missed.

She even felt it necessary to share how they'd "consummated" their love on the beach.

By then, Sage's eyebrows were reaching for her elevated blond ponytail and the stymied waitress had come over twice to take our orders before hurriedly scurrying away when she was denied.

Murphy just kept sipping his ice water. His ears weren't even red. I had to think he'd probably gone to his safe place inside his head.

For me, there were no safe places left.

It wasn't a surprise when Sage apologized about needing to go because our friend was having a baby and she really, really, really had to visit her in the hospital. I'd known she was close friends with Kelsey, but not Rylee as much. Though to be honest, she probably would've said she needed to line up for a firing squad rather than hearing personal details from my mother.

Such as tidbits about her recent wax job, and how'd she gone totally bare for the very first time.

And it had *changed* her life.

Just as mine was changed from this dinner conversation and enduring it with poor Murphy sitting across from me.

God help us all.

On the bright side, once Sage left, my mom actually seemed to settle down and let Burke talk.

Make that talk *a little*. Not enough to say much more than his line of work and that he enjoyed a spirited round of golf.

Or perhaps she settled down due to a food coma from the huge order she made that Murphy insisted on paying for as a wedding gift.

God, he was so sweet, but I'd be making him cookies by the truckful for months to make up for his generosity. Our whole night had been shanghaied and now he was paying for the privilege.

At least dinner was delicious. I'd gone for a shrimp and rice dish, while Murphy and Burke had opted for steak. My mother ordered three wine spritzers and a fisherman's platter big enough to sink the table.

At least she seemed more understanding after the third wine spritzer, so when she brought up that "joke" I'd told about how I met Murphy, her eyeballs didn't pop out and roll around the floor as I nodded cheerfully.

"Yes. I put up a post on Facebook, looking for a man to inseminate me without a relationship."

Burke coughed and my mother thumped him on the back. "Why would you want a baby though? Isn't the whole point of a hookup hoping you *won't* get pregnant?"

Murphy dabbed his mouth with his napkin, his expression saying all I needed to know.

Want me to handle this? I will.

I'd never had someone who had my back before. It made my chest feel too tight and the ache I'd carried in my throat since laying eyes on my mother vanish. I didn't need him to defend me or my choices, but knowing he was there if I needed him made all the difference.

"I wasn't looking for a hookup, Mother. If I wanted one of those, they're easy enough to find. I want something more out of life."

"By shackling yourself with a child so another man might not want to get chained down with you and your offspring?" She glanced at Murphy. "Is this just about a good time for you, son? Because I can't claim to understand how this benefits you."

Murphy sat back in his seat. "Veronica is very important to me. It's not about benefiting me. She thought this plan through and when we begin to try to have one, I have no doubt we'll figure out our way through it as we've figured out our way through the rest."

"A-ha! So, you're actually dating, not just trying to have a kid. That makes more sense. It's an ingenious way to snag a family-minded man, VeeBee." She patted her updo. "I have to give you props."

Props? Lord save me.

"I'm not trying to snag Murphy. I would never set up a scheme to do that. I'm not you, Mother. You're the one who gave me tips on meeting rich men when I was thirteen."

She let out a tinkly little laugh. "What's wrong with wanting your daughter to aim herself toward a successful man? By the way, Murphy, what is it you do again?"

"He's a carpenter. I'm supporting him with my baker's salary. And when we have our brood of illegitimate babies, we'll probably have to put up posts on Facebook asking for hand-me-downs. Will you please excuse me?"

Before anyone could stop me, I slipped away from the table and booked for the door.

Let no one say I couldn't make an exit.

SIXTEEN

Cabin Fortress: You suck.

OKAY, HE DIDN'T REALLY SAY THAT TO ME. AT LEAST NOT THAT I knew of, because I didn't even have my purse. Or my phone.

Nothing but my tattered pride and hot tears of shame.

Leaving this way was the ultimate act of cowardice. But I just couldn't deal. And with the way my emotions were spiraling all over the place, it was probably better for my mother and Burke that I'd taken off.

And Murphy. Jesus, would he ever want to speak to me again? I'd fled and left him to handle all...that.

Blindly, I pushed my way through the guests in the foyer and through the doors. Stepping out on the porch into the now chilly October night stole my breath. I stumbled down the steps, dodging other patrons, my destination fuzzy and indistinct. All I knew was I needed to get away from the restaurant and I wished like fuck I'd worn a jacket tonight. This wrap dress was not going to cut it when it couldn't have been more than forty-five outside. Served me right for being fooled by our temporary fall warmup.

Then again, annoyance and anger and personal disgust worked well at keeping the chill at bay.

As I charged up the street, I realized the breeze didn't make me cold. It gave my irritation fuel. Like I was righteously indignant and there was even a wind machine to blow back my hair just like in the movies.

Booyah.

I detoured off the sidewalk to the long pier that stretched toward the lake. Jabs of guilt assailed me with every step, but I kept moving because I had no choice. If I stopped, I'd go back, and I really didn't think I could handle any more of my mother tonight.

It wasn't even all her fault. Sure, she said and did inappropriate things, but worst of all, she didn't behave the way I'd always believed a mother should. She'd left me chasing after her for far too much of my life.

I stopped at the end of the pier and faced the miles of dark rippling water, my heart in my throat. Was it any wonder I hadn't wanted to chase after a happy relationship too? I'd just tried to find a practical, non-emotional way to build a family for myself without wishing or hoping for any of the intangibles.

Like, oh, love.

Or romance.

Or maybe finding a best friend who also happened to turn me on and make me laugh and make me crazy in all the best ways.

Like Murphy. Murphy was already so important to me, and that scared the fuck out of me. Because even without the baby goal between us, I enjoyed his company far too much. And that meant he had power over me.

The power to change my plans. The power to leave. The power to claim to send a postcard that never arrived and break my heart with a smile.

"Veronica."

Oh, God, his voice. My name barely carried over the rush of the wind. My pulse sped up and I gripped the steel railing around the pier until the cold bled through my palms straight to my bones.

Then he said it again, louder now.

"Veronica."

I swallowed hard and turned around, shivering as the stiff breeze blew my hair straight back.

With one glimpse of him, so strong and proud in his dark vest and crisp white shirt, his white sleeves billowing a bit in the wind, I wanted to run to him, bury my face in his chest, and never leave.

I fought the impulse for a minute, maybe two, as we stared at each other. Then I moved toward him and sighed in relief when his arms encircled me tightly.

"I'm sorry," I mumbled into his throat. "I'm sorry I ran off and left you with my mess."

"It's our mess now."

I eased back to look up at him, laughing and sniffling, and he gave me a wry smile. "I mean, what mess?"

"Yeah, right. That was a *Meet the Parents* sequel if I've ever seen one."

"Pretty sure they've had a couple of them."

"Yeah, and tonight would've qualified to join the list." I swiped at my chin. "I swear, I'm typically not much of a crier, but my emotions are all over the place lately."

"She sprung information on you that you weren't expecting. You're entitled."

"Oh, yeah? And was I entitled to run off and leave you hanging?"

"Yes." He brushed back a strand of my windblown hair. "Because that's the only way you'll ever believe I'll always chase after you."

"Aww, Murphy." I glanced up at him, swallowing deeply at the reflection of the lights surrounding the pier shimmering in his hazel eyes. Such trustworthy eyes. Such broad shoulders, capable of carrying the weight of what mattered every day and not faltering.

Steadfast. True. Honorable. That was Murphy.

And he was everything I wanted, more than I ever could have guessed.

He was the exact opposite of my mother. The word *flighty* had no space in his vocabulary. He was the sort of man who would stick—for life.

If I was brave enough to take the chance and let him in.

"I don't deserve you," I whispered.

"Don't I get to decide that?" His hand molded to my cheek. "I get to say who I want and what I want. If I'm lucky, you'll want me back."

"I do. God, I do. So much. But I didn't tell you about my baggage."

"Baggage like what? A secret lover stashed away somewhere? A prison record? Maybe a hidden past on the run?"

My lips trembled into a smile. "No. More like I have commitment issues. I get really fucking bitchy when I get PMS and on days one and two of my period. And I probably wanted a baby to have someone to love, and someone to love me back, which shows I may not be good parent material at all."

His hand firmed against my face. "What makes a better parent than that?"

I didn't have an answer for him. Or myself. I was questioning everything right now.

Except how I felt about him. That was a warm, wild beat in my chest that never waned for even a second. It was growing more intense with every passing moment.

He turned me toward the railing and wrapped his arms around me from behind, setting his chin on my head. His solid column of warmth at my back made me feel more secure than I'd ever felt in my life.

And more scared.

"I believe in you," he said after a couple of minutes of silence, broken only by the lapping water and the soft murmur of the voices around us.

Despite the chill, it was a nice night and lots of people were out and about. None of them existed as far as I was concerned.

There was just Murphy.

"I believe you know your own heart and mind. You made the decision that was right for you, and I gotta say I'm glad for it. Without that post, we might not have ever spoken beyond 'Eight petit fours to go, please, ma'am'."

I snorted and turned my head to speak over my shoulder. "You never ordered eight."

He pretended to suck in his stomach. "Gotta act cool in front of the hot chick."

"You think I'm hot?"

"No."

I pretended to pout as he turned me toward him again and imprisoned me against the rail with his muscled arms caging me in on either side. "I think you're the loveliest woman I've ever seen in this life or any other."

I blinked at the sudden sting in my eyes. Damn wind. "Oh, is that all?"

"No. Not even close. You're also smart and funny and make the best brownies I've ever tasted. I even like the peanut butter swirl ones now."

"You didn't used to?"

"Nope."

"Hmm. Maybe it's my magic new ingredient." I leaned against his chest and grinned up at him.

He twirled my hair around his finger. "What's that?"

Love.

I nearly said it. Nearly clued him in to the truth inside me.

Instead, I mumbled, "White chocolate chips," and reached up to yank his head down to mine.

I kissed him hard and he kissed me back with matching desperation, his fingers streaking into my hair to cup the base of my head. I bit his lower lip and he made a hungry sound in his throat, one that echoed in my belly and directly south. Just the insistent rub of his tongue against mine had me reaching down to grasp his belt buckle in a firm grip that told him in no uncertain terms I wanted my hand around more than metal.

"I want you." Shamelessly, I panted it into his mouth between kisses.

"Veronica, we're outside."

"I know. I feel the cold railing against my ass and your hard cock against my pussy. Well, not quite, since you're the size of a damn giant compared to me, but that's where I want it."

"Jesus. Oh, Jesus." He was swearing in a continuous stream now, and it was pretty damn funny as well as hot as hell.

I barely got out a giggle before he was seizing hold of my hand and tugging me up the pier, dodging pedestrians with his typical politeness if not his usual moderate speed.

"Sorry, excuse us, in a hurry, sorry, coming through!"

I hurried to keep up with him, my wrap dress whipping against my chilly legs in the breeze. Murphy had warmed me right up though.

Inside and out. Especially between my breasts in that spot no other man had touched before.

No one else.

"Where are we going?" I asked between choppy breaths, scarcely able to hold back my laughter. It filled me up inside, squeezing out everything else.

Maybe this was what joy felt like.

And falling in love.

"My cabin. Or your apartment. No, your apartment is closer."

The apartment I rarely spent time in these days, since I spent every free moment with Murphy at his place. I didn't want to go there now. It was small and already felt empty, as if I no longer lived there.

I'd already begun to move on to my future.

I squeezed his hand. God, I hoped.

He drew me up the street to where his truck was parked near the bed and breakfast. Even in his rush, he didn't just unlock it and move toward the driver's side. Oh, no, he opened my door first and would have waited while I got inside and belted in.

If I hadn't climbed in and turned to him standing beside the open passenger door, then reached for him with my arms and legs, wrapping both around him while he let out a startled "oof," and met my mouth with his own.

I lost track of time. Of place. I barely felt the cramps in my inner thighs from the awkward way I'd coiled around him like a horny snake. But I didn't miss how his hand anchored in my hair or the firm press of his lips as he matched my eagerness and returned even more.

My Murphy, who wasn't into PDAs, was definitely giving as good as he got tonight.

Somehow I pulled back to pant against his throat. "Drive up the street. Pull off by the Paulson's boat launch."

He didn't argue with me, just stepped back to touch his fingers to his mouth where I'd practically kissed him raw. His smile made me smile back stupidly, before he tucked my dress around my legs and gently nudged them inside. I still hadn't reached for my belt when he shut my door.

Or when he came around to start the truck. I wasn't quite able to move.

I was in some kind of dazed love-pre-sex coma and could only keep right on smiling as he drove the short distance up the street and pulled over where I'd indicated near a shady grove of trees.

Wasn't the stealthiest of makeout spots—or let's be real, fucking spots, because I wasn't intending to stop with just copping a feel—but it would probably do without us getting arrested.

And if I was wrong, I'd pay that fine with pride.

He shifted toward me and I covered his mouth with my finger. "Ease back your seat."

No arguments once again. Hallelujah.

Once he had, I climbed astride his lap more than a little awkwardly. The windows were already getting foggy, and I was glad no one would be able to see me try to be seductive as I wedged my ass on his lap and tried to shift so the steering wheel didn't bruise me to shit.

And oh, hello there, happy cock. I missed you.

"Did you just call my cock happy?" His laugh was strangled.

"Was I talking out loud? Whoops. More like your cock makes *me* happy." I kissed him and rubbed up against it without the slightest ounce of hesitation, sliding my dress up between us so he could feel just how wet I was. Since my panties were basically a scrap of nothing and I was suddenly very pleased with that fact.

"Jesus."

"That again?" I grinned and steadied myself on his shoulders, watching his face as I rocked up and down. "Do you have condoms?"

He nodded and tipped back his head. "In my wallet. Back pocket. If I move, I'm probably going to come, so not doing that."

"No, you aren't." I nipped his lower lip and savored the sound he made.

I could live on each one of them. Just store them up like oxygen.

"You have one?"

"Nope." I did, actually, and would use it if he wanted me to.

Oh, wait, no, I didn't. My purse was back in the restaurant. I frowned. Oh, crap.

Then I looked at the backseat and saw it lying there, as if it had been thrown onto that spot. Not by me.

"You saved my purse."

He nodded. "Grabbed it on my way out after apologizing to your mother. I tossed it in the truck on my way to find you. It was just blind luck thinking you'd run for the water." He craned his neck to glance into the backseat. "I hope I didn't break your phone."

"Don't worry. It's sturdy."

Just like me. I was sturdier than I'd ever given myself credit for, because even though I was scared of this—so terrified—I wasn't running away.

I was grabbing onto Murphy with both hands and holding on for dear life.

"So am I. And if you keep wiggling against me like that, I can't promise not to—" He took a shuddering breath when I rubbed against him that much harder.

"Maybe come in my mouth?" I leaned down and playfully licked his lower lip, my eyes never leaving his. "Better yet, maybe I'll ride you and *then* you can come in my mouth."

"Veronica."

"I don't want you to wear a condom this time. I also don't want you to come in my throat. But I very much want to suck all of this." I reached between us to squeeze him, the slide of my fingers stimulating me too.

I wasn't sure which of us moaned louder.

"It's your choice." I made myself still my movements so that he focused on what I was saying. "Wrapped or unwrapped, I'm here for it."

He reached up to cradle my chin in his big hand. "I want it too. I want every bit of you, Veronica Dixon."

I kissed him, undoing his zipper with no finesse whatsoever. I wanted to press my lips to his pecs and his abs and his dick—and everywhere in between—but the need inside me was far too great. Not just physically. I wanted him in a way I hadn't known was possible.

I fumbled him out of his boxer briefs and swiped my thumb over the swollen head, then I set him against me. I couldn't wait.

But Murphy would never be the guy who didn't think of foreplay, even if I was hot enough to come from a strong breeze. He cupped my breasts and rolled his thumbs over my tight nipples, his hungry expression more than enough to send me over all on its own.

Then he leaned forward and dragged his tongue up the side of my throat. "You're the only girl I've ever had sex with outside of a bed."

It made me laugh. And ask probably the worst question ever. "Not even Sage?"

Right. Because now was the perfect time for my inappropriate feelings of jealousy to rear up yet again.

He shifted his head and nailed me with a far too perceptive glance. "I never slept with Sage. We never even came close. We just dated a couple of times, that's all."

"Mmm-hmm."

He frowned, but then he smiled so wide I almost would've slugged him—if I hadn't been gripping his cock like a joystick. "You're jealous of her. You're jealous of her and me. Even though you have absolutely no reason to be."

"What? Me? No." I looked at the roof of his truck. "Maybe a little. But you can probably fuck it right out of me."

"Oh, can I?"

"Yes. You can."

He reached down between us and slipped aside the little panel of material that kept us apart. Then he lined himself up, locked his gaze with mine, and drew me down on top of him, so freaking slowly that my breath escaped on a hiss.

"Oh, God." The feel of him inside me bare was...

There weren't words. Just groans. Grunts. The sounds of us moving together and making the truck fucking rock.

"Veronica." His thumb brushed my lower lip and I sucked it into my mouth, every bit as hard as I was drawing him into my body.

He threw back his head, the cords in his neck tensed and outlined in the sliver of moonlight sneaking inside the fogged-up windows. "This isn't going to—fuck, I can't last."

"Me either. God, me either."

I bucked against him with no skill whatsoever, moving so jerkily in the confined space that my head bumped the ceiling and I just did not care. I barely even noticed, but he reached up to hold my head in both his hands, shielding me from my own need while his hips rose to give me everything I craved.

He did all the work and I just absorbed.

Basked.

Moaned with every delicious, dragging stroke.

My nipples tightened and I raced against him faster, rubbing at the spot that hit me just right. Enjoying every inch of him, tucked so deep inside me. "You can pull out," I gasped. "Finish in my hand. My mouth."

I wanted him to have every choice. Now and always.

He leaned up to speak close to my ear, his breath warm against my lobe. "And miss filling you up? Not a chance."

His primal, possessive tone made my body quake. I cried out as I felt him jerk inside me, and that sensation was all I needed to go flying. Knowing he was inside me, with me in every way that mattered. His release spilling deep within me, taking us both where we were meant to go.

If we were meant to. And if not, that was okay too. Because neither of us were alone anymore.

Not anymore.

"Veronica." He cupped my head and drew it to his shoulder while I rode out the last of my shudders. He was shaking too, and knowing he'd experienced just what I had was more powerful than any orgasm.

We could've created a life just now. And if we didn't? We were creating one anyway.

Ours. The one meant for us to live together.

"You're the only woman for me." His voice was guttural. Raw. "The only one, ever."

I shut my eyes and curled around him, kissing the side of his throat where his pulse beat so fast and hard.

For me.

For us.

"You're the only man for me, Murphy." I eased back to frame his face between my hands. "Okay, wait, that's a lie." His brief frown was worth it as I added, "Well, you and Cabin Fortress."

He laughed and smacked my bare ass, then rubbed it gently before pulling down my dress. "Get back in that seat, girl."

"Afraid we'll be arrested?"

His gaze connected electrically with mine in the near darkness. "No. I'm taking you home so I can get you pregnant the right way."

SEVENTEEN

VEE:

Fortress, I have breached your walls. I'd say
I'm into you, but I'd prefer you get in me
again. Very soon.

My truck bounced over the gravel drive up to my cabin. The cab of the truck was quiet and still smelled of her. For fuck's sake, her scent was still on my dick. I was a damn mess.

The fact that I still wasn't done with her, that was the part that scared the fuck out of me.

It didn't feel one and done.

It never had with her.

And now, she'd let me inside of her without a damn condom in my fucking truck. That was not the way I wanted to do that the first time. Not that it was our first time. No, that had been definitely out of the ordinary as well.

Freaking kitchen counter.

We had only been involved for a short while, but it felt as if we'd been already been together forever.

As usual my life was spinning out of control when it came to this woman. It had happened the very first day I saw her and now...

Now our lives might be changing forever. She'd come at me like a siren with a purpose. I'd crashed into the rocks and drowned happily.

I'd drown daily if she let me.

I glanced over at her as I slapped the gear into park. "So, that happened."

She smoothed her hand over her skirt. "Which part? The part where my mom interrogated you, or the part where I jumped you?"

"Both."

She tipped her head. That damn head tilt was going to be the death of me. "You charmed the pants off my mom. Then me." She gave me a wicked grin. She toyed with the hem of her skirt. "Well, panties. And I think we should practice a little more."

I groaned as I tried to straighten my skewed tie. My little hellcat left me as disheveled as a horny teen after prom. Then again, my prom hadn't ended nearly as well as our crazy truck escapades.

I climbed out of the truck and came around to her side, opening the door and undoing her buckle before hauling her into my arms again.

"Murphy." Her voice was startled, but the light in her eyes told me she was onboard. I couldn't take all of this too seriously or she was going to bolt.

She might not need me anymore after our little interlude.

My grip tightened on her hips as I backed up with her in my arms. I held her tight against me and she wrapped her legs around my waist. "Damn, girl. You make me think all sorts of ungentlemanly thoughts when you give me that look."

She looped her arms around my neck. "Which look would that be? I'd like to memorize it so I can pull it out of my pocket whenever I need you."

"Need me for what?"

Easy, asshole. Don't scream 'I am half in love with you already' in her face.

Especially since I was pretty sure half had been a foregone conclusion before I'd even messaged her the first time. Add in a few weeks and I was about as gone as you could get.

"This." She bounced up with the incredible—sweet loving mercy —strength of her amazing thighs. This woman was my match in so many ways.

I stalked up the walkway. And even with Veronica's serial killer talk in the back of my mind, I never remembered to lock my damn door. There was nothing precious enough in my place to worry about. At least there never had been before now.

I juggled her slightly so I could get my hand on the doorknob before I kicked the door open and slammed it shut. Her eyes went bright with excitement and my boots made a sharp click on the hardwood as I bypassed my living room, kitchen, and went right to my master suite.

"Man with a purpose."

"You're goddamn right." I tossed her into the middle of the bed, and she made a squeak that turned into bawdy laughter.

She rolled onto her knees. "Murphy Masterson, what got into you?"

I unbuttoned the tiny freaking buttons of my vest and stripped it off. "A certain woman attacked me in my own truck."

She put her hands on her hips. "And you're offended?"

"No." I slowed myself down. Stared her down as I undid the buttons at each wrist. "I just feel the need to show you who's boss."

She threw her head back with a laugh. "Not you, sir."

"Strip, Veronica. If that dress isn't off before I get to my belt, you'll be wearing one of my shirts home tomorrow."

Her laughter dried up and for a moment I thought I went too far. Instead, she went for her little tie at the side of the wrap dress and it slid free. "Better hurry up with those buttons, Fortress."

I was too wired to deal with the little plastic disks that made me insane on a good day. Then again, I rarely got dressed up. But for her,

I did. Right now, with her creamy skin on display, I had no hope of being dexterous.

I jerked my tie to the side as she tucked her fingers into the shadows of her dress to find some magic hook or string and the whole dress unfurled. She was perfect. And she drove me to distraction.

A rainbow of colored T-shirts with one of Macy's racy slogans on them made her look sweet and about the age of a coed. In a dress?

Nope.

Nothing coed about her.

All woman with her perfect breasts pushed up by a pale purple bit of lace that I'd only gotten a brief glimpse of when she'd been riding on top of me. She'd barely let me breathe before getting into my zipper.

But not now.

Now I could take my time and make sure she was full to the fucking brim with my...

Jesus, since when had I had these caveman impulses to spread my seed?

Since a certain rainbow-tipped blond came into your life, buddy.

She shrugged off the dress and cupped her hands over her breasts. "You're lagging behind, Fortress."

I don't know why that name made me crazy. But it was like a secret just between us. No one knew this side of me besides this woman. Not even former girlfriends, and there had been very few. I was too quiet, too reserved, too...friend-zoned.

But not with her.

Her gaze raked down my chest as I whipped the tie out of the collar of my shirt. Her lips parted. I arched my eyebrow as her gaze drifted to the silver and blue tie around my hand. I wrapped it around my palm and made a quick slipknot.

Her eyes widened and she licked her lips.

Well, that would be one way to keep her from moving this along faster than I wanted.

"Do you trust me?"

She swallowed hard and nodded quickly.

"I need the words, Veronica."

She lifted her hands, wrists up. "Oh, yes."

If my dick hadn't been pulsing behind my zipper before, now it was a full-on throb. I looped the tie over her hands and gently tightened it over her wrists, before I brought them both up to my lips. I nipped at the fragile skin, then followed it up with a soft kiss.

I knelt on the bed and urged her back on my quilt.

Don't think about the fact that Aunt Milly made the quilt for you, asshole.

Nope.

All I could focus on was this woman. This moment.

And maybe, just maybe, planting a baby inside her. One that I'd cherish just as much as his or her mama. If only she'd let me.

I reached behind her head to tug her twist out of the pretty barrette thing she had it in. I needed all her blond hair on my pillows. Spread out for me so I could take all of her in.

I straddled her thighs to lift her arms up between the pillows to the slats of my headboard. I only looped it once and tied a knot that could be released easily. I didn't want her completely at my mercy. I loved how she reached for me. Always.

She never held back.

It was one of the things I loved about her.

I closed my eyes.

Love had come so quick. As much as I wanted to put it in a box at the back of my brain, it just wouldn't be denied. For right now, I wouldn't fight it.

Tonight, I'd show her exactly how I felt since I couldn't say it quite yet.

I tugged the tails of my shirt out of my pants and found the patience to undo each button. Mostly because she looked at me as if she was starving and I wanted to hold onto this moment. Maybe if I made her realize just how good we were together, it could be more than just a transaction.

Because, to me, it wasn't.

Not by a longshot.

I didn't think about my own body issues, or that she was so damn small under me. Her green eyes shown in the shadowy light of the night. Only a lone light shone in the corner to let me see her. But it was more than enough.

Part of me wondered if I should back away and stoke the fire for her. She looked amazing in firelight, but I didn't have the strength for that right now. The heat we made together would have to be enough.

She bucked up under me to get me to move up. I stripped off my white dress shirt. "Still trying to control this particular situation, Veronica?"

She rolled her lower lip behind her teeth with a little shrug. "Can't fault a girl."

I reached behind my head for my undershirt and tossed it on the floor with my shirt.

"Why is that so hot?"

I grinned down at her. "Pardon?"

"You have no idea how amazing your body is."

I swiped my hand across my belly self-consciously.

"So strong and you literally have those notch things at the top of your belt. I mean, how? It's just wrong."

I glanced down at my belt and laughed. "What?"

"The romance novel things. You know. The sin lines. I didn't think they were real, but my God, there they are." She lifted her head. "I want to lick them. If you'd crawl up here, I'd lick all sorts of things like a lollipop, Fortress."

"Jesus."

"Nope, just me. Jesus can wait his turn—wait. You know what I mean."

I couldn't stop the quick laugh. I was in the middle of seducing her and she said the craziest things. And yet, it made it even better. More real to a level I'd never had before. It didn't feel forced and like I was putting on a show for her.

Like I was going to get shot down for being ridiculous.

I drew my fingertip down the little dip in her chin to her throat. "There's nothing between us tonight. On a number of levels. That you trust me with that humbles me, but most of all, I just want to please you."

"You do."

I followed the light trail of my fingers with my mouth. She wore a little pendant with a whisk and a heart. I nudged it aside to get to her deliciously perfect breasts. I detoured around the firm curve of her breast to the tip of her nipple that poked against the lace. I watched her face as I found the center clasp of the bra and freed them.

Soft and warm, her skin beaded up with a wash of goosebumps as I dragged my scruff across one, then another before doubling my attention on her tight nipples. She arched up off the bed and tugged at her restraints as I sucked one deep into my mouth.

My name was a disjointed sigh ending in a sweet little purr as I let her nipple free. I drew lazy circles around her belly until she was writhing between my legs. Each wiggle reminded me that there was only a fine layer of wool between us.

But I needed to take a second and taste all of her before I got rid of that barrier.

Knowing I could slip inside of her with no condom again gave me the strength I needed to extend this moment. She was worth the strangled cock.

I propped myself up with a hand next to her neck. I was careful not to pin her to the bed by the hair. Of course that sort of backfired on me since that left her hair vining around my arm as I hovered over her.

I lowered my mouth to hers, just as I slipped my fingers under the scrap of lace she called underwear. Her tongue stroked along mine as my fingers found her soaked slit. Knowing that it was a mix of us there made my dick even harder.

I'd never come inside a woman before her. Even longstanding girlfriends, we'd always been careful to use double the protection. Young and unwilling to tie myself to anyone, I'd been careful all my life. Because I knew a baby meant a lifetime. I wasn't wired any other way.

Knowing she wanted this from me already had me tied to her, whether she knew it or not. We'd had the discussion about me being part of the baby's life, but for me, she was a package deal.

Forever.

Even if that meant I would be sidelined if she grew tired of me.

She was it for me.

I tucked two fingers deep inside her and touched my forehead to hers as she rode my hand without restraint. As she took what she needed from me without a moment's hesitation. Her name was a strangled groan on my lips as she shattered under me.

I stretched out on her as she shamelessly rubbed herself along my cock. "Off. Get these pants off," she panted against my neck. "I need you. All of you."

Me?

Or just my swimmers?

I believed it was more. She'd indicated it was. But God, it was so easy to wonder if maybe she wanted one part of me more than the rest.

I shut my eyes before she saw the questions blinking in my brain like a neon sign. I quickly rolled off the bed and shucked my pants, underwear, boots, and socks. Until there was nothing between us.

I reached above her head for the tie, groaning into her mouth as she kissed me and scrambled into my arms when I released her.

She tore off the tie and threw it on the floor, and then she was in my arms. Her warm skin pressed against mine as she knelt on the bed. I followed her into the middle of the wide mattress as we faced one another. Her multi-colored hair was wild around her shoulders and all she wore was her necklace.

We were thigh to thigh, my cock jutting up between us. I was beyond hard for her. It felt like my skin was too tight for my body, but especially my cock. She reached for me and I hissed out a breath. She swiped her thumb over the head and her pupils went wide with lust.

I'd never had a woman look at me like she did.

She gently stroked down my length and rubbed the head along her lower belly. She had such gentle curves and a narrow waist that made me feel clumsy and too big for her, but she was fearless.

It seemed like she was fearless about everything.

Where I was cautious, she was running ahead with wonder and bright colors. And for the first time, I wanted so much to follow her light. Not to hide in the shadows like I usually did. Where it was safe so I could watch and not put myself out there.

She turned, pulling me on top of her on the pile of pillows so she was propped up under me. As if she wasn't the smallest, most fragile woman I'd ever known this way. No, she took me in hand and then into her body.

Her bright green eyes fluttered shut as I slowly stretched her to accept all of me in one fluid thrust. I had to fight back the urge to take her. To imprint myself on her. It wasn't about that right now. It was a connection I hadn't allowed myself with a woman before.

I undulated my hips against her, giving her the long, slow strokes I didn't know I was capable of. Her eyes popped open as every part of me rubbed against hers from the tip of my cock to the very base of my shaft. I widened her thighs to take me deeper.

She clawed my back and I blew out a slow breath as I did it again and again.

She was the one made for me in every way.

I tipped her hips slightly and growled out her name. She clasped me so damn tight, her body welcoming me and pushing against me at the same time. My strokes grew faster and her grip on me grew tighter. Slow and steady was replaced with desperation. There was nothing between us, not even air as she gripped my torso with her knees, her arms around my back and her mouth on mine.

Even if I'd wanted to stop, I couldn't.

My body wasn't my own.

It was hers.

She wrung me dry in heart and mind.

I sealed my mouth over hers and swallowed her cries. She reached up between us to frame my face and I was gone.

So far gone.

I emptied myself inside her. The room fuzzed out of focus except for her. Her eyes were as wild as the storm-tossed lake I loved and had to be next to. How fucking fitting.

I curled my arms under her to hold her close and at the last minute, I tipped her hips up to keep me inside her. Not just for the animalistic side of me that wanted to fill her with my come, but for her.

The woman who wanted a baby so very badly.

I only hoped I could be the man she needed too.

I lowered my mouth to hers once more. Riding the afterglow had always been more like hunting and foraging in the kitchen. There was something about ramen noodles after sex to refill the well, but with her? I didn't want to let go.

I didn't even want to sleep.

Talk about gone for a woman, Moose.

She cupped my face. "Think we made a baby?"

"Maybe." I kissed her languidly. "Practicing is going to be fun if we didn't."

"That's the truth." She stretched her arms over her head and rubbed her calf along the back of mine. "I've never enjoyed sex this much in my life."

"Is that right?"

She winced. "Probably shouldn't say that."

"Why?" I nipped her lower lip. "I'm good with that moniker."

For now.

She wiggled under me. "Sex machine?" Her laughter spiked. "Your ears. I can't."

I frowned. "What about my ears?" I touched one and hoped the heat was from post-coital bliss.

"I love when they get red when you're embarrassed."

"Great." I rolled off her and took her with me to sprawl across my chest.

She propped her chin on her stacked hands on my shoulder. "It's adorable."

"Can we pick a few new adjectives?"

Her eyes glittered in the low light. "It's hot that you know grammar."

"Shut up." Her laughter took the sting out of my embarrassment. I tucked one of her wild locks of hair behind her ear. "What are you doing next weekend?"

"Not sure. Probably just working."

"Think Macy would let you take Sunday off?"

"Begrudgingly." She wrinkled her nose. "She'd work me every day if the labor union didn't get up in her business."

"Really?"

She laughed. "No. I'm kidding. I just usually work on the weekends because Jodi and Ellie also work at Robbie's on the weekend."

"Pizza is very important to the Cove."

"You're telling me. Next to coffee anyway." She tilted her head. "What's next Sunday?"

"My brother, Penn is coming in from New York, plus Travis and my niece Carrington—"

"Her name is Carrington? Isn't that a soap opera name?"

"Her mom's...interesting."

"That sounds like a story." Her eyes were heavy and her face soft with half-sleep. She yawned. "Is this like a family dinner?"

"Something like that." I didn't want to scare the crap out of her with my huge family, but after meeting her mom, I figured we should do the same with mine.

"Are you showing me off to your people?"

"Maybe."

"Maybe I like it."

I settled her against me and stroked her hair until she fell asleep. I sure fucking hoped so.

EIGHTEEN

Fortress,

Just how big is your family? I was going to bake for them,
but I'm not sure how much to make. Does your mom like
flowers? Maybe I shouldn't go after all. Can I call in sick?

YOURS IN TERROR, VEE

"My family's not *this* big, you know." I opened the door to
the small backseat of my truck and slid out the large pastry box with a
grunt. In truth, I probably could have used tie-downs in the flatbed
for her box of treats. Cinnamon goodness had been teasing me the
entire ride over. "Did you bake snickerdoodles?"

"Maybe."

"I'm going to have to row an extra twenty minutes for this."

"I like watching you row." She grinned at me across the hood of
the truck. "Especially the early morning ones where the lake is all

misty. Goodness the sweat on your shoulders this morning just did something to me."

And me when she attacked me as I was putting my kayak away. She'd warned me that she was on her "good week" whatever that meant. And well, we'd both been enjoying a full week of sexual hijinks.

She couldn't get enough of me—and vice versa.

However, it was becoming apparent the dual purpose of our rigorous sex life was at a fevered pitch right now. And while I was enjoying the babymaking adventure we were on, I was getting a little raw. I wasn't complaining—much. Because in all honesty, we were acting just like a new couple who couldn't get enough of each other.

But Veronica was a little demanding when it came to certain preferred times to get busy. Something about temperatures and prime ovulation time.

However, the kayak interlude this morning had been a surprise. I swallowed hard, willing my dick to behave. I could not go hug my mother with a freaking boner. Last night, I'd wondered if I could keep up with her.

This morning, well...the proof was in my tweaked back and her moans echoing across the lake.

I was pretty sure my kayak rack wasn't built for the kind of stress we'd put it under this morning. We were both wearing a few new bruises, but it had been worth it. I'd be rowing in the morning a whole helluva lot more if that was my reward.

She fluffed a dark red sunflower looking bloom in the center of the huge bouquet of fall flowers we'd stopped in town for on the way to my parents' place. They lived on the far side of Crescent Cove, where the upper middle class could afford a little more land. The lakefront properties were going up in price with each passing year.

I'd been lucky to get a plot before the developers started driving up the costs. My father was forever trying to convince me to sell and move closer to them. I loved my family, but I didn't need them to be my neighbors. The twenty-minute drive suited me just fine.

Veronica came around the truck to meet me. "Are you sure these are okay?"

"My mom's going to love them. You'll win a dozen points just with the flowers. Add in these?" I hugged the box closer to my chest. "You're going to make us all look bad."

"That's not what I meant to do." Her huge green eyes went even wider. "I can put them back."

"No, no." I scooped her in close to me. "I'm just teasing."

She poked me. "Well, don't. I've never done this before."

"Never?"

She looked down at her black strapped shoes that reminded me of a schoolgirl's—*wrong, Moose. Don't go down that road.* It was bad enough that I found every part of her sexy as hell, I didn't need to add in a schoolgirl fantasy. Especially since I'd never had one before her.

It was probably the braids.

Her colorful hair was wrapped up in one of her crown braids with little bits curling around her face. She looked impossibly young and way out of my league. She was wearing one of her colorful dresses. It reminded me of the poppy fields I'd seen in books. She matched her flowers, for God's sake.

I was lucky I'd remembered to wear khakis instead of jeans for Sunday dinner.

My girl looked like she was coming from church. And I was not having churchly thoughts.

"Okay, let me just go over the names again."

"The only one who counts is me."

I turned at the deep voice behind me and handed the box to Veronica. "Jesus, it's good to see you, man." I gave my older brother a bear hug, lifting him off his feet.

"Christ, what have you been eating?" Penn slapped my shoulders. "You're a beast."

I let him go and stepped back with a half-laugh. I tugged down my shirt and took the box back from Veronica. "Just the same old stuff."

Penn gave me a once over. "I think not. Are you sure there aren't steroids involved?"

"No, definitely—"

Veronica stepped in front of me. "Actually, he's been eating very sensibly. Even trying to change my terrible diet. And he rows every morning."

Penn laughed. "I stand corrected." He glanced from Veronica to me. "I'm just impressed. Gotta look after my little brother. I'm used to the softer, gentler version, not this fit tank." He slapped my midsection. "Putting us all to shame, Moose." He nodded to Veronica. "Who's the little pit bull?"

I rolled my eyes. "Veronica, meet my oldest brother, Penn. Don't hold his shitty manners against me."

He *tsked*. "Swearing in front of a lady. What would Mom say?"

Veronica peered up at him. Penn might be a little shorter than me, and all lanky muscle, but he was still well over six feet. His dark hair was long and shaggy. It was probably a four-hundred-dollar haircut knowing my brother. She tipped her head slightly. There was no playful light in her eyes.

No, they were flat and assessing. Finally, she held out her hand. "Pleased to meet you. I think. I'm still reserving judgment."

Penn laughed. "I like her. Way more interesting than the women you usually date, little bro." His eyebrow lifted. "Way more interesting."

My eyes narrowed. It wouldn't be the first time my brother tried to lure a girl away from me. He'd even managed to do it a time or two. In his words, it was to protect me. One of the women had earned Penn a black eye.

The other girl I'd been dating hadn't been right for me from the jump. I wasn't entirely shocked she'd picked my brother over me. Everyone chose Penn. It was one of those things I'd been used to all my life.

Penn was wild and reckless. He'd been looking for a way out of this town since he turned seventeen. He'd even gone so far as to take his tests and graduate early so he could get to art school. It was all he'd cared about.

That and bedding whatever willing female caught his eye.

So, yeah, I didn't want him looking at Veronica. Even a little bit. Not that I had any reason to believe she'd go for him. Even if virile male pheromones trailed behind him like Pepe LePew.

Asshole. But hormones are what she wants though.

"Murphy."

I looked down at Veronica.

"Don't crush the box before your mom sees what I made for you guys."

Penn snatched the box from me. "I wasn't sure if it was your girl or the box that smelled so sweet."

Instead of swooning like most women did, Veronica rolled her eyes. She handed me the flowers and snatched the box from Penn. "Hands off." She did an about face and stalked toward the house.

Penn's eyebrow arched. "I really like her."

I sighed and followed the two of them to the front door. The sounds of my family were usually comforting, but there were a few more nerves attached to this Sunday. The shrill scream of Carrington made Veronica shoot a worried glance my way.

"Welcome to the Masterson house." Penn snatched the box away from her again and sailed through the door. "Ma! I'm home."

"Is he always like that?"

"Afraid so." I lowered my mouth to hers for a quick kiss. "Please don't hate me." I handed her the flowers and ushered her inside.

Carrington came running down the hallway, my mother on her heels. The little girl's lemon-blond hair flew behind her in frazzled curls. Shrill screams dissolved into giggles as my mom hooked an arm around her and scooped the giggling five-year-old up off the floor. She had a beater clutched in her little hand and what looked like mashed potatoes smeared across her face.

"I didn't finish the potatoes, young lady." My mom blew her bangs out of her face. "Can you...?" She handed Carrington to me.

"Unca Moose!"

"Hey, Cari Bobari." I curled my arms up until I could kiss her belly. She squealed and twisted until I had no choice but to toss her over my shoulder.

"Higher!"

Forever the refrain when she saw me. All she wanted me to do was throw her in the air, in the pool, in the bouncy house. The girl was a daredevil and had me wrapped around her finger. Even worse, she knew it. It was growing to be a theme in my life.

"Hey, Ma."

"Hi, baby." She pulled me down by the ear to kiss my cheek. "You said you wouldn't be a stranger when you got that cabin. Your check-in calls do not include any of the good stuff. Nope, I have to get all that at Suzanne's when I'm getting a cut."

Before I could open my mouth, she turned to Veronica.

"So, you're the one causing such a stir in town."

She blinked at my mom, then held out the flowers. "Depends on the hour of the day, I suppose. But if you're talking about my baby project, then yes, ma'am, I'm sure people are still talking. I'm Veronica Dixon, but my friends call me Vee. Well, except your son." She peered up at me, her eyes going from fierce to soft. "He likes to call me by my full name."

I caught her hand in mine.

My mom didn't miss that. I knew she wouldn't. Her gaze narrowed, but she took the flowers. "Well, come on in before the boys eat all my food."

"I'm more worried about the cookies," I muttered.

"Cookies?" My mother perked up. She had a sweet tooth as legendary as each of her boys. It was second only to my little sister, Maddie. She was pretty much made of sugar. And vinegar.

A head peeked around the corner. "Who made the cookies?"

"See. I knew they weren't safe. Don't you eat all those." I set Carrington down and she took off like a shot.

"Cookies? Can I have one?"

"Not before dinner," my mother shouted. "I'm JoAnn, by the way."

I flushed. "Sorry, Veronica. This is my mother, JoAnn."

"Pleased to meet you, Mrs. Masterson."

My mom waved that away. "You can call me Jo or JoAnn and that's about it."

"Right." Veronica beamed a smile at her. The fierce Veronica was back in her box and the sweet one who won over everyone in the town was back. "Your home is beautiful. Thank you so much for letting me intrude on your family dinner."

"Considering you're thinking about adding one to our numbers, it's only right."

Vee opened her mouth, then shut it. What exactly could she say? My mother was just as much a force of nature as Veronica was. Her hold tightened on my hand as we headed into the living room.

My parents had one of those cookie-cutter houses that was all open space and windows for the majority of the downstairs. The other half was the kitchen. My mother's domain in all ways.

The television was on and my father was in his recliner. Veronica's plate of cookies was already being plowed through. I'd probably overstated the whole too many cookies thing. All my siblings had a bottomless pit for a stomach. My father was even worse than we were.

He spotted Veronica and the footrest slammed down as he got up with the quickness. "So, you're the one who's finally going to give me another grandchild."

Veronica's eyes went wide as her neck craned back.

My dad didn't give her a chance to even say hi, he just scooped her up in a big hug. "You might be doing things a little backward, but I like you already."

"*Oof.*" Veronica gave me a startled glance, her face buried in one of my dad's flannel shirts.

"Hank, put the child down. There's no bun in the oven yet." My mother's eyes narrowed. "Right?"

"No, Ma."

Not that we knew of anyway.

She gave a little grunt and headed for the kitchen, but not before I caught her burying her nose in the blooms. My mom might have to be a hardass thanks to the men in her life, but she loved flowers. I should have thought about bringing her some myself. Veronica was always the thoughtful one for all occasions.

My dad dragged her into the living room.

"Tell me about yourself, sweetheart." He set her in front of the couch, then sat on the edge of his chair, turned toward her.

She sat down gingerly and smoothed the skirt of her dress. "I'm a baker at Brewed Awakening."

My dad held up a hand. "Not that part. We know that part. Who are your people?"

She blinked. "Pardon?"

"Family," Penn said before licking the pads of his fingers with an absurdly loud groan. "These cookies are from heaven. I don't care who your mom and dad are. I just want dozens of these to bring back to New York."

Veronica flushed. "Why thank you."

Penn winked at her. "Maybe I'll just take you with me instead."

I crossed to the couch and sat between them.

"*Ow.* Fucking hell, Moose."

"You keep that city trash talk on the train, young man," my mom hollered from the kitchen.

Penn frowned and punched me in the kidney. I didn't give him the satisfaction of grunting even though my eyes nearly crossed. His bony-ass knuckles always hurt. I aimed a well-placed elbow into his ribs, and he flicked my ear.

"All right. Take it outside or cut it out." My dad reached for Veronica's hand. "I'm sorry about my sons. They have no manners."

"I didn't do anything." Christian reached for another cookie from the coffee table.

"Because you didn't even introduce yourself."

"Everyone knows who I am." Christian nodded at her. "Nice to see you again, Vee."

"Officer."

Christian tapped his chest. "No badge today, hon."

"She's not your hon."

"Aww, look how growly Moose is getting." Christian snagged two more cookies. "Don't worry, I'm not looking to knock up the hot baker."

Veronica's cheeks flushed.

My dad flung the remote at Christian. "Manners, boy."

"Hey. Why are you all ganging up on me?" He leaned down to pick up the remote and lobbed it back at my dad.

"Because you have about as much sense as a wildebeest." Maddie came in the room and popped him on the back of the head. She held her hand out to Veronica. "I'm Maddie. Somehow I'm related to these idiots."

Veronica shook her hand. "I'm Vee. I think I've seen you in the café."

"I'm pretty sure the whole town goes to the café. Well, except Dad. He only likes Folgers." She shuddered.

Veronica wrinkled her nose. "You should really come in, Mr. Masterson."

"Hank. And I don't need to be paying three dollars for a coffee, thanks."

"Try eight in the city. And that's for subpar coffee." Penn tossed a corner of a cookie into the air and of course it landed right in his mouth. Everything came up roses for my damn brother.

My dad reached for a cookie.

"If you ruin your appetites, I will tan all of your hides."

He sat back with a little snarl on his lips. "I swear that woman has eyes all over the house."

"She could. Big Brother is out there." Penn pulled a pencil from behind his ear and twirled it through his fingers.

My father ignored him. "Tell us about you, Vee."

"I moved to Crescent Cove to work with Macy at the shop. We had a small coffee truck for a while, but when she found the storefront here, we both decided to move. And it's been amazing." Veronica laced her fingers through mine and held on tight.

"And your folks?"

She squeezed my hand harder.

"Dad."

"What? I'm just being conversational."

"You're being nosy." Maddie plopped into her well-used beanbag chair. "Interrogations are for second visits."

"No, it's okay." Veronica gave him her brave smile.

Was it any wonder I was already head over heels for this woman?

"I moved around a lot with my mom. She recently came for a visit, but she's off to Australia with her new husband." She shrugged. "Long story."

That was the truth. Andrea Dixon had whirled through our first official date with a whole lot of revelatory bombs. I still hadn't fully recovered from meeting her.

My dad frowned. "Is she some sort of airline stewardess?"

Veronica laughed. "No, that would be too sensible. She just finds a new adventure and goes for it."

"Sounds like you." My dad laced his fingers over his slight paunch. "Going off with that Macy girl."

"Dad, Macy is one of the most successful women in our town right now. And most of it is because of Veronica. You can't keep your hands off her cookies."

"That's what she said," Penn muttered.

I stomped on his steel-toe boot.

Penn just chuckled. The bastard.

Veronica nudged me with her shoulder. "Thanks, Fortress. You don't have to stick up for me. I know that my lifestyle isn't conventional. He's right to ask questions."

"Well, if you do have a baby with my son, I just want to know if we will have to chase you down to see our grandchild."

"Dad."

"It's not an outrageous question."

Veronica patted my hand. "No, it's not. And while my quest for a baby might be a little unconventional, I've found my home here in Crescent Cove. I've been looking for a real home for a long time. And I want nothing more than to raise my baby here."

I wasn't aware that my entire body had tightened until she said that. I wrapped my arm around her and hauled her close. "Now can you stop with the questions? I don't want to scare her away."

She turned her face into my shoulder for a moment and gave me a grateful smile.

"Would someone set the damn table?" My mom's bellow came from the kitchen.

I rose and tugged her with me. "We'll do it, Ma."

"I'll help!" Carrington came into the dining room with a stack of plastic bowls with napkins inside.

I came up behind her and she immediately climbed onto my boots as we shuffled around the table so she could reach. She rattled off the extent of her day at Kindergarten in excruciating detail, but I didn't interrupt her. My niece was adorable as hell despite her father's truly craptastic taste in women.

Speak of the devil. Travis came through the sliding back door with his helmet under his arm.

Carrington wiggled away from me and shrieked her way across the room to him. Travis dropped the helmet and caught her mid-leap and hoisted her above his head. "Munchee-chee. How goes it?"

"Travis, wash your hands and help me with the salad." My mother was a no-nonsense woman. Especially when one of her kids came in late for dinner.

"Right." He set his daughter on the floor gently, then scooped up his helmet. "Hellooo." On his way up, his eyes followed the petite lines of my...what? Girlfriend? Possible future mother of my child? I didn't even have a decent label for her.

We didn't talk about them. Somehow I wasn't supposed to toss her over my shoulder and keep her up in my cabin.

The stack of dishes I was shuffling around the table clanked together.

"Veronica, meet my perpetually late brother, Travis."

He reached up to ruffle his colorful mohawk. "Look, we match, darlin'."

What the hell was it with my brothers? Didn't they know how to speak to a woman without an endearment attached?

Veronica grinned. "So we do. What did you use for color?"

Travis shrugged. "They stick me in a chair and put goop on my head. Then I go in front of a camera. That's all I know."

"Travis is a model. Ish." Christian stole Travis's helmet. "Don't hold it against him. We don't. Mostly."

"You're just jealous because I get paid to have beautiful women crawl all over me."

"Really?" Penn flicked the long ends of his hair. "Last commercial I saw you in, there were more suds on you than pretty girls."

"Even men have to do dishes, jerk."

"Not if you have a maid."

"Well, there are no maids here, so I appreciate the free products that Travis sent me from the set." My mother came in with a huge platter of chicken. "And for that remark, Penn, you get to do dishes tonight."

"Ma. I came all the way from—"

"I don't care where you park your butt at night, Penn Michael Masterson, you come in this house and you're just my son. And if you think you're too good to get your hands dirty in my sink, you can skip my dinner too."

"Jeez, Ma." Penn crowded into her and dropped a kiss on her cheek. "I'll do the dishes. Just don't take away my chicken."

"Go on now. Get the potatoes."

I felt a small, cool hand curl around my fingers. "Can you come outside with me for a second?"

I frowned down at her and curled my arm around her back. "Everything okay? They didn't scare you into leaving, did they?"

"No. I love your family. They're so real."

"Real is one word for it."

She tipped her head up. "Just for a second."

I put the last two plates down. "Sure. We'll be right back, Mom."

"Don't be too long, the food will get cold."

"Go ahead. We'll be right back."

"I don't know that it's fair for Moose to get to go outside to make out with a pretty girl. That should be my job," Penn hollered.

My jaw tightened.

"More scooping, less talking," my mother shot back.

I followed Vee outside. She led me to the edge of the deck, then urged me down two steps. "What's up?"

She turned me to face her. With the height of the stairs, she was almost to my eye line. She framed my face with her hands. "Relax, Murphy."

I frowned. "I'm relaxed."

She smoothed her hands to my shoulders and gripped them. "Really? Because there's a lot of tension going on here and here." She released my shoulders to smooth the pad of her forefinger between my brows.

"My brothers always make me crazy."

"I don't know how it is to live with siblings, but if it's anything like me and Macy, I understand they know how to push your buttons."

I blew out a breath. "Yeah."

She laced her fingers along the back of my neck. "I only care about one Masterson man in that house. While your brothers are charming and funny in their own ways, they aren't my Fortress. And that's who I'm here with and want to be with."

I lowered my mouth to hers and kissed her hard. The kind of kiss that marked her as mine. The kind of kiss I'd never felt the need to give a woman in my life. There were so many tangled emotions inside me when it came to me and Veronica.

Knowing how much more interesting my brothers were than I was had always been a sore spot for me. Women always chose Penn and Travis, and even Christian had people running after him like he was built out of chocolate.

Me? Not so much.

Vee plastered herself to my chest and sighed into my mouth. "Just you."

I lifted her up as I walked us back toward the house. I set her down just outside the door. "Not sure I like that you handle me, Veronica Dixon."

She bit her lower lip and slid her hand under my Henley to score her nails lightly along the skin of my lower back. "I think you love how I handle you, Fortress."

I groaned and dropped another kiss on her smirking lips. "You may have a point."

"Now let's eat so we can go home." She grinned. "Then I'll show you just how much fun it is to be handled by a Dixon girl."

"I definitely like that idea."

NINETEEN

MURPHY:

I thought I'd bring home dinner. Save you a
night cooking. What would you like?

Two and a half months later

I STARED AT MY PHONE.

What did I want?

Hmm, that was a good question. Not a particularly hard one
either.

I wanted what I already had.

Happiness. Definitely had a butt load of that lately. So much that
I usually walked around with a perma-grin. Macy scowled when I got
too "love-dippy", but I knew she was happy for me.

Us. Because we were definitely an us.

Love was another thing I'd always wanted, and I had that in
spades. Even if we hadn't quite said the words. I hadn't yet, and

neither had Murphy. But I knew how I felt, and I was almost positive he was on the same page.

One covered with lots of hearts and initials and fat-cheeked Cupids.

Good thing because Valentine's Day was only a month away, and this year, I would actually have a special someone in my life.

I also wanted a beautiful home, one spacious enough that I didn't feel cramped but that also seemed cozy. I had that too. Though I hadn't officially moved in with Murphy, I stayed over almost every night. His cabin was ours now. He'd told me multiple times to add whatever I liked or to change the décor if it suited me.

So far, I'd just added a few paper-mache bats in the kitchen at Halloween that had stuck around. I was too used to a Halloween all year atmosphere at work because of Macy, so making up a batch of lemon-blueberry muffins with beady-eyed bats staring at me from the eaves of the stove just made the place feel homey.

Even if it was January.

I wanted the cutest dog ever known to man, who was currently sleeping on my feet as I worked on the laptop by the fireplace in the living room. Every now and then, he would look up at me adoringly until I leaned down to give him a pat and cooed to him that he was Mama's favorite.

He was also Mama's only baby, but whatever. Latte enjoyed being loved on as much I appreciated the cuddles.

I rubbed the slight ache in my lower belly. Especially today.

I had to go to the bathroom, due to far too much coffee while I answered emails from new people who had heard about the baby club support group. We'd actually named it Baby Daddy Wanted and set up an LLC and all that, at Murphy's lawyer's urging.

Yes, my boyfriend had a lawyer, because he already had a gaming company and from what I could tell, money out the wazoo although he wasn't the least bit ostentatious.

But the baby support group and far too much of Macy's coffee blend weren't why I didn't want to go to the bathroom.

I didn't want to know if I'd gotten my period—again. But I was almost sure I had.

Cramps, I hate you.

Not because they hurt. Because of what they signified.

So, yeah, I had gotten so many of the things I wanted. More than I'd ever dreamed of. Just one thing was proving elusive.

What had led me to Cabin Fortress—and Murphy—in the first place.

It was early days yet. So early. We'd only been trying for a few months. It was just that Crescent Cove had been built up to be this great mecca of unplanned pregnancy, and here I was, planning the shit out of it, right down to the times I was supposed to be ovulating. I'd even visited Murphy for lunch at his work site with a sandwich and an edible thong.

Three times.

And so far?

Nada.

Which was why I was working on emails and chatting in our newly created Facebook group for Baby Daddy Wanted, that went along nicely with our new website. Along with all the other facets of our growing business that Murphy was working on in his spare time.

He didn't have much, what with his now three jobs and his very horny, very desperate to be knocked up girlfriend. But the guy did not complain.

Like ever.

He was basically perfect, and I so was not. Too bad a girl could only use the PMS excuse for why she was being a raging emo-ball so many days out of the month.

I didn't want him to know I was freaking out about the pregnancy thing. It was too early. I knew that logically. In my heart? I was a big ol' mess of stress.

A knock sounded on the door and I glanced guiltily at my phone before I tucked it into my pocket. I would reply to Murphy soon. Once I was sure I could say something like *bring home Chinese, please* rather than *I have my period and I need chocolate and a million hugs.*

Murphy wouldn't blink if I blubbered all over his shirt. I'd done it before, usually related to my period. But I was trying not to burden him. He had so much on his shoulders, and he was so amazing. The last thing he needed was a meltdown from me.

Neither did whomever was at the door.

I whisked my thumbs under my eyes as Latte scampered up and ran over to the door, barking up a storm. I was halfway to the door when I heard Macy's very distinct response.

"Hear all that? That noise is why I'm a cat person."

I was laughing as I scooped up Latte and tucked him under my arm so I could open the door. On the other side of it stood Macy and Rylee and the cutest baby unicorn I'd ever seen in my life.

Here I'd been bored half the day since I had it off, and little had I known my friends were planning a sneak attack.

"Hayley!" I squealed so loudly that Latte looked at me in alarm as he was passed to his aunt Macy—who did *not* hate dogs, despite her cat-loving stance—and then I reached for baby Hayley. I hadn't gotten to see the baby since shortly after she was born, and I couldn't wait to get in some snuggles.

Rylee eagerly shifted her into my waiting arms. "God, I need a drink." Though she hadn't been to Murphy's cabin before, she breezed past me and right down the hall into the kitchen. "You gotta have a beer, right?" She opened the refrigerator. "No beer?"

"She's having a rough mothering day," Macy explained, rubbing noses with Latte. She was always happier cradling fur babies, no matter how she snarled.

"There's a couple hard ciders on the door," I called, smiling down at little Hayley with her bright blue eyes and long dark lashes.

Seriously long.

"Wow, she's a beauty," I murmured as she smiled up at me, as angelic as a Gerber baby, for pity's sake.

And Rylee was finding it rough being a mother? My heart

lurched. I knew it wouldn't be as easy as it seemed from the outside. Of course not. But I wanted so badly to experience it for myself.

Yeah, it probably wasn't the best day for a visit.

I dragged my gaze from Hayley and grinned at Macy snuggling my dog. "Let's sit down."

We'd just dropped onto the long couch when Rylee came back in and passed around the hard ciders.

"You're not nursing?"

Rylee looked at me as if I'd grown a horn to match the one on the top of Hayley's unicorn onesie. Freaking adorable. "I pumped like a champ ahead of time just so I could drink today. Macy promised there would be alcoholic beverages."

Macy rolled her eyes. "And so there are. Now hush."

Rylee sat down on the other side of me and kicked out her legs while Macy bent to pick up Latte's bright green toy squeaky bone and flung it wide. Latte went running, skidding on the hardwood floors, his tiny nails scrabbling for purchase.

We all laughed, except for Hayley, who was already wiggling for her mother.

Rylee tipped back her cider, took a long pull, then put it aside to take back her daughter.

"She's probably the most beautiful baby I've ever seen." I adjusted Hayley's little unicorn rainbow onesie as Rylee preened.

"She totally looks more like Gage, but I'm going to take it as a win anyway because she has my nose. See? Tiny button." She flicked the body part in question and Hayley giggled.

"She's cute for a human baby," Macy said grudgingly. "Just don't think I'm giving you any more baby showers if you have more."

"Girl, shush. This body is solo occupancy for a few years at least."

"You hear that? Before it was, *oh, this will probably be our only baby.* Now the kid's a few months old, and it's *oh, not for a few years.*" Macy shook her head. "Baby fever is everywhere in this town."

"C'mon, we make stupendously cute children. We can't deny the world our progeny. It would be cruel." Rylee grinned and adjusted her hold on her daughter so she could reach for her cider. "Just gonna fuck like bunnies until if and when. Once the doctor clears me anyway. I was stitched up like a damn Velveteen rabbit."

I winced. There was an image.

"Speaking of baby fever." Macy reached for the paper bag beside her purse. "I got you something."

"We got you something," Rylee corrected. "Who saw it first and mentioned Vee?"

"She's such a glory hound. Here." Macy pushed the bag into my lap.

Already my stomach was knotting with dread. Anything baby related probably wouldn't go over well with me right now. I was so happy for Rylee and the rest of my friends with babies—even Sage, who had become a good friend over the last few months—but I was just a little tender today.

Every day lately.

I set aside my untouched cider and pulled out a tiny gray dinosaur onesie with little spikes on top of its head. And had to swallow a sob.

Later, I promised myself. I'd have a good cry in private. And I wouldn't burden Murphy with it either.

"Oh, how cute is this."

"Gender neutral." Macy poked one of the spikes. "Any kickass Dixon-Masterson kid would love this, right?"

"Absolutely. Thank you so much. It's perfect." I didn't even sniffle as I gave her a one-armed hug, then did the same with Rylee.

"No bun in the oven yet?" Rylee tipped back her bottle again. "Not for lack of trying, I bet, what with how Murphy looks at you."

It made me smile despite the tears that were hovering. "Lots of practice. No results yet."

Macy shocked me by rubbing my back and not making a smart crack. "It'll happen."

"Until then, we have Latte." I smiled at the puppy currently curled up protectively over his bone. He'd fallen asleep mid-chew, as he often did.

"And you have Baby Daddy Wanted. Look at that, already in business together. Mace said you practically live here too. Bet this won't be far behind." Rylee tapped her own ginormous ring and yet again, tears hovered.

Jesus, Dixon, get it together. You've only been dating for a few months. Next, you'll want a pony too.

The crazy thing was, if I said I wanted a pony, Murphy would've probably built on a paddock and bought me one. He did anything to make me happy. Which was a big part of the reason I was scared I couldn't fulfill my end of our happy family bargain.

Yes, it was early. No, neither of us had been tested. We weren't even married or engaged or any of those things, so trying to start a family was probably nuts anyway.

But what if years passed and I still never got pregnant? And what if Murphy with his big family and traditional values started to feel like he'd missed out?

Then what?

I was putting the buggy before the kid. Intellectually, I knew that. But I'd never had even a glimmer of this much happiness before, and I was so terrified of somehow messing it up.

Somehow not being enough for this wonderful, incredible, perfect man I'd found.

By the time they left a short while later, I was ready to take a shower and just hide from the world for the rest of the day. Murphy was bringing home Chinese takeout and we'd binge on Netflix tonight.

A good way to escape from the reality I hadn't been able to deny once I'd finally gone to the bathroom.

I wasn't pregnant for another month. And I was okay with it. Or I would be. I'd take a nice hot shower, put my hair up and slip into a nightie, and I'd greet Murphy the right way with a welcome home blowjob before dinner. It would reheat, right?

But before I showered, I had a phone call to make. I'd put it off for almost three months, and today seemed as good as any for making amends. God knows she'd called and texted me enough times.

Biting my lip, I hit the speed dial for my mother.

"VeeBee. Thank God." The relief in her voice was palpable as soon as she answered. "I didn't think you were ever going to forgive me."

I blinked. Say what? My mother never asked for forgiveness.

Then again, neither did I.

"I'm sorry too. I shouldn't have run out on dinner. I was just overwhelmed."

"Of course you were. What kind of mother springs her marriage on her daughter like that? And I didn't know it was a special date for you and your gentleman. I messed it all up for you."

"You did?" I actually pulled the phone away from my ear. "Is this really Andrea Dix—I mean, Newman speaking?"

She laughed, but it was a softer, gentler laugh, not the loud, seemingly false one that always grated on my nerves. "Yes, it is. And it's a new year, so I guess you could say I've turned over a new leaf. Trying to anyway. It's hard teaching an old dog new tricks, even if she wants to learn."

I didn't say anything. I didn't know how to respond.

"How are things going with you and your young man?"

"Good. They're really good."

"I'm so glad to hear it. He's a decent man. After you told me that Facebook post story, I was prepared for him to be some kind of pervert."

That was so the opposite of my Murphy that I had to snort out a laugh.

"But that night at the restaurant after you ran off—and deservedly so," she added before I could interject, "why, he sat there and just about flat out said he was in love with you and you were the best woman he'd ever met."

My throat grew tight and hot. "He did not. Did he?"

Not that it came as a huge shock, since he proved his feelings to me every damn day. But telling a woman's mother how you felt was big.

Especially since she'd acted wackier than a lawn appliance during dinner and he'd been left on his own to fend them off after I'd split.

"He sure did. And that he didn't know if he'd get to be the father of your babies, but if he did, he'd think he'd won the damn lottery. I just can't imagine anything sweeter than that. Right then and there, my opinion changed. Plus, he has manners too. To be honest, I'm not even sure he's fully human. You don't think he's one of those cyborgs, do you?"

I rose to put away the cider I'd barely touched. Latte trotted behind me to the kitchen. "Pretty sure he's not."

"I know I screwed up some stuff for you growing up. Us moving around so much, never really setting down roots... I know it had to be hard for you."

I stopped with my hand on the refrigerator and my dog circling my legs, begging to be picked up. "Since when?"

"Since Burke talked some sense into me." She sighed. "It took some time."

"I just bet."

"Why didn't you ever tell me, VeeBee?"

"Tell you what?"

"That you weren't happy. That I was messing everything up. Here I thought you liked that we were friends, that you had more freedom than the other girls at school. But that was never what you needed."

I stared hard at the heart photo magnet on the fridge of our little family, taken just a few weeks ago in the backyard. It was after the first real snowstorm of the season, and Christmas lights glimmered behind us. Latte was wearing a little green jacket and he'd licked my chin just as the timer on the camera went off, so I was laughing while

Murphy hugged me. I would have been anyway, because we were stupidly happy.

Swallowing hard, I glanced down at my flat-ish belly. Or we would be, if not for this one thing I kept trying to force.

For someone who was all about fate and what was meant, I sort of sucked at letting nature take its course.

"You're right," I said finally, setting the cider inside the refrigerator and shutting the door. "I wanted a real home. A family. Security. Stability."

"Of course you did. And I'm sorry I didn't see that."

"It wasn't all bad. Or even most of it. You did the best you could. I know that. We had fun, and I got to have experiences traveling at a younger age than most of my friends. Just I would've liked seeing you more as I got older." I lifted Latte and juggled him and the phone. "But that's all water under the bridge. You're happy now, and so am I."

So much. And I was not going to mess it up with neuroticism.

I hoped.

God, I hoped.

"I am happy, darling, and I'm so glad you are. I was thinking maybe Burke and I could come for a visit for your birthday?"

That was a few months from now. I could handle anything in the future. Besides, she really seemed to be trying, and I only had one mother.

I didn't want this distance to remain between us. So, if she was making an effort, I would too.

God help us.

"We'd love it if you visited for a few days. We'll make arrangements as it gets closer, okay?"

"Okay. I love you, sweetheart. Don't ever forget that. No matter what a jackass your mom is sometimes."

I smiled through the veil of tears that wanted to break free. "I love you too, Mom."

We hung up a little while later. Then I fed a demanding Latte before rushing upstairs to take a quick shower, spreading lotion over every inch I could reach. I wasn't sure if I was in the mood for any sexy times—even ones focused strictly on him—but it never hurt to look as nice as first day cramps allowed.

After I'd tugged on one of my cuter nighties and swept on some mascara and lip gloss, I hurried out to make sure Latte hadn't eaten a table leg along with his chunky kibble.

He was contentedly gnawing on his green squeaky bone, his face the perfect picture of innocence—until I found the purple Converse he'd dragged into his lair. Luckily, he'd barely chewed on it, but I still pretended to scold him until he scampered up my leg for a hug.

Yeah, my kids were probably going to run wild in the streets, since Mama didn't have a disciplinarian bone in her body.

I carted him over to the couch, about to sit down for some serious snuggles, when I noticed the folded papers tucked in the side of the planner I'd been halfheartedly working on recently. Kelsey and Sage and Ally were all into planner stuff, decorating their weekly view in their calendar and all that jazz. I was mostly just dipping a toe in, but with all the charting I'd been doing for my pregnancy planning, having a central location for it all helped.

Carefully, I set down Latte on the sofa and yanked out the papers. I didn't need to know the best times for fucking for the foreseeable future. We would be together when the urge struck, not when my basal body temperature flashed the green light.

I tore up the papers and crossed the room to toss them into the fireplace. I flung the last of them into the fire just as the front door opened and Latte went flying off the couch, barking like a maniac.

Awesome timing, Dixon, as always.

"Hiya. How was your day?" Pasting on a smile, I dusted off my hands and turned to Murphy, whose arms were full of our dog, the plastic sacks that meant our favorite Chinese place, another brown paper sack that made me think of ice cream, and a huge stuffed brown bear.

I thunked down on my ass.

"You okay?" Murphy set down Latte, who immediately barked to be picked up again. But Murphy seemed to notice the bear in his arms and let out a half laugh. "Oh. This. This is for—"

"You think I'm pregnant, don't you? Is this for the nursery?"

I wasn't going to cry.

I so wasn't.

"Are you pregnant?" His gaze sharpened and the joy I glimpsed in his expression both thrilled and hurt me, because I wanted it too. I wanted to give him that baby. Give it to us.

But it wasn't just about me. It was about him too, and timing. And if now wasn't the time, it just wasn't. Maybe it never would be.

"No." I drew my knees up to my chest. "You can keep the bear for someday if you want, but maybe it's better off going to Goodwill for someone else to enjoy because I don't know if I'm ever going to be pregnant."

"Okay."

"Okay? Did you hear what I said? I don't know if I'm ever going to get pregnant, Murphy."

"I heard you just fine. Have you been granted some future forecasting ability I should be jealous of?"

I almost laughed. Almost. But the frustration won out. "No, I'm just being real. We've been trying, tracking everything, and it's just not working. Yes, it's early, but who's to say if it'll ever work? So, it's better if we're just realistic and stop fooling ourselves."

"Is that what we've been doing?" He set down his bags and the bear on the coffee table and crouched down beside me to poke at the fire with a poker. "What are these papers in here?" He pried out the corner of one that hadn't burned fully yet and frowned over his shoulder at me. "You tossed out your tracking charts? What happened?"

"I got my period, that's what happened. And I don't want to get my hopes up every month. Even worse, I don't want to get *your* hopes up. You're bringing home bears for the nursery, for heaven's sake."

"No, I brought that bear home for you. I knew you'd gotten your period because of the day and because you asked for Chinese. You always do that on the first day."

"You know when I get my period?"

He nodded as if I was slightly slow. Which I was, because I'd dragged him into every part of my reproductive cycle. He'd just been paying more attention than I gave him credit for.

I never gave him enough credit.

"So, you knew I had my period, so you brought me Chinese and a bear." I shifted my sitting position so Latte could climb onto my lap. I cuddled him close, burying my face in his soft fur.

With him, I'd never open my mouth and shove in both feet and both hands.

Probably.

"Don't forget the ice cream that's melting on the coffee table." Murphy smiled and set down the scrap of paper he'd retrieved. "The bear's name is Sir Mix A Lot, by the way. I was hoping he could watch us have sex tonight."

A laugh spilled out of me, the sound so loud that Latte's huge brown eyes grew wide before he dove off my lap. "You've developed a thing for grumpy women on the rag?"

"I've had a thing for *this* woman for forever, and that's what the shower is for." He scooped a hand over my wet hair. "Though you've been enjoying it without me."

"Not like that." I sighed and turned my face into his hand. "Why are you so good to me?"

"Because I love you, Veronica." His throat moved, the firelight flickering over his tense features. Tension I'd put there. "I should've said it before now. Maybe then you wouldn't be torturing yourself."

"Oh, God." His words caused me to bury my face in my hands. "I love you too."

"Really?"

"Really."

Gently, he pried my hands away from my face. "Can you say that while you're not hiding?"

I smiled and reached up to cradle his jaw. "I love you, Fortress. So much. And I think it's made me nuts, or more nuts, because I'm so determined for us to have this little picture-perfect family, and that was never your dream anyway, it was mine. But you've given me literally every other thing I've ever wanted. I guess I'm getting greedy by thinking I can have this too."

"You're all I ever wanted. Just you. You and Latte," he added, who barked, probably hoping his name would lead to the proffering of a treat despite the fact he'd just had dinner. "I would love for us to have a baby. Or three babies. Because I love you, and I want you to be happy. Not because I need them for us to be complete. We're that already, aren't we?"

"Yes." I nodded, my eyes filling. "I just want you to have everything too."

"There's no baby that could be more everything for me than you are." He took my hand, kissing my fingertips. "You're the best thing that ever happened to me."

Latte barked again, and Murphy laughed as he glanced at the dog. "You too, buddy."

We both were quiet for a moment, staring into the fire.

"We never know what will happen. We don't," Murphy repeated, squeezing my hand. "But if in a few years, we decide we want to expand if it hasn't happened yet, we can always adopt."

"Yeah. There are so many kids that need families. That would be a blessing to them, and us. Even if we had our own, maybe we could."

He nodded, smiling at me. "We can do anything we want to. We can always make a way."

"You're right. I don't know what I was getting so worked up about."

"Me either. Since I got worked up when you said we'd been fooling ourselves, and I thought you were going to say you didn't need me if there was no kid."

"What?" Genuinely shocked, I stared at the side of his face. "How could you think that?"

"Maybe because you're not the only one who feels like they've failed. And that's just insane. We've been trying for a couple of months. We aren't even married yet."

"M-married?" Even with as traditional as Murphy was, that word made my vocal cords seize up. "Us?"

Mainly because I'd never hoped that big in my life.

"Stranger things have happened." He rubbed his thumb over my knuckles.

"That we're sitting here at all is strange in the very best way, considering how we got here." I gave him a soft push and he fell out of his crouch back onto his ass. I straddled his lap and wrapped my arms around his neck. "I could never want anything more than I want this right here. You and me and...the dog," I whispered, darting a glance to where Latte had finally fallen asleep, head on his bone.

Even with his eyes closed, Latte cocked an ear.

"I could never ask for more, but I do."

"So do I. I'd love to have a baby with you. But I'd also love to keep right on practicing, just for the hell of it."

I smiled and tipped my forehead to his. "Me too."

"We don't know what the future holds. I just know I want to keep holding onto you." He wrapped his arms tightly around my waist, fitting us together as if we were meant to slide together just that way. Puzzle pieces that locked just right.

"And I'll keep holding onto you." I glanced over his shoulder at the bear watching us innocuously from the coffee table. "But we might have to work up to the bear thing."

TWENTY

I WASN'T EXACTLY LYING TO HER.

Nor would I ever lie.

But she didn't need to know exactly what I was doing. The fact that she even had to question if I loved her enough to be happy without a baby made this little trip into Rochester even more important. Juggling my schedule and hers to find a time for me to sneak away was like herding feral cats.

My passenger side door opened, and Gideon's bearded face ducked in enough to show me just how annoyed he was. "Why am I here?"

"Just get in."

He sighed. "My one day off in a month and you want to go shopping? Dude, you have a girlfriend for these things."

"Soon to be fiancée."

"Oh, shit. Another one bites the dust." Gideon climbed in and gave a little grunt when I took off before he even got his seatbelt on. "What's the freaking rush?"

"We're heading to Rochester."

"God, why?"

"Jeweler friend."

"Let me out."

I laughed. "I'm already nervous enough, give me a break."

Gideon slouched down in his seat—as much as a six-foot-three guy could anyway. "You suck. This is the kind of thing you drag your sister to do, not your best friend."

"I cannot deal with Maddie today. She'll hit me with a barrage of questions and squeals. Have you ever heard how high-pitched a seventeen-year-old girl can be?"

Gideon gave me a bland stare.

"Right. Sorry."

Not many people knew Gideon had a seven-year-old daughter. He kept that part of his life private. An ugly divorce had left him gun-shy about introducing people to Dani and that included people he dated. Not that he dated much. It was one of the reasons we got on so well. We understood the need for a solitary lifestyle.

Gideon could turn on the charm for customers, but when they were gone, he was work first, talk later.

And that quiet steadiness was exactly what I needed right now. I was usually the steady one, but I was freaking the fuck out.

Gideon tapped his fingers on the door handle. "Marrying her? You sure about that? Was that part of the contract?"

"I never should have told you about it."

"Hey, I get it. Having a kid is awesome. Hard work, but awesome. But marrying her? Sure about that?"

"Yes."

"Decisive answer. I like it."

"Was that a test or something?"

"Maybe. I asked Jessica on a whim."

I turned down the radio. Gideon didn't talk about his ex much. "I assumed it was because of Dani."

"Nah. We were wild for each other. But not the right kind of wild. It was sex and adrenaline. We had shit-all in common. Once I started getting paraded around to her famous friends, I should have gotten out. That wasn't the life for me."

"Everything about Veronica fits me."

"Then I guess we're getting a ring today."

I nodded. "Yeah. Yeah, I am. I could have gotten her a ring the first week. I just knew."

"Then you're one of the lucky ones, pal. For me, everything is about Dani and that's the way it needs to stay." Gideon looked out the window.

Talk about a decisive statement. The rest of the trip was quiet. Classic rock filled in for the lack of conversation. I didn't know what was up with Gideon lately, but I knew something was bothering him. He'd spill it after he figured it out.

The one thing women didn't understand about guys was that we didn't want to talk it out. We wanted to figure it out, then fix the problem.

And right now, I was going to fix mine by making sure Veronica knew I wanted marriage and babies if they happened. But the most important part was marriage. That I wanted her forever, no matter what.

I rolled up to the family-run jeweler that my father used for my mother. Every Christmas, we went in and got her a little something. It was tradition. A good one that I intended on keeping.

We strode up the walkway to the store. Gideon was walking slower than usual with his hands fisted in his pockets. I held the door for him. "Still pouting?"

"I hate shopping."

"Look at it this way, you can get Dani's birthday present while you're here. Shopping all done."

"She's seven," he grumbled.

"And little girls love to have something special." A statuesque blond came out from behind the glass case.

Gideon glowered and took a spot near the wall just inside.

"Murphy," she said warmly and kissed my cheek. "I was surprised you called. It's not like you to come in after November."

"I know." I rubbed my palms down my thighs. "Bit of a special request."

"I pulled out all my favorites based on what you told me about your special woman."

"You're a lifesaver, Cara."

"We love all the Mastersons. Especially since you each choose such special pieces." She held her arm out. "Come this way and we'll find something perfect for her."

Two hours later, I was sitting in the chair deciding between the final two rings. Cara had wandered over to see Gideon and had finally gotten him to actually look at the dainty necklaces made for little girls. He had one wrapped up in a sparkly unicorn bag before I could even get mine done.

Bastard.

In the end, we both walked out with little bags.

The car ride back was just as quiet, except this time it was me who was pensive. The ring was important of course. But this was Veronica. She didn't care about jewelry or the sparkly things most women did. She had one necklace she wore, but it was more because it was a gift from Macy when she'd graduated from pastry school.

"Where's that restaurant place we use?"

Gideon gave me a look. "Just outside of Laurel."

"We've got one more stop."

"Dare I ask? Are you going to put the ring on a cookie sheet or something? Bake it in a pie?"

"Fuck off."

Gideon smirked. "You two are weird." He pulled his phone out. "Good thing I specialize in weird."

No, I wasn't going to freaking bake a pie. That was her

wheelhouse. But I could make sure she had everything she ever needed to start a life with me. Including a kitchen befitting a master baker.

Unfortunately, shopping for large appliances was a bit trickier. They didn't exactly have them in the back to take home, no matter what size truck I had.

Thankfully, Gideon knew everyone, and it got me an in with the supplier. We cut a few corners and bypassed the showroom slick lights and salesmen. Instead, we went right to the source. The owner of the supply store managed to pull some strings and get what I needed rerouted to the store.

We backed my truck up to the loading dock and met Matt on the platform.

Gideon jumped out and extended an arm. "Thanks, man. This crazy idiot had a wild hair and I knew you were just the man to help us pull it off."

Matt lifted up his hat and scratched his mostly bald head. "Gotta say this is a first for me. It's usually a wedding present, not an engagement gift."

I climbed up on the platform and peeked into the cardboard protection. "My girl is a pastry chef."

"Well, that makes a little more sense. All I know is if I brought a double-wide refrigerator home, I'd be spending a lifetime riding the couch."

"If I know my girl, that won't be the case for me."

"You say so."

I shook Matt's hand. "Thanks so much."

With the help of a pallet jack, the three of us managed to get it into my truck.

Once we got back on the road—and after I bribed Gideon with a burger as big as his hand—he finally relaxed enough to lighten up. He popped a fry into his mouth. "You know this means we have to use Lucky to get it into your garage."

"Crap."

Gideon laughed. "Your scheme has holes. Not my fault."

"Yeah. Well, hell." I stabbed my display and found his number. The phone rang through the speakers of my truck.

"Yo."

"Want to make a quick hundred?" I asked.

"Depends. Does it require clothes? And do I get baked goods?"

I don't know what it was about Lucky, but he made me want to smash my fist into his teeth. Maybe because he reminded me of my brothers too much.

It's for the greater good.

It's for Veronica.

To make Veronica happy.

The chant evened me out. "I need to move a fridge."

"Oh. Yeah, no problem. I still require baked goods."

"Handy for you, Veronica made a fresh batch of chocolate croissants last night."

"Man, you might not even have to pay me if I get all of them."

"Deal."

"Wait, I said might."

"Nope. Meet you at my cabin." I hung up.

Gideon laughed. "I don't know what it is about this girl, but she's good for you. I guess marrying her isn't the worst idea in the world."

"Damn straight."

She made me a better man in every way. And I was going to spend the rest of my life proving it to her.

Half an hour later, I pulled up my drive to find Lucky and my dog cozying up like they were long lost pals. I stepped out, my boots crunching on the gravel. I squinted at Latte. "Traitor."

"I can't help it if everyone likes me except you, Moose."

"I don't dislike you," I growled.

"It's okay. I thought it was because I'm naturally loved, and you were jealous."

"God, no."

Lucky lifted the dog up into the air and made little kissy faces at his scruffy little face. "Nope. It's just because I was snuggling up to your girl. I told you it was because I wanted to turn the screws, but really, it was because she's the perfect girl."

I curled my fingers into fists at my sides.

"For you." Lucky set Latte down to scamper off to chase the squirrels. "That girl is too sweet for me."

My fists relaxed.

"I'm happy for you, man. Not to mention she makes us bomb-ass lunches since you guys got together." He slapped my shoulder. "So, let's get this beast off the truck and get you a wife."

Gideon laughed and released the tie-down. "You're something, Lucky. Good thing Murph is so easygoing."

Murph.

More and more people were calling me that because of Veronica. Not the big, silent Moose who was clumsy and awkward.

Not the lonely guy in a cabin anymore.

Between the three of us, we muscled the fridge into the back of my garage. I pulled out the slats of ash I'd been working on for the last few weeks. I'd wanted to do a remodel of the cabin the more time I spent with Veronica.

This was just the final step I needed to stop thinking about it and actually do it.

For her.

To change my life so it was ours, not just mine.

"Dude, you are so whipped." Lucky wiped his brow with his forearm. It might've been the tail-end of January, but we'd all worked up a sweat moving the industrial appliance off the truck.

I opened the refrigerator door and put the little black box on the top shelf, then closed the door and set the rainbow-stained wood against the stainless-steel monster. "Yep."

"Now what about those chocolate bits of heaven?"

I laughed. "How about a beer with them?"

Lucky nodded. "That sounds like a plan to me."

The three of us polished off a six-pack of beer and Lucky cleared out the leftovers in my regular fridge. He took Gideon home for me and I put my nervy ass in the shower.

Maybe I wasn't doing enough.

Maybe the fridge and a new addition to my—*our*—cabin wouldn't excite her much.

I scrubbed a layer of skin off before I calmed down enough to get out of the shower. Then I stared into my closet. Should I dress up, so she knew something was up? It seemed like an asshole move to wear the track pants I normally did when we were hanging out at night.

"Fuck it." I grabbed a white Henley and her favorite vest with dark-washed jeans and my dress boots. She might look at me funny, but she'd know I wanted to take the time.

For her.

Always for her.

Latte started barking his fool head off and my stomach tightened.

"Fortress?"

I smoothed my hand down my shirt and made sure it was tucked in all the way around. "Hey, you're home." I came down the hall with a smile.

"Hey." Her crown of braids she wore for work looked a little more lopsided than usual after a shift. Latte was wiggling to get down and she let him free. "At least you'll want some of my kisses." Her smile was tired, but still bright and beautiful.

"Always." I crossed to her and drew her up on her toes for a kiss. Cinnamon and vanilla and Veronica. The best parts of my life would be forever linked with those scents. And I was so very okay with that.

Her eyes were a little fuzzy and soft by the time I set her back down on her heels. "Well, hello there. Were we supposed to be going out?" She toyed with the buttons of my shirt. "You look amazing, but I really wanted to just stay in tonight."

"We're not going anywhere."

"Oh, good." She tilted her head and gave me a dreamy smile. The one that meant I would have a handful of cuddly female tonight. Some days she came at me like I was the last bit of water in a desert, other times she was like this. Just soft and sweet and so very mine.

"What were you up to today?" she asked.

"You'll see."

"Oh, will I?" A sparkle dented the tired in her bottle green eyes. "Does it have something to do with your very yummy smell?"

"Side benefit."

She wrinkled her nose. "I smell like burned cookies and baby drool."

I buried my nose in the little bits of hair that escaped her braids. "You smell amazing."

"That's only because you love me."

"I do." I straightened. "So very much, Miss Veronica Dixon."

"Oh, what did I ever do to deserve you?" She gripped my arms and smiled up at me. "I'd love to just have soup and toasted cheese and watch something blow up in a movie I've seen a million times."

"Sounds pretty perfect. And I'm the lucky one, believe me."

"Let me go take a shower and then we'll turn off the world."

I grabbed her hand before she could escape. "Wait just a second."

"I'm filthy."

"It'll just take a second. I want your opinion on something."

She sighed as I drew her over to the back door. "Okay. Do I need my coat?"

"Here." I went back to snag her shawl off the back of the couch before returning to her. I settled the worn, soft wool over her shoulders and gathered her into me. "We're going to the garage."

Not about to miss a trick, Latte scrambled down from his perpetual perch on his stack of pillows and shot between our legs to get outside.

"Why are you acting so weird?"

"I'm not."

"You so are."

I laced our fingers together and opened the side door to the garage. Latte scooted in first and I almost stepped on him. "I'm a little nervous." I turned on the light and she pulled away and ran to the huge fridge.

"Oh my God. Is this for me? For us?" She tried to wrap her arms around the steel frame, but she couldn't quite reach. Her purple sneaker bumped into the panel of wood when she opened the door. "It's perfect." Her hands flew to her mouth. "Oh, Murphy."

"I want to build a home with you, Veronica. A whole life. I thought maybe we could make the cabin a little more suitable for a pastry chef of your caliber. A kitchen you've always dreamed about."

"I don't need those things." She closed the refrigerator door and gripped the ring box as she brushed a few tears away.

I moved over to her. "I didn't mean to make you cry."

"No, these are good tears. No one has ever cared about me enough to want to try to make me happy. You already do that every day, Fortress. But...all this?"

I took the box from her. "I just need you to know I think about our future. About us and all the things we can have together."

"I don't need things," she said again.

"I know." I went down on one knee, then flicked the box open. "But I want to give them to you. I want you to know it's not just about babies. Babies and more fur babies are the cherry on top for me, but it's always been about you. About the two of us forever. Will you marry me?"

Her shawl floated to the floor and Latte jumped up between us as she curled her arms around my shoulders. "Of course I'll marry you."

"Thank Jesus." I wrapped my arms around her waist, pulling her down until we were on the cold floor in a laughing heap. She grinned and drew Latte between us, and he showed us that he approved by licking both of our faces from our foreheads to our chins.

It wasn't the most traditional proposal in the world, but it was perfect.

Perfectly ours.

Tears and happiness mixed into our kiss—kisses, plural—and she held me just as tightly as I was holding her.

I would never let her go.

Latte tried to chew on the corner of the box, but I managed to free it enough to pluck out the pear-shaped solitaire ring. I slid it on her finger, then I tossed the box so he'd go attack it.

Better to lose the box than the ring, and if it kept him busy while we got busy...

Well, a man had to do what he had to do.

"Oh, Fortress," she said against my mouth.

"I'll forever be your safe haven. I can't imagine my life without you. Don't want to."

She straddled me and wrapped her arms around my neck now that we were alone for a moment. "Forever sounds pretty amazing to me. I love you so much."

"I love you too, Veronica."

And I was going to enjoy proving it to her for the rest of our lives.

EPILOGUE
VEE

Sometime in May...

Good thing I loved my husband more than anything on this earth. Okay, equally as much as our little guy. I stroked the soft, springy fluff on Latte's head as I scrolled through my to-do list. Well, Murphy's updated to-do list. It was time to do my monthly checkup on the website to make sure it was all running smoothly.

If it wasn't, he'd step in and do his computer stuff. I didn't understand all the coding and backend things he mumbled about. All I cared about was making sure the women and men who wanted to make a family could find each other. And it was working beautifully.

A little too well, actually, because my life was positively stuffed with to-do lists lately.

I flipped back and forth from my work calendar tab to my personal one. Between the website and the café, I was getting a lot of use out of my paper planner to keep it all in check. Handily, Ally and Sage had pulled me even deeper into their planner girl circle with Kelsey and a reluctant new convert, Rylee.

Now that the wedding was taken care of, there was more time for work. We'd gone over the top with our ceremony on St. Patrick's Day and had even ended up getting matching shamrock tattoos and a little baby shamrock for Latte—on each of us, not him, since dog tattoos were not yet a thing, thank God—to commemorate him as part of our family.

Ten days in Colorado for our honeymoon had been one hell of a way to start our marriage. Seriously, the Rockies were as impressive as I'd hoped.

Life was settling into a pretty amazing routine. I still pinched myself pretty much hourly that I'd gotten so lucky.

The ever-present snick of Murphy's nail gun was the only thing that I'd change. Since we'd gotten home, he'd been working on our new addition—the secret addition that I sort of knew about but wasn't allowed to see until it was done. And really, how could I fault the man I loved for wanting to do something sweet for me?

Especially when it would end in a professional baker's dream kitchen.

At least that was what I figured based on my one clue.

I was learning that my even-keeled Murphy was very stubborn about certain things. I forgave him because it was all about me. Hey, I could be selfish too. When he asked to watch me bake in the café kitchen was when I got really excited at the prospect.

I'd always dreamed of a personalized workspace. I'd even caught him designing an under-cabinet mount for an iPad Pro.

For that alone, I'd attacked him to show him how appreciative I was. He hadn't exactly known what I was thanking him for, but it didn't stop him from enjoying himself. It was for a good cause. He was so excited to design the whole thing for me that I couldn't ruin it for him.

Even if I did want to string him up from the beams for all the dust and noise that invaded our quiet little cabin most nights.

I flipped back to my personal calendar and skimmed through our handful of personal appointments. Things like a few couples' dinners with Sage and Rylee and their spouses, a movie night with Macy, and a birthday party for Jodi that I'd agreed to bake a special cake for. A girl only turned eighteen once.

My finger slid past the small pink color code I used for...

Wait.

I paused, then glanced down at my watch.

I was six days late.

I'd been keeping track of my cycle. We'd decided to just live and let live about the baby thing. The stress we'd put ourselves under had almost cost me Murphy.

Or it might have if he wasn't so damn understanding.

I curled my hand between Latte and my flat belly. Well, mostly flat. We'd done a lot of indulging in Colorado. Ice cream was truly evil. Especially the Murphy-sized bowls I'd been eating.

But could it be true?

I fumbled for my phone and swiped for the baby app I'd deliberately buried in a folder where apps went to be forgotten.

I will not obsess.

I will not obsess.

I will not...

The app date blinked red as soon as it opened.

Missed period.

I dropped my phone and Latte yelped when I shoved my chair back. I set him in my seat and ran to the back of the house. I halted at the large black zippered tarp barrier my husband had put up. "Murphy!"

The music was blaring. I raised my voice and called his name again.

When the volume lowered, his disgruntled voice came from somewhere back in project land. "I'm not falling for that again. You cannot come back here."

"I have to. Murphy, you don't understand."

"Yesterday you told me it was an emergency because you had ideas for the size of the oven."

"I know, but it's not about that. I mean, I still think you should check with me about what oven you're buying, but it's about something else." A whole different oven. My oven and the possible bun in it.

"I'm almost done with this one thing." He let out a grunt. "Then I'll be right out, I promise."

"It can't wait."

He blew out a breath and I heard a thud, then his voice got closer. "Are you bleeding?" He unzipped the tarp and tugged a dusty face mask down as he shouldered his way through the small opening.

"No. And that's the problem."

He frowned down at me. "Babe, you're not making any sense."

I pressed my lips together. His exasperated voice was so cute. It was even cuter when he slipped and called me babe. He didn't do that too often. I secretly liked it a lot.

But right now, even the cuteness factor of my incredibly adorable and super-hot husband could not trump a baby. I grabbed his hand and dragged him away from the construction zone.

"This better not be a trick to get a look. If you're going to try to bribe me, I prefer the hot pink teddy."

"You already ruined that one, buddy."

"I know. I didn't mean to rip it." His ears pinked up. "But I already bought you a new one. It came yesterday."

"You did?" I smiled up at him. "You *really* liked that teddy."

"Um, that would be a fact."

In fact, he'd ripped it on our honeymoon during our first night at the swanky ski lodge he'd booked for us. Not that we actually skied at said lodge, but it was gorgeous. I'd put on the teddy and stood in front of the huge windows in our honeymoon suite with the mountains behind me and the only light coming from a few candles and a roaring fireplace.

It had been one hell of a night. Maybe it had happened then.

Our baby. If there was one.

Gah.

"As much as I'd love to see a fashion show starring you and lace, I was putting up tiles. I swear, it will only take me another hour to finish and then I'm all yours for the night." He tugged me closer by the little pocket of my yoga pants. "I can strip these off and we can shower off all the tile dust I'm covered in. We might even make it through a movie if we try really hard. Though I do prefer when you distract me from the screen."

I laughed. That was my Murphy and all his perfect domesticity.

Latte came barking around the corner at the sound of his voice. Murphy was our baby's favorite person.

Fur baby.

Knowing my luck, it will be true with our real baby as well.

But I had to take a test first. If he'd just cooperate.

"That all sounds amazing. But I think we need to do one thing really quick. It should only take five minutes. Maybe three. Depending on how many I take."

"Take? You are making no sense. If I hurry up, I can finish putting up the tiles, then they can cure, and I won't even work tomorrow night. How's that sound?"

"Murphy Mitchell Masterson, will you shut up about the tiles?"

He blinked. "Did you have to use my stupid middle name?"

"Yes. I need you to come with me right now. Do not argue with me. Just do it."

He linked our other fingers together. "All right. I'm sorry. Where are we going?"

"To the linen closet."

"Do you need me to change a light bulb?"

I snorted. "No."

"Get something you can't reach?"

"Maybe."

He laughed. "Lead the way."

I turned and led him through the living room to the current kitchen, then down the hallway toward our bedroom. I glanced back at him just before we got to the closet. "So, this might be nothing, but I just... Oh, Murphy it might be something."

"Is everything okay?"

"Maybe," I whispered.

My fingers shook as I reached for the doorknob. I opened it slowly and pointed at the white bin on the top shelf. "Can you get that down?"

He reached up and pulled it down to hand to me.

"My hands are shaking too badly. Can you open it?"

He wiped his hands on his canvas pants. "You sure you want me touching any of your things? I'm all dirty."

"You won't hurt the box."

He unclicked the side locks and tugged the top off. His eyes widened then his gaze crashed into mine. "What? Are you sure?"

"Six days late," I whispered.

"Six?" He hustled me around until he could kick the door closed. "Holy shit."

"Yeah. I was looking at my calendar for the monthly checklist for the website and...just can't believe I didn't notice. I stopped paying attention...mostly."

"I did too. You'd get upset every month when we were first together. I just hated to see that disappointment in your eyes." He blinked fast and his eyes got red. "I don't want you to be disappointed again if this is wrong."

Ever worried about me. God, I loved him. "I know. Maybe I should have taken a test first."

"No." He covered my mouth with his, giving me a hard kiss. "We'll do it together."

My eyes stung and I tried to laugh around the rock in my throat. "I didn't even think about taking the test without you. I literally ran right to get you." I blinked away the tears threatening to flow like Niagara Falls. "You're the other half of me."

He lowered his forehead to mine and covered my hands on the bin between us. "We'll do this together too. No matter what."

"Maybe I can pee alone? I mean, sometimes I sneak in and pee when you're showering if I have to go really bad, but I mean, you know, there's this whole stick thing. Awkward."

"I get it." He laughed and hugged me closer. "Maybe take two?" He dug into my stash of tests. "Did you buy these in bulk?"

"Maybe."

He shook his head. "Okay, maybe three. Just to be sure."

"Right. Taking more than one is better. Sensible."

"Right." He set the bin on his bedside table and ripped open a box.

I'd read all the instructions online and knew what each one required. The main theme was to pee and me hoping like hell that I didn't get it all over my hand.

Did I have to pee enough? Maybe I should drink some water.

I wandered into the bathroom to fill up the Dixie cups we kept in there.

"Wait. You're doing it now? I didn't finish reading the instructions."

"Already read them," I said between swallows. "I just have to make sure I can pee enough for all of them. Dammit, I just went twenty minutes ago. I should have stored it up."

"You didn't know." He leaned against the doorjamb with three white plastic sticks in his hand. Two were all white and one had purple accents. "So, this one does the plus sign and this one says the actual word—"

I took them from him gently. "Yes, I know."

He gnawed on his lower lip. "Okay, yeah. I'm sure you do." He swallowed. "Okay, so I'll just be out here while you pee."

I started to close the door.

"Maybe I should stay in here with you. You know, solidarity."

I pressed my cheek to the door. "I love you, Murphy."

He blew out a breath. "I love you too."

"I'm gonna pee now, okay?"

"Right. Yes. Pee away. I can't believe I've said pee so many times in the space of a minute. Okay. Right. I'm going."

"I'll just be a minute. Or three."

Nerves jangled in my belly. I was actually nervous enough to have to do what we'd been discussing—at length.

So much for needing to store up. *Thanks, anxiety.*

I plucked out a bunch of tissues for the counter and set them on top then quickly pressed the stopwatch feature on the new watch Murphy had bought for me. I couldn't even pretend that I had the dexterity for my timer.

"Veronica?"

"Coming." I washed my trembling hands and opened the door. "Okay, just a few minutes."

"How many?"

"Five minutes."

"Okay, I can totally do that." He shoved his hands in his pockets. "*We* can totally do that."

I curled my fingers around his wrist and tugged one of his hands free. Suddenly, my nerves weren't quite so scary. Even if the test wasn't positive right now, it would be all right. There were tons of babies who needed homes. Maybe even a slightly older child. And if we didn't go that route, we'd just have a bunch of cats and dogs.

I went onto my tiptoes and cupped his cheek. "Kiss me, Murphy."

"I'm dirty."

I smiled against his mouth. "Why yes, you are."

He untucked his other hand and curled his arms around me. "You know what I mean."

I did. And I would continue to enjoy the dirty side of my husband. During my extensive research, I'd found out that some pregnant women wanted sex a lot. I had every reason to believe that it would be the same with us. From the stories I'd heard from Sage, I'd be crazy for it, at least during the second trimester.

Except there was one problem. I was already crazy for this man.

He lifted me against him, and the kiss was so sweet and thorough. The definition of Murphy in every way. He lowered me to the floor and pressed his cheek to mine. "I love you so much. And even if it isn't positive this time, we'll keep trying, I promise. Well, not officially trying, but...trying."

"Yeah. I know what you mean." I sighed as I glanced at my watch. Just about time.

I took his hand in mine and we went into the bathroom together. Thankfully, the room was extra-large, thanks to my very handy husband.

We both stood in front of the counter.

"Hot damn!" He lifted me off my feet before I could even focus on the tests. He spun me around and kissed me soundly. "Holy shit, we're gonna be parents."

I didn't even have to look down at the tests. I trusted his reaction and the rightness I couldn't deny.

"You're going to be the best dad." I dashed away my tears when he put me down.

"And you're going to be an amazing mom."

"Team Masterson in the making." I laughed and held on as he spun me around again, then set me down and went down on his knees in front of me.

"You stay in there and do your job for your mom. She's perfected the art of baking." He covered my belly with his big hands and smiled up at me. "We'll see you in about nine months and not a minute sooner."

I grinned through my tears. "This baby is right on time."

WANT A LITTLE MORE VEE AND MURPHY?
Go to our website for a bonus story!

Also, turn the page for more Crescent Cove goodness! Ivy thought one wild night with a stranger would add some excitement to her life. Oh boy, was she right.

Next up is Rory & Ivy's story!

Rockstar producer & writer Rory is happily single...until he gets Ivy in the family way. Now making her—and his baby—his are all he wants.

For character charts, reading order list across all of our series—including spoiler free versions—please visit our website at tarynquinn.com.

We appreciate our readers so much!
If you loved the book please let your friends know. If you're extra awesome, we'd love a review on your favorite book site.

Now...turn the page for a special sneak peek of ROCKSTAR BABY now.

ROCKSTAR BABY
CHAPTER ONE

Fuck me running.

I peered through the windshield at the blur of white coloring the world around me. The *thunk-thunk-thunk* of the wipers didn't do a thing for visibility. The sound just pissed me off.

If the plane hadn't been delayed, I would've traversed these back roads in the daylight. Or closer to it. Of course Kellan hadn't seen fit to tell me that he lived in the middle of nowhere.

His hometown was probably rustic and lovely in the summer. In this hell they called winter? It was complete shite.

Add in something called lake effect on the weather report—what the heck was that?—and I was already over Turnbull, New York before I'd even reached it.

My cell rang through the audio system of my rental car. *Kellan McGuire.*

The reason I was even here. The guy was lucky I liked him.

"Kellan, I'm almost there."

"Are you?" He didn't sound as happy as he should have considering the thousands of miles I'd traveled.

Hello, *I* was the pissed off traveler. He was the bloke sitting on his living room couch and twirling a pencil while he pretended to be productive.

"I think so. Maybe."

"What mile marker did you pass?"

"Come again?"

"There's mile markers on the side of the road. They're to help during winter conditions since we get some travelers passing through to Syracuse and Rochester."

I squinted into the snow slanting down in front of my headlights and wondered why I hadn't hired a driver.

It'll be more of an adventure this way.

Turnbull isn't far from the airport.

When else am I going to see the quaint bits of New York?

I was a fucking moron.

"I can't see a bloody thing out here," I muttered.

"They're there, trust me."

"I've been driving a good while and I haven't seen a damn thing but snow. What the hell is lake effect? I thought being near bodies of water was a good thing."

Kellan let out a low laugh. "Not this time of year around here. Look, it's getting late."

I glanced at the time. Past ten. Jesus. I hadn't realized I'd been driving this long. As it was, I'd be in town barely a day before I hopped on the red eye back to LA tomorrow night. Kellan and I were working on a song together and between both of our hectic schedules, a day was all we'd been able to carve out.

The hours were ticking by and I was driving in circles in a blizzard. It was a miracle I'd even made it across the country to New York when flights were being cancelled right and left.

"You're right, it is. My GPS says I'm on North Hollow. Isn't that the road I'm supposed to be on?"

"If you're headed to Turnbull, yes, but I'm just outside Turnbull. Remember I told you it was easier to go to Crescent Cove then program it for my address? Otherwise the GPS takes you the other way."

"The way with no mile markers?"

Kellan laughed. "Essentially. Sorry, man."

For God's sake, I could see nothing out here. Even a deer would be welcome company. And where were all the other vehicles? Surely someone else had to live in this godforsaken backwoods area.

Maybe not. Maybe this was where they'd find my body. I'd become the subject of one of those tragic dead guy music specials. Did they even do those anymore?

Fuck, I'd have had more sex if I'd known this would be my last stand. I didn't even have on proper footwear. The autopsy pictures would show my beat up Jordans with the hole in the heel and everyone would murmur about how I must have spent all my money on wine, women, and song.

More like beer, pizza, and recording equipment.

"Look, you're closer to Crescent Cove than you are to my place. With the storm, why don't you go back to town and get a room for the night? By morning, the storm should be easing up so you can make it out here. Or better yet, I'll come to you. Just text me where you're staying."

It took me a moment to decipher what he was rambling on about, since I was currently trying not to slide off the road in my small sedan. I should have demanded a truck at the very least. This car had no traction whatsoever.

"You must be joking."

Kellan cleared his throat. "It's late, man."

"So you already said. Is it your bedtime or something? Need I remind you that I traveled across country to help you with your first solo single? You're the one who wanted to make sure it was a success."

Kellan had basically begged me, but I wouldn't remind him of that yet. Unless he gave me no choice.

I was hotly in demand. It was simply a fact. If I took the time to work with someone, they had serious chops and there was a good likelihood of our collaboration being a hit. Or someone had requested a favor. That was rarer, because I didn't make a habit of putting myself in that position. I didn't like to be beholden to anyone. Ever. Or for anyone to be beholden to me.

Life was less messy that way.

"I did. I do. But Christ, man, we just got Wolf to sleep. He's the fussiest sleeper on the planet."

"Look, mate, I feel for you with your issues with your pet dog, but—"

Kellan laughed long and hard, filling the car with the sound. "Wolf's my son. Nice one with the dog though."

I frowned although he couldn't see me. "I didn't know you had any of those."

"Yeah, well, came as a surprise to me too, but it's a been a couple of years and here we are."

"I'm happy for you, but I'm not happy for me. For one, I can't even find a lane to turn around in." Or anything but trees. And snow. And darkness. And snow.

"If you're on North Hollow, go up to the old, closed Heaphy's gas station. Turn around there then follow North Hollow back to a 4-way stop and take a left. That'll take you right into Crescent Cove in about twenty miles or so."

"Twenty miles? Why can't I just program the GPS from here?" I didn't see any gas station. Of course it had to be an old, non-functional one when I'd just noticed my tank was stuck near E.

So much for the rental car place making sure the car was set to go. Sure, no problem, I can stop for gas out in the middle of the woods. Why not?

"You can but the amount of woods in this area sometimes gives it fits. Just follow my directions and you'll be fine. In this weather, you don't want to be taking the scenic route the GPS will try to take you on."

"Scenic, is it? Is that what they're calling this?"

Kellan heaved out a sigh. "Look, man, I'm sorry about all this. Try to find the gas station. If you can't, call me back in an hour and I'll come find you. If I try to leave now, Wolf will hear it and Maggie will pitch a fit."

It was my turn to sigh. "Along with the son, you have a girlfriend too?" It was only logical, but I didn't get too personal with the people I worked with if I could help it.

I was focused on the music. *Only* the music. I didn't give two figs about who was waiting—or not waiting—at the dinner table.

"Wife. Didn't we discuss all this already?"

We probably had, but I tended to tune out when it came to family and all that. It was a potential job hazard in my line of work. Not that I had any looming entanglements on the horizon, but I also made sure not to cultivate them. My happiness was found in the studio, not in building family units.

I'd spent enough time trying to put an ocean between me and mine.

My old man didn't get my love of music versus a good stable job like he had in the fields. My mum wasn't much better. She'd stayed home with her children and thought that a family was the cornerstone of life. My younger brother Thomas went his own way, as did my younger sister Maureen. Yet my mum behaved as if we were living in a Norman Rockwell painting. Even if her marriage didn't seem particularly happy and her kids weren't close, the idea of home and hearth was all she cared about.

Not me. I wasn't doing anything for the sake of tradition or appearances. And I was lucky enough not to have to please anyone but myself.

"Don't remember, sorry." I shrugged it off. "I won't be your best friend, but I'll help you get that hit single you're looking for."

"Fine by me. I've already got a best friend and no particular fondness for the warm and fuzzies myself." Kellan paused. "So, give me that call if you can't find your way back to the Cove, or else text me in the morning and I'll meet you before we come back here to use my studio. Hope you can find accommodations. See Sage at The Hummingbird's Nest if all else fails."

I grunted and disconnected the call. *Thanks for nothing.*

Goddamn rockstars. Always thought the world revolved around them.

The sad part was they were usually right. Especially the successful ones like Kellan McGuire. As the frontman for the rock band Wilder Mind, he made the girls scream and his songs climbed the charts. Until one of the members had quit and Kellan had gotten the itch to play on his own on the side.

I played music now and then, sitting in with bands for my own entertainment or if a song needed something the artist couldn't provide. But I was a part-time rocker at best. I treated music as art, but I also kept an eye on the business end. Whether or not my pop believed my work to be "artsy fartsy", his words not mine.

I kept driving until I found the gas station Kellan had mentioned. I didn't entirely trust his directions, and they were hard to follow in this inclement weather in any case. It was practically impossible to see anything. But somehow the huge sign for Heaphy's still partially worked, a couple of the letters gleaming in neon in the darkness.

After making a U-turn, I went back the way I'd come from. I drove and drove and drove until I was about to turn to the GPS out of desperation. I didn't see any 4-way stop. Maybe Kellan had been drinking. Maybe I'd become snow blind.

Struck incapable by lake effect, whatever the flying fuck that was.

Then a stop sign appeared out of the darkness like a battered red angel. The sign was moving in the wind. I would've said that didn't seem possible, but my rental car was too.

Definitely getting a truck next time. Or a battering ram.

I made the left turn. Barely. The car fishtailed and the ditch on the side of the road came frighteningly close before somehow the tires bore down and gripped the road.

Heart in my throat, I soldiered on at the brisk speed of...eleven miles an hour.

This place was a hellhole. I was not ever returning. I didn't care if Kellan bribed me with a million dollars and a lifetime of producing credits. I'd just stick to sunny California, thanks. When I needed a taste of cold, I'd go home to Ireland or visit my sister in Cheltenham.

It felt as if I was driving forever, although that might've been due to my reduced speed. I didn't trust this car. Certainly didn't trust the road. Weren't they supposed to be out sanding or salting or something?

They probably would've been had it not been approaching eleven now. No one was driving out here but me.

A colossal idiot.

When the small green sign for Crescent Cove swam into view, coming out of the snowy dark like an oasis in the desert, I nearly wept.

Sweet bleeding Christ, I was here. I'd found it.

Now to acquire lodging for the evening.

I peered through the windshield at the rows of tidy buildings and storefronts as I passed them, most of them dark and closed up for the day. Kellan had mentioned an inn. I'd have to turn on the GPS for that one. Small town or not, there were enough side streets that I didn't want to be circling around all night.

Assuming I didn't end up sleeping in my car. I'd probably freeze.

I scratched my chin. Huh, that'd be a new experience. Maybe I could get a song out of it.

One I wouldn't give to Kellan. He was on his own.

A sign labeled Main Street came briefly into view and I grinned. Thank God. The place Kellan had mentioned was probably near here.

I hoped.

My stomach growled as I slowed to a crawl near the famed lake Crescent Cove was known for, at least according to Kellan. The snowstorm made it seem like a huge dark bowl of wind-whipped water with spots that were flat and dense. Likely parts that were iced over. I squinted at the festively lit gazebo and tried to imagine this quaint little spot festooned for Christmas. Probably quite pretty, if one was into small towns. I'd grown up in one and had been eager to leave it as soon as I turned eighteen.

What was quaint to some seemed like a strait jacket to others. I'd had no desire to live in a snow globe, with or without the flakes.

A sign caught my eye not far from the pier that led down to the gazebo. The Rusty Spoon.

My stomach rumbled again. That would do just fine.

Small rural towns often had diners. And thank God for that. What else would be open at this time of night? Other than possibly some swanky place probably down to a dessert and drink menu at best.

I'd take my chances with the grease and a corner booth—after I found the inn.

It took me another fifteen minutes to find it via GPS and then to locate parking. I was tempted to do a sideways tilt off a snowbank but figured that probably wouldn't ingratiate me to this perfectly lovely town.

That I could not fucking *wait* to leave.

The Hummingbird's Nest bed and breakfast was church silent as I crossed the wide porch to the door with its cheery little bell. That might've been because of the innate quiet of a good snowfall or due to the lateness of the hour.

Going inside didn't change my assessment. I saw absolutely no one in the foyer, or the little gift shop to the left, or the fancy restaurant closed off behind pocket doors to my right.

Then a blond popped up from behind the wide cherry counter. "Hi, you look peaked!" Her curls bounced to match her infernally perky voice. "Weary traveler?"

I blessed myself because Jesus Christ, my heart had nearly stopped at the sight of her. "You could say that. Room?"

"Like room at the inn? Sure thing. What's your name? Do you have people in town? What brought you this way in a storm like this?"

Far too many questions, offered in a rapid-fire style that made my ears buzz. She was like a living white noise machine. Except her noise was pink, to go along with her brightly colored dress. "Come again?"

"I'm sorry, you must think I'm wacky."

That was one word for it.

"I'm Sage Hamilton. My husband and I own The Hummingbird's Nest—where you're standing," she added, as if I'd failed to notice the sign on the door. "We don't get a lot of out-of-towners this time of year, and definitely not this time of night during a storm. But your reasons for being here are none of my business. I'm just a nosy sort." She smiled and her looks veered from pretty into downright stunning.

"I was meeting an acquaintance near Turnbull but the storm delayed my flight. Then his baby was fussy and I didn't even know he had a baby. Named Wolf no less. Who names their child that?"

"Mine is named Star."

"So, it's a small town thing then." Made sense.

"Possibly." Her smile grew as she tapped keys on a sleek computer system. "So, how long are you here for?"

I glanced at my watch. "Twenty-two hours give or take."

"Aww, you're going to miss the Sap Fest."

I hated to be redundant, but... "Come again?"

"Maple syrup. You came at the perfect time to try some of our tastiest local concoctions. Like maple ice. If you're a fan of icees from the gas station, you've got to try these."

"Um. Shame to miss that."

"You have no idea what I'm talking about, do you? What country are you from anyway? I can't place the accent."

"America."

Rather than becoming offended, she laughed. Gaily. As if I wasn't a rude fucker who'd invaded her happy hushed sanctuary at damn close to midnight.

"Point taken. I have a nice room for you. The last one we have with a fireplace. Good for a night like this."

She leaned forward and tilted her head, peering over the counter at my hands. At least that was what I assumed she was looking at. Maybe my lack of gloves? Surely she couldn't see the hole in my sneaker from that height. It wasn't a big one. It hadn't even been the shoe's fault. I'd met a nail and lost. And stubborn fool that I was, I'd refused to stop wearing my favorite pair.

"No luggage?"

"A bag in the car." I gestured vaguely out the door. "I wanted to make sure there was room for me before I brought in my belongings."

"We always have room at The Hummingbird's Nest." Her voice was sober as she tapped her name tag. I'd not noticed it before.

And lookee there. It actually said that exact sentiment.

We always have room for you at The Hummingbird's Nest. You're not a friend, you're family.

"I'm not even a friend, but I'll take the goodwill. Let me go get that bag—"

"You haven't finished checking in yet. I'll send my assistant out to retrieve it for you." She pressed a button on the phone. "Yo, Hamilton, we've got a live one."

My eyebrows lifted. Was she truly having someone get my bag or would my rental car end up at the bottom of the lake, never to be found again?

Was this small town really like the one in the Richard Marx song? I was a bit west of the setting of that one, but there were crazies everywhere. Possibly ones with shiny blond curls and doe eyes.

A talk dark man in a business suit—at midnight?—came down the sweeping staircase a moment later. He said nothing to Sage, just cocked his head at me. "Vehicle make and model? And may I have the keys?"

"You say hello first." Sage let out a long breath. "He's not new here, but he acts it. Oliver Hamilton, this is...what's your name?"

"Rory."

"Last name?" When I hesitated, she tapped her keyboard pointedly. "Unless you're checking in with an assumed name, I'll find it out on your credit card. Unless you only have cash. Hmm. You don't seem like the miscreant sort. Are you in trouble with the law?"

"Don't mind my wife. She claims I'm the one with no manners, but sometimes she puts me to shame." Oliver held out his hand and I gave him the keys.

"Blue Honda parked in front of the flagpole at the white house down the street. Bag is in the boot. Trunk," I corrected automatically.

He nodded, moving in close for an instant as he passed me. "But if you touch a hair on her head while I'm occupied, I'll use your own vehicle to end you."

NOW AVAILABLE!
Ebook, Print, & Audio

Check out our website: tarynquinn.com

Have My Baby

Claim My Baby

Who's The Daddy

Pit Stop: Baby

Baby Daddy Wanted

Rockstar Baby

Daddy in Disguise

My Ex's Baby

Daddy Undercover

Wrong Bed Baby

Lucky Baby

Daddy on Duty

Cop Daddy Next Door

Protector Daddy

Baby, Be Mine

Daddy by Design

Driven Daddy

Second Chance Baby

Sweet Baby

Daddy in Hiding

For more information about our books visit

www.tarynquinn.com

For more information about our books visit

www.tarynquinn.com

USA Today bestselling author, Taryn Quinn, is the bestie combo of bestselling authors Taryn Elliott and Cari Quinn. We've been writing together for years and decided to combine forces under one name.

Do you like...

✓ Ultra sexy romance with a side of sweet and funny.
✓ Quirky characters.
✓ RomCom shenanigans that usually involve crazy families.
✓ A crazy baby town that has exploded into a few side series.
✓ Office romance.
✓ Rockstar romance.
✓ And one BIG promise. If you love found families, you're guaranteed to find ones you wish were your own by the end of our books.

☕ Pour a cup of coffee and join us. We're glad you're here.

For more information about our books visit
www.tarynquinn.com
Email us: tq@tarynquinn.com

facebook.com/TarynQuinn
instagram.com/tarynquinnauthor